11-18-98

A CRIMINAL
APPEAL

A CRIMINAL APPEAL

D. R. Schanker

ST. MARTIN'S PRESS
NEW YORK

Design by Nancy Resnick

Library of Congress Cataloging-in-Publication Data

Schanker, D.R.
    A criminal appeal: a novel / by D.R. Schanker. —1st ed.
        p.   cm.
      ISBN 0–312–19253–3
      I. Title.
    PS3569.C332616C75   1998
    813'.54—dc21   98–21583

First Edition: September 1998

10   9   8   7   6   5   4   3   2

For Suzanne
her heart and bones

It is with great pleasure that I acknowledge the perseverance of Laura Blake Peterson, the insight of Reagan Arthur, and the kind assistance of Becky Noller and Elizabeth Roberge. This work was made possible by the love and support of Suzanne Buchko and Cheshire Schanker.

A CRIMINAL
APPEAL

1

If I were a self-help book, I would be *The Big-Boned Syndrome: Hardy Women Who Can't Leave Well Enough Alone.* If we had a twelve-step program I would be the first to stand, and I would say, *My name is Nora Lumsey and I am a big-boned woman and my intentions are good but I keep fucking up.*

I was made too big. I am built like the proverbial brick shithouse, and this awful outsized quality I have—of never being sure of where I begin and end—has sent me teetering through the world, bumping hard into people, smashing things as I go.

Clumsy Lumsey.

This is a story about blundering in.

In the *Indianapolis Standard*—our only daily newspaper—the whole sad mess was distilled into three neat phrases: the *elderly white lady,* the *two black boys,* the *good citizen.*

It happened at 1:30 P.M. on a clear, sunny spring day, dry and warm, at a corner bus stop in the white residential section of Indianapolis known as Meridian Heights. The elderly white lady was waiting for the downtown bus, on her way to St. George's Episcopal Church, where she was to play the organ for a choir rehearsal. The black boys drove by in a beat-up green Plymouth Reliant. The back driver's-side window was covered over with a yellow plastic garbage bag.

As the *Standard* told it, the black boys pulled up to where the elderly white lady stood clutching a shiny black purse and a leather portfolio stuffed with sheet music. As the car slowed to a stop, she held the portfolio tight to her chest, pressed against the buttons of the thin white sweater she wore around her frail body.

A small brown hand reached through the rear passenger-side window, grabbed the bottom of the purse, and tugged. The lady uttered a sharp cry and tugged back, twisting the purse in an effort to wrestle it out of the brown hand's grip. But the brown hand was tenacious. The battle of wills ended with a gunshot.

The bullet entered the lady's forehead just above her right eye. She fell backward, and the purse slipped from her fingers.

The car screeched into motion as the woman hit the sidewalk. Her portfolio sprang open, and pages of sheet music fluttered across the curb and into the gutter, lifted by the tailwind of the Plymouth as it raced away.

There were two witnesses to the crime: a driver who approached the intersection at the moment the gun was fired, and a woman in a nearby house who heard the gunshot and ran to her window. She saw the car speed away and called 911.

The driver—a young white man on his way to a game at the RCA Dome—gave chase, taking care to note the Plymouth's license-plate number. He saw the face of one of the black boys pop out from a passenger-side window and peer back at him. Then he saw a hand with a gun emerge and fire a shot. His windshield shattered. He slammed on his brakes as glass showered over him.

The man's sense of civic duty landed him on the front page of the *Standard,* his photograph in full color next to a family snapshot of the victim. The city's political and religious leaders, black and white, condemned the crime and called for racial unity.

The next day the *Standard* reported that the car, which had been stolen, was found abandoned downtown.

A few days after that, the *Standard* informed the city that the purse was found in a Dumpster a half-mile from the murder scene.

Three weeks later, the *Standard* reported that an arrest was imminent based upon fingerprint identification, informants in the black community, and the good citizen's eyewitness account.

One day after that, the murderer's face appeared on the front page of the *Standard* for the first time. It was the face of a black child. With bony fingers he held the placard with his prisoner number across a scrawny-looking chest.

His name was Dexter Hinton. He was ten years old, and he was deaf.

Seen daily in the *Standard* and nightly on the TV news, the mug shot of the boy's face became a logo for the murder and for the city's fears.

In response to the drumbeat of news stories and editorials decrying *the credo of violence embraced by young blacks,* our governor appeared on television with several black clergymen to urge reason and restraint in the boy's prosecution. The governor implored anyone with information concerning the crime to come forward.

On the editorial page of the *Standard,* the governor was derided as weak on crime, more concerned with political correctness than the safety and security of the public.

Five months later, the boy was tried as an adult, convicted of murder, and sentenced to fifty-five years in prison.

The murder weapon was never found.

The city, satisfied that the menace had been subdued and justice done, turned its attention to the next tragedy.

Like everyone else, I put the child's terrified expression out of my mind, forgot all about him.

Until thirteen months later, when the child's eyes burn up at me from a page buried in the middle of a trial transcript that comes across my desk.

And then the child's fate entwines with mine, and his life becomes mine to fight for.

2

I am a ghostwriter for justice, a midwife of the appellate court, a handmaiden to the law.

I am—to give the job its prosaic title—a law clerk, and in that capacity I serve Judge Carter Albertson of the Indiana Court of Appeals. In his name I write opinions addressing the complaints of those who lose at trial—the criminal defendants found guilty, the civil litigants denied satisfaction. It's a position intended as a one-year apprenticeship between law school and the legal profession, and if I were writing a book about this job, it would be *A Young Lawyer's Introduction to the Scum of the Earth*.

My first case was a conviction for child molestation. A four-year-old girl testified that her daddy got into bed with her and stuck his "hot dog" into her, then took a yellow toy shovel and pushed it into her vagina. And there in the trial transcript was state's exhibit C, the child's crayon drawing of the bloody shovel, the back-and-forth strokes of yellow carefully speckled with red. The defense attacked the child's credibility by showing her the drawing and asking whether the father had pushed the handle or the business end of the shovel into her. The child did not remember, or did not understand the question.

On appeal, the defense asked for the father's conviction to be reversed on the ground that the trial court had erred in ruling that the child was competent to testify.

First lesson for new lawyers: There is no argument too shameful to make in defense of one's client.

The next few weeks of my professional life are filled with thefts, assaults, rapes, more child molestation, drunk driving, murders, cocaine dealing, more child molestation. Every appeal is a story of perversion, desperation, stupidity, malice, or all of the above, and the stories always end the same way—another defendant, another victim, and another long journey through the justice system.

I have been at this job for ten weeks, and my life has come to be haunted by the characters in these dramas, and by the terrible and pathetic things they do.

There's the man who bites off another man's ear in a brawl at a gas station. There's the man who imprisons a woman in his house, superglues her eyelids shut, repeatedly rapes her over a period of two months, then murders her. There are the teenage boys who dump a truckload of manure into a neighbor's pool. There's the woman convicted of theft for changing the price on a package of steaks at the supermarket. There's the drunk who shoots his business partner, paralyzing him, because he thinks he's his wife's lover. There's the guy who mails packages of cocaine from Florida to Indianapolis once a week for a year before he's caught. There are the two young men who beat their high school teacher to death with a ballpeen hammer and steal two dollars from him. Their defense is that he had made "homosexual overtures."

Homosexual overtures. And they got off with twelve-year sentences, which in Indiana means six years with good time.

My fondest wish for those two is six years of torture with a ballpeen hammer.

Big-boned women have compassion to spare, but not a drop of pity for murderers with excuses.

Lock-em-up Lumsey.

I work at a desk in a large green room within Judge Albertson's chambers on the third floor of the Indiana State House. The walls of this room are lined with bookcases containing volume after volume of case law from Indiana and its neighbor states. This room is a cocoon of law, and in the middle of one of its walls is the door to the judge's office, a creaking green-painted wooden door that is always kept shut.

I share this room with Tammy, the judge's secretary, a decidedly small-boned woman, and Larry Haberman, the judge's senior clerk. Haberman has been the judge's clerk for seven years, having decided that he prefers the quiet anonymity of writing opinions for the judge to the stress of life as an attorney.

Haberman is tall and bearded and pear-shaped, and he has a deeply religious nature. Sometimes I think he's in love with me—he argues with me like he's got something to prove. On this cold afternoon in mid-October, Haberman is attempting to engage me in one of our periodic debates on God and justice.

"Think about it, farm girl," Haberman says—he is from Chicago, and he must constantly assert the innate superiority of the city-born—"doing justice requires a certain leap of faith, a belief that the difference between right and wrong matters. If that faith doesn't come from God, where does it come from?"

"The law," I reply. "The law defines what's right and wrong."

"But without the moral authority of faith, the law is arbitrary, an empty vessel."

"The law *is* an empty vessel," I respond. "That's what makes it fair. When judges start consulting God, the justice system will really be in trouble."

"We are all accountable to a higher power," he insists, smiling. "Even judges. Even you."

"Tell that to the judge," I mutter, and at that moment we hear the judge slowly turning the doorknob within his office. "He thinks we work for him."

The judge steps into his doorway. He looks around the room silently, taking too long about it, as Haberman and Tammy and I stare at him. I wonder if he's been drinking. It's 2:00 P.M. and he's been holed up in his office since returning from lunch with his cronies, a cadre of fellow judges.

Judge Albertson is a short man with a fringe of snowy hair and rubbery features. He is thin, almost gaunt, having lost much weight on a crash diet over the summer. His face is flushed. He touches the doorway to steady himself.

"Nora," he says without looking at me. He pauses, twists his head, birdlike, then says, "Come in here. I've got a case for you."

I rise, surprised to be summoned into his inner sanctum. Usually we take our cases from a stack of file folders tucked among the volumes of the Indiana Code. To be handed a case personally is a rare sign of approbation, and it is my first time.

I feel Haberman's eyes fix worriedly on my back as the judge ushers me into his office.

It is a dark-wooded room with a high ceiling. The walls are lined with glass-enclosed bookshelves, above which hang photographs of the judge with a number of prominent Republicans, most notably Richard Nixon, in whose campaign he had worked at the beginning of his career, and Indiana Governor Edgar Whitcomb, who appointed him to the bench.

Like me, the judge is a child of southern Indiana, farm-born, and he has been a judge for twenty-six years, the third longest tenure among the fifteen judges on the Indiana Court of Appeals.

He motions to the worn leather chair opposite his desk. I slide into it and wait as he opens a blue appellant's brief, his fingers trembling with age.

"It's a damned bothersome case," he begins, and now, five feet away, I can smell the scotch on his breath. "Pathetic story. The crime made some news. You may recall it. The appellant is a black youngster named Dexter Hinton."

I shake my head. The name doesn't ring any bells.

"Who shot a white woman named Cora Rollison in a drive-by robbery."

I shake my head again.

"There was quite a bit of hubbub at the time because he was such a young offender. And the boy is deaf. Ten years old when he committed the crime, and because of the nature of the case, they tried him as an adult." He pauses and looks at me, eyes steady for the first time.

"There was a black preacher making noises to the press during the trial, the Reverend John Jones, up at a place called the Lord's Light Christian Church. He even got the governor involved, if you remember. It cost the governor a good deal of support. We haven't heard from the Reverend Jones recently, but I am concerned that when the opinion is handed down, the whole damn controversy will resurface."

He stands, rubs his hands together as if drying them, then goes to the window. "I've read the briefs, and I've decided the conviction should be affirmed. There will be publicity surrounding this case, so it's especially important that our work remains confidential." He smiles, then turns away. "But if my name were to get into the paper, I would like the court to be seen in the most favorable light. People need to believe that we're doing our job."

I nod; it couldn't be clearer.

"So it's an affirm. Nothing fancy. The main issue concerns the admissibility of a videotaped confession that was later recanted. Your job is complicated by the fact that the brief is *pro se,* apparently written by the boy's grandfather. He must have gotten some help, though. I'll be damned if he hasn't made a good argument of it."

"Sounds interesting," I say.

He moves unsteadily back to his desk, sits, and points to a large box on the floor by the wall. Upended in it are seven or eight clasp-bound volumes crammed with papers.

"That's your transcript," he says. "It looks like a lot, but there's not much to it. And here are the briefs."

He hands me the thin blue appellant's brief and the much thicker red state's brief. "The state's done its job," he says. "The attorney general's not taking any chances with this one."

I glance at the briefs. The printing on the appellant's brief is faint and uneven; it has obviously been typed on an old manual typewriter. The state's brief is crisply word-processed in Times Roman type.

The judge licks his index finger and flips through his desk calendar. "Today is the fourteenth of October. I'd like to get a draft opinion from you by the end of the month. That way I can get it to the other judges in November and hand down the opinion by Thanksgiving. We've got Judges Waldron and Johnson on the panel. I've discussed the case with them and I think we've got their votes."

He glances at me quickly, then pulls a stack of papers toward him. "All right, Miss Lumsey," he says. "Go to it."

I put the briefs on top of the box containing the transcript and carry it out of the judge's office.

Haberman narrows his eyes and pouts theatrically. It's evident he's burning with envy, having accustomed himself to being the judge's favorite. He must really be suffering, I think; it's not like him to keep his mouth shut.

I throw Haberman my sweetest smile as I put the box on my desk, shove it aside, and ignore it, if only for the pleasure of watching Haberman burn.

3

The judge leaves the office at 4:00 P.M., a half hour before our quitting time. Tammy disappears promptly at 4:10, allowing just enough time for the judge to clear the building.

Haberman stares at the clock until precisely 4:30, then turns off his computer and exits with a poisonous glance in my direction.

I remain. I do my best work without Haberman breathing down my neck, and there is nothing for me to hurry home to but frozen pizza. So I stay.

I take the appellant's brief from the top of the box and open it.

> This appeal constitutionally presents due process rights under bill of rights unnecessary search and seizure of confession, and respectfully pray the court in its discretion to overrule trial verdict which was wrong and contrary to law and against evidence. I pray this appeal be granted because my grandson is no murderer and should get a new trial. He was only a boy of ten when the killing happen and he would not harm anyone but he was scarred and under the spell of some older boys. He would of confessed even for crimes that happened before he was born, that's how scarred he was. His sentence is more harsh than I

can bear a boy cannot under God go to prison for the whole rest of his life that is not justice. He did not do the horrible act he was accused of and if there is no one else to help him then me and his Guardian Angel must try to save his life. We pray to this court, we beg you, look at the terrible unfair trial this boy had, the inethical acts of the police officers and linching he got on TV and in the papers.

And it goes on. I flip through the brief and try to get a sense of the argument, which appears to have to do with the confession having been coerced. I wonder what the judge had meant when he said that the grandfather had made a good argument of it.

I pick up the state's brief and skim it, hoping the attorney general's office had made my job easier by translating the grandfather's stream-of-consciousness prose into a coherent legal argument.

Of course they had. With crisp contempt, the deputy attorney general had gleaned the issues the grandfather had labored to express, and had redefined them.

The Appellant raises two issues, which we restate as (1) whether the trial court erred in admitting Hinton's confession, and (2) whether the trial court erred in admitting evidence seized through the execution of a search warrant at Hinton's home.

I read the statement of facts in the state's brief, and as the story of the crime is related, vague memories of news reports about the case surface in my mind. The *two black boys*. The *elderly white lady*. The *good citizen*.

I lay the state's brief aside and pull the first volume of the trial transcript out of the box. I thumb through it quickly, through page after page of documents—the search warrant and probable cause affidavits, the witnesses' statements, the charges filed, appearances, pretrial motions, continuances. They are all potentially important—these leavings of the judicial process—but I have no patience to sift through them now.

It is the confession I am looking for, the boy's statement to police. I want to read the boy's own words, to know how he managed to say that he shot an old woman in the head for the sake of a few dollars.

I slip the first volume back into the box and pull out the second. I let the pages fall a few at a time, expecting to find among the pages of court testimony the usual densely-typed form for statements taken by the Indianapolis police.

But in the middle of the volume falls a plastic insert holding six photographs—the photo lineup—six faces of black teenagers arranged sideways on the page, three on top, three on bottom. The bottom-center photograph is ringed in red crayon.

The boy's deep-set eyes glare aggressively from beneath his high forehead, and I remember now the whole of it, the time in my life when his case was news. It was the beginning of my third year of law school. I would arrive at the library early to study before my first class, but instead I would fritter away the time drinking coffee and reading every inch of the *Standard*. The boy's trial was in the news for months, but it might just as well have been taking place in a foreign country, far from the world of courses to outline and cases to parse, for all the impression it made on me. And it could hardly have cut through the awful anxieties I suffered that fall over my grades and my future.

But that face. I remember that face, and I remember thinking that face was evidence of the sorry state of the world, a reason to be cynical. It wasn't pretty. It wasn't sympathetic. It wasn't remorseful. It was angry, obnoxious, rude. I remember feeling threatened by the boy's wildness, his seeming lack of moral restraint.

The face before me glares unhappily, the cheeks, forehead, and nose shining white, striped by the photographer's light, like war paint. It is an unforgettable face, a criminal face, a face that would get picked out of any lineup.

I find the child's statement to police in the third volume. Unlike the usual narrative confession, it is six pages of dialogue between Sergeant David Castle of the Indianapolis police and Beth Warren, a sign-language interpreter. The conversation is as crisp as a play, unflustered and eerily unequivocal.

Q. You wish to make a statement at this time, right?

A. Yes.

Q. I'm going to read the waiver form. "I have read this statement of rights and understand what my rights are and I am willing to make a statement and answer questions. I do not want a lawyer at this time. I understand and know what I am doing. No promises or threats have been made to me and no pressure or coercion of any kind has been used against me." Do you understand that?

A. Yes.

Q. Now you go ahead and tell us about it.

A. Do you want me to tell you the whole plan?

Q. Right.

A. Okay. My brother Joe and me wanted to get some ice cream cones at the Baskin-Robbins because there is a girl there my brother likes. But we didn't have any money. My grandfather gives us money but he was at work and he doesn't keep any money at home because he thinks we would steal it. I mean a couple times I did steal some money from him and now he hides the money at home.

Q. Where's your brother Joe now, Dex?

A. I don't know.

Q. What happened on the day you wanted some ice cream?

A. We didn't have no money, so Joe says to wait for him, he'll go out and get some money and come back and we can go out later for ice cream. So he goes and I stay home watching TV and he comes back an hour later with a car and he says get in we'll get ice cream. I said did you get some money? He said I didn't get any yet but we can get some now. And then he goes under the seat and gets a gun and hands it to me.

Q. Where'd Joe get the car?

A. I don't know.

Q. What about the gun?

A. I don't know.

Q. You didn't ask him?

A. No.

Q. How do you talk with Joe? Does he understand sign language?

A. No, I have to point, show him.

Q. And how do you understand him?

A. I just do.

Q. What do you mean?

A. I read his lips sometimes, and he doesn't say much anyway.

Q. What happened next?

A. We drive around. He said, we got to find some woman who is walking alone. When nobody is around. And all you got to do is point the gun at her and take her bag real fast and get back in the car. And I'll drive away. So we drove around and we didn't see nobody until there was a lady standing at a corner. So we drive up real close by the sidewalk. She was right there, next to the car, so I didn't even have to get out. She didn't even see me coming until I grabbed it. But then that bitch didn't let go. So I shot her so she'd let go.

The confession sits on the page, inert and unfelt, like a description of a day at work, except, maybe, for the way the boy's machismo is expressed in that word *bitch*.

But I've got to give the kid credit. No excuses: *I did it. Here's why.* It's a sick fucking world.

I thumb impatiently through the remaining volumes. The last volume contains the record of the sentencing hearing, along with a presentence report and dozens of letters to the court, about two-thirds of which were written on behalf of the boy.

> If you want to know what a fine young man Dexter Hinton is I can tell you. I go to sunday school with Dexter and even though he is only ten and I am fourteen he understands everything better than I do. Once I did not understand what God meant when he said that we must endure a fiery furnace in Psalms. Dexter understood that faith cannot come without suffering. Being deaf, he had his fiery furnace built in. He was wise for his years and he wouldn't kill no white woman or black woman.

And on the other side:

> The tragic, senseless death of Mrs. Rollison was a blow from which her friends, family, and community can never fully recover. This is the day of reckoning for the young person who killed that kind, lovely woman, and it is time the justice system made people take responsibility for their actions! Nobody made Dexter Hinton pull that trigger! He should pay the price! The fact he is ten should not matter! We are sick of the self-pity of cold-blooded murderers!

I close the volume and put it back, suddenly weary at the prospect of sifting through page after page of these anguished, angry voices.

I pick up the blue appellant's brief and look at the cover, the caption neatly typed, the letters unsteady and showing the effort of their production. Then I look at the bottom of the page, where the names of the attorneys usually go. Here, there is the name of the defendant, Dexter Hinton, "by his next friend," Carl Hinton, apparently the grandfather, and below their names it says, *pro se,* for himself.

Below that is the address.

I look at the address once without reading it and then I look again. The address is 2913 Rutherford Avenue.

I live at 2907 Rutherford Avenue—three houses south of the Hintons.

4

Indianapolis is a black town, and it is a poor town. It is called the Circle City, having at its center a war memorial—an obelisk—ringed by a traffic circle. And for fifty blocks in every direction from that monument it is a black town. Of course there are pockets where white people live—mostly in extremes of rich or poor—within that area. But Indianapolis is more than predominantly black. It is a black town.

I did not know this when I moved here, having been raised in the southeastern corner of the state, in Louisville's orbit, and I was easy prey to the sly euphemisms of the Realtor's trade.

Just two weeks out of law school at the time, I still lived in Bloomington, an hour to the south of Indy. I was occupied studying for the bar exam, which I would take in July before beginning my job with the court. I had three thousand dollars left from the money my father gave me to help with law school expenses, and I hoped it would be enough for a down payment on a small house in the city.

I contacted a Realtor, a middle-aged woman named Fay, a Hoosier if I ever saw one, a blonde with a peacock puff above her forehead and straight blond hair like a curtain around her pert, blue-eyed face. She had a forceful and knowing air, and despite the paltriness of the home I could afford, she took me enthusiastically to several homes in the neighborhood she deemed to match my needs and income.

The neighborhood is called Riley-Harrison, after James Whitcomb Riley, the folksy Hoosier poet, and Benjamin Harrison, the president who made his political career in Indiana and who lived in one of the Tudor-style mansions that line the neighborhood's eastern border.

When Fay drove me into the neighborhood for the first time, I gaped at the prettiness of the brick and stone facades, the stained-glass windows and green-copper trim above the front doors. The lawns were crowded with trees, and on that sunny afternoon in late May the street was shady, quiet, and cool.

As she drove, Fay advised me that the neighborhood was "up and coming," that it was "artistic" and had a "gritty urban charm."

We looked at several homes she had selected. I was amazed at what I could afford. These houses, built in the twenties and thirties, were small but uniformly beautiful; they had hardwood floors and crown molding, stone fireplaces, and built-in china cabinets with leaded glass doors.

Then Fay cleverly took me to the city's northern reaches and showed me the kind of home I could expect to buy in the suburbs for the same money—a condominium made of ticky-tacky, overlooking another condominium.

On our second weekend of house hunting, I signed a contract offering to buy the house at 2907 Rutherford. It is brick and stucco, built in the style of an English cottage, with stained glass windows throughout, a sunken living room, and creamy smooth plaster walls. It was, I thought, a tiny masterpiece, and from that place I could be at my future office in ten minutes.

I gave Fay my deposit money and returned to Bloomington to cloister myself in the law library, where I would spend the next eight weeks learning the essence of torts, contracts, criminal law, wills, trusts, and the rest of what I needed to know for the bar exam. I did not see the house again until the closing, which took place a week before the exam.

On that day, with my newly acquired keys in hand, I stopped at the house and walked through its empty rooms with the satisfaction of having moved a few steps upward in the world. I was now a lawyer— or would be, once I had passed the bar—and a homeowner.

When I stepped outside, I noticed a black man mowing the lawn next door. He nodded at me and smiled. I smiled back, wondering if he worked for some lawn-care company. But I didn't see any lawn-care truck.

Then I looked around me at the other homes on the block and across the street. People were out working on their lawns and in their gardens, fixing their cars. People jogged by and walked their dogs. Kids played in driveways. And every one of them was black.

I stood on my front step, panic-stricken and awed at my stupidity, my mind crowded with fears for my safety and for my investment. I took a few shaky steps toward my car when the man next door stopped his mower, took off his cap and wiped his brow, and came striding toward me.

He held out his hand and smilingly introduced himself as Elston Cumberbatch. I smiled and shook his hand, and as I said my name I noticed others noticing Elston and me and stopping what they were doing to watch. Within seconds an impromptu welcoming committee had selected itself, seemingly, and had begun to move toward my lawn. I soon found myself shaking hands with several of my new neighbors, many of whom appeared to be in their late fifties and older.

I do not remember Carl Hinton among that crowd.

Over the next weeks I get to know some of these people, even venturing on some evenings to sit on a neighbor's porch at dusk for conversation.

There are the Williamses, who raised seven children and whose home, across the street from mine, began as two bedrooms and was expanded over the years to something the size of a mansion. There is Mrs. Perkins, my next-door neighbor to the north, a high school phys ed teacher who is raising her seven-year-old twins on her own. There are the Colemans, who live down the street in a pretty house similar to mine, and with whom I have long talks about the incomparable craftsmanship of plasterers in the twenties. And there's Mr. Cumberbatch, whose family came to Indianapolis from Jamaica in the forties, and who still speaks with a lovely island lilt. I once asked him why his family forsook paradise for the inhospitable Midwest.

"Economic opportunity," he said.

I have taken my place on this block as the émigré white woman with the pickup truck—the vehicle of choice for big-boned women— and I have come somehow to belong without belonging.

I never thought much about race until I moved here, and I did not know what racism meant, not in my gut, not until I sat in pleasant conversation with a black man and woman and felt a nervous anxiety burbling in my chest and the word *nigger* forming loudly in my mind, shouted almost, and I had to force myself, like a sufferer of Tourette's syndrome, to keep from screaming the word out.

Blame it on my upbringing, and on the white-trash hillbilly genes I carry around.

Where I come from, there are no black people. I was born and raised in a town called Unity, the county seat of Unity County, a town built by farmers and farmwives. It is a place of pastoral plainness, religiously oppressive, a place so fiercely opposed to flamboyance that it is a wonder the corn has the courage to grow.

There are no black people in Unity County because the residents of that place have endeavored since before the Civil War to maintain the racial purity of their community. In 1837 there were twenty-three families who owned all the property in Unity County. They were Southern Baptists, every one of them, and through succeeding generations they have sold their properties to none other than Southern Baptists, of whom there have always been plenty, members of churches in surrounding counties, eager to move into this enclave.

The Klan was there too, of course, although it was hardly needed, and it served more as an outlet for expressions of race hatred than as a deterrent to black families wishing to buy property in Unity County. In truth, there wasn't a damn thing for the Klan to do, being that

20

there were no more than a few scattered negro families in that corner of the state, the Klan having succeeded perhaps too well in creating an atmosphere of hostility to strangers.

Yet the Klan was a defining force in the identity of those people, and participation in it is still a rite of passage among the hilljacks I grew up with, although the last time I saw a Klan uniform was a summer afternoon sometime in the late seventies, when I was exploring the attic cedar closet in my Uncle John's house. I fingered the slippery fabric and the crosswheel with no more than passing curiosity. It didn't mean a thing to me then. In fact, I don't know if I had even seen a black person at that point in my life, except on TV or glimpsed through the grimy windows of my father's truck on trips into Louisville, when I would ride along with him to buy presents for Christmas.

But there's much I haven't told.

My father raised us, all four of us children, after my mother left. I was eleven. And it would be unfair to say that he was merely a racist. He was that, as we all were down there in Unity, but he was more.

5

I take the briefs and two volumes of the record home with me. It is
after 7:00 by the time I reach my block, and I am eager to be inside
with two fingers of whiskey, but I drive past my house and stop in
front of the house where Carl Hinton lives. It is a house much like my
own, but somewhat larger; where my rooms are all on one floor, the
Hintons' home has a second story. The house is dark but for the
shifting blue light from a television in the front room.

I watch for a moment, chilled by the thought of the grief in that
family, then I drive around the block and go home.

I sit with my whiskey in my living room. I hold the record on my
lap and think about my ethical obligations.

It would violate the judicial code of ethics for a judge to decide a
case where the judge had even the appearance of a conflict of interest, financial or otherwise. As clerk to the judge, I am bound by the
same rule, and if I were to have any contact with Dexter Hinton or
his family, I would risk losing my job, getting disbarred, and possibly
even criminal prosecution for obstruction of justice. Which would
certainly not be good press for the judge.

I remind myself that I have never even met the Hintons, but I am
uneasy; I know what I'm capable of, and right now it's scaring me
shitless.

I open the volume containing the sentencing hearing and turn to the presentencing report, a three-page form, filled out by the county probation officer, encapsulating the history and future prospects of the defendant about to be sentenced. It is, in all the criminal cases I've worked on, the place I go for comfort for my doubts, a place to assuage my uneasiness over affirming a conviction; a defendant's protestations of procedural error ring hollow when the presentence report shows that he's been convicted of the same crime twelve times before.

The presentence report on Dexter Hinton, filled out by a probation officer in the juvenile division, shows under the heading "Identification" that his height is four-foot-six-inches, that he weighs ninety-three pounds, that he is black, slender, and of dark complexion. Under the heading "Family" it is stated that his father is John Hinton, thirty-six, whereabouts unknown, and his mother is Diana Baker, thirty-three, with a last known address in Sacramento, California. Dexter is listed as living with his grandfather, Carl Hinton, and his half-brother, Joseph L. Baker, aged sixteen. It is noted that a warrant has been issued for the arrest of Joseph L. Baker in connection with the offense and that the whereabouts of Joseph L. Baker are unknown.

The section headed "Previous Record" notes two juvenile offenses, one for shoplifting, the other for criminal mischief.

Under "Personal History," the report says:

> The defendant has been a deaf-mute since the age of three and a half following an illness. He attended the Indiana School for the Deaf since then until the present. He has had little contact with his mother since age five or with his father since age six. From age six to seven he lived with an aunt in Lexington, Kentucky, where he was enrolled in a deaf-mute school, but was returned to Indianapolis when the aunt divorced.
>
> Test results indicate that the defendant is within the

high normal range of intelligence. His sign-language skills are slightly above grade-level average.

The defendant stated through an interpreter that he loves his grandfather and wants to stay with him. He stated that he likes his school, particularly his teacher, Ms. Braxton. When asked about his mother and father, he shrugged and did not sign anything.

When asked about the instant offense, the defendant stated that he is very sorry. In signing this statement he appeared calm and unemotional. The defendant stated further that "she should have let go [of her purse]."

The defendant stated that his hobbies are basketball and football. He likes video games and television and comic books.

Under "Evaluation and Plan," the probation officer wrote:

After reviewing the defendant's background, it is a fact that he does have a history of criminal activity and, in this officer's opinion, is in need of corrective and/or rehabilitative treatment which can best be provided by long-term commitment to a penal facility.

Further, this officer feels that the imposition of a reduced sentence or the presumptive sentence would seriously depreciate the seriousness of the offense and further the victim of the offense was 72 years of age. This officer feels this was a brutal, senseless killing and that the defendant has earned and deserves the maximum penalty provided by statute.

Further, it is recommended the defendant be assessed court costs in the sum of $254.84.

I feel no relief here, no comfort for my doubts. Yes, it seems likely that he did it. The previous convictions. The shattered family. And the fact that twelve jurors sat with this child in front of them as they heard the evidence and felt sufficiently certain of his guilt to convict him.

Yet I feel a damned hard pull at my heart. Call it idiot compassion, call it whatever you want.

6

The morning is dark and drizzly, and the Indiana State House glows faintly against a gray sky as I drive past the security guard and park behind the building. Built of pale white limestone mined in southern Indiana's famous quarries, our classical, copper-domed State House is the repository of political power in Indiana. On the first floor, the governor and secretary of state have their offices; the second floor houses the General Assembly and the chambers of the Indiana Supreme Court; and on the third floor reside the judges of the Indiana Court of Appeals. It is either fitting or absurd that these politicians and jurists—mostly male, ambitious, and single-minded—come to work in a setting of such extraordinary beauty. How many of them stop to appreciate the vaulted skylights, the pink marble columns, the chandeliers like inverted floral arrangements, stems twisting gracefully into glass blossoms? Has the governor ever noticed that above the center rotunda, the dome's false ceiling of stained glass is a summer sky arrayed with a subtle embellishment of stars?

Sometimes I go out of my way to walk past the governor's office, hoping to catch a glimpse of our governor, who is a youngish man, good-looking and blond-wifed, conservative, popular, and thus far scandal-free. I have not seen him yet.

Ringing the octagonal second-story balcony of the rotunda are eight statues representing art, industry, commerce, literature, religion, medicine, justice, and law. Some mornings I stop and regard the figure of Justice, a big-boned, heavy-breasted woman like me whose weary arm unflaggingly holds the scales aloft.

But on this day I am late. Fearful of pissing off the judge, I run through the rotunda and up two flights of marble stairs.

As I enter the chambers, Haberman is sitting at the judge's work table, the two of them chatting like old college friends.

"Look who's tardy," says Haberman. "Good morning, farm girl."

"Come in, Nora," says the judge. "I'd like you to run through the issues in your case with Larry."

I quickly shed my coat, sneak Haberman a nasty look, and smooth back my hair, which is so stringy and fine that on wet days I resemble an otter.

I carefully lay out the details of the Hinton case. Haberman shifts childishly in his chair, jealous of the judge's attention.

"The defendant was taken to the police station, where he signed a waiver and made a tape-recorded statement through a sign-language interpreter in response to the detective's questioning. Then the defendant's grandfather arrived. After consulting with his grandfather, the defendant made a videotaped confession. The trial court admitted the video, but suppressed the preconsultation statements. Now, on appeal, the defendant contends that the video confession was tainted by the prior admissions and that there was no incentive *not* to cooperate after the admissions had been made. The state says that the video was admissible regardless. I don't know what the answer is yet. I haven't had a chance to look at the case law."

"I can tell you," Haberman snorts. "It's admissible unless coercion was involved."

"Maybe," I say, nodding deferentially, "but for juveniles the parental consultation is as important as the Miranda warning is for adults. If a kid doesn't get the consultation, a confession isn't admissible."

"That's not quite right," Haberman insists. "If the juvenile is Mirandized and there is no coercion, it's admissible."

"Of course," the judge says, and it's clear he doesn't want to hear another word about it. "What's the other issue?"

"It has to do with the search warrant. The police were led to the defendant's home when they found the fingerprints of the defendant's brother Joe on the stolen car. There was no information linking the defendant to the crime until the police conducted the search and found the defendant in the home. The police also found some marijuana in Joe's room, which they seized. The search warrant lists only Joe Baker as a target of the search. The defendant argues that the warrant was invalid as to him because it did not specify him individually, did not authorize a search of his room." I look at the judge, hoping for approval. "This argument is obviously without merit, as the police search of the *house* was supported by sufficient probable cause."

Haberman shrugs and the judge looks at me silently. After a moment he closes his eyes slowly, wrinkling his face like a cat, and nods sleepily, apparently bored of our colloquy.

I return to my desk, irritated at the judge and Haberman and furious with myself for not making a better argument on the consultation issue. It doesn't matter whether or not the boy had been Mirandized; a child is presumed incapable of understanding the Miranda rights. In fact, the whole purpose behind the "meaningful consultation" requirement is to ensure that the child knows that a confession, once made, becomes evidence.

I look again at the sequence of events—the search, the arrest, the questioning, the boy's confession, the summoning of the grandfather, the grandfather's arrival, the consultation, the videotaped confession.

Now I understand what the judge meant when he said the grandfather had made a good argument of it.

Haberman was right about one thing—in the adult context, the U.S. Supreme Court held that statements given to police after a suspect had received the Miranda warning would be admissible despite the suspect having been questioned before the warning had been received, unless coercion had taken place—"or other circumstances calculated to undermine the suspect's ability to exercise his free will."

But in the context of a child confessing to a crime, doesn't the absence of a parent or guardian automatically undermine his ability to exercise free will? Doesn't the very fact of his being a child affect that ability?

I knock firmly on the judge's door. He answers with a sharp "yes," and I enter. I tell him that there's a chance we may have to reverse Hinton's conviction on the consultation issue.

He looks at me skeptically.

"In the juvenile context, you can't assume competence. That's the law. If you put any ten-year-old on the stand, you have to prove the kid knows the difference between the truth and a lie. In this situation, where you have the kid questioned by cops and locked in an interrogation room without his parents involved, you've got to assume that the kid was scared and intimidated. That's enough. Just subjecting a kid to that is coercion."

"That may be true, Miss Lumsey," he says evenly. "But the fact is, the grandfather did arrive and did have consultation of more than a half hour. None of the child's statements made before the consultation were admitted. Only the postconsultation statement got in. I don't have any problem with that."

"Still, I'd like to see what other states say about whether the post-consultation admissions are tainted under these circumstances."

He sighs, deeply annoyed. "It's clear that Hinton is the perpetrator. Remember that a jury of twelve citizens found him guilty at the conclusion of a long judicial process. This is a minute point of law, a technicality, and it is a technicality of the sort that the public finds infuriating as a justification for overturning a conviction that has been attained at great cost to the state."

"I understand that, but isn't it our job to—"

"Remember that the decisions of this court sometimes have an impact far beyond the parties involved and far beyond the confines of the law. This is one of those decisions. It's an important decision for many reasons, and I chose you to draft it because I have faith that you will do it clearly, concisely, and as instructed."

I swallow hard. "Judge, I'd just like to do it right."

"Of course, Miss Lumsey, but it is an affirm, understand?"

I understand. Every fiber of my body is rebelling against it, yet I understand.

I don't have a choice.

7

I spend the day reading the transcript of Dexter Hinton's trial. The prosecution's opening statement begins in classic style:

> May it please the Court, ladies and gentlemen of the jury. You hear a lot about rights these days, constitutional rights, this right and that right. Everybody has rights, and sometimes it seems that criminals have more rights than the rest of us. But nobody can say that Cora Rollison was not within her rights to stand at a bus stop on a spring day without the threat of harm. And that's what this case is about: an elderly woman's right to stand and wait for a bus, unharmed, unthreatened by a couple of young thugs looking for easy money.

A few pages later:

> The evidence will show that Dexter Hinton confessed to shooting Cora Rollison, only to recant that confession upon the advice of counsel. But it was too late. He had confessed and the confession will be introduced into evidence. The evidence will further show that in Hinton's recantation he alleges that a third person was in the car,

a nameless person who fired the shot that killed Cora Rollison. The evidence will show that there was no such person.

A third person? I can't recall having seen reference to a third person in the grandfather's brief.

I flip to the defense's opening statement, which matches the prosecution for oratory:

> May it please the Court, counsel, ladies and gentlemen of the jury. It's often harder to disprove something than it is to prove it, particularly when you're talking about a violent crime. So you as jurors must remember that the burden of proof is with the prosecution. It's their job to convince you beyond a reasonable doubt that this defendant, this young man Dexter Hinton, committed the crime of murder. You will hear about an alleged confession. The evidence will show that not only was this child's confession coerced, but that he was actively encouraged by police to lie. You will be given an opportunity to picture the scene in the police station for yourselves: a ten-year-old child, deaf, alone after having been taken from his house following a search by a battalion of police. The evidence will show that this deaf child was denied his basic constitutional protections from the get-go, that he is being scapegoated in order to cover up police incompetence, and that he is innocent. He did not do the terrible deed that is the subject of this trial. He did not kill Cora Rollison. That heinous act was done by a third man, of whom you will hear in testimony by the only true eyewitness to the crime who is here today—the defendant himself.

Surprised to see reference to testimony by the defendant—a gutsy move on the part of the defense attorney—I look at the table of contents to find Dexter Hinton's testimony. I find it near the end of the transcript, on the second day of the trial. It is preceded by the court's swearing in of the sign-language translator—an Owedia Braxton, who had been the defendant's teacher at the Indiana School for the Deaf—and a statement by the prosecution that it waives any objection to the use of a translator with a prior relationship to the defendant.

Q. How old are you, son?

A. Eleven.

Q. But you were ten at the time this crime was committed, isn't that right?

A. Yes.

Q. Were you in the car with your half-brother that day?

A. Yes, I was.

Q. Did you go with your brother to rob someone?

A. I went, but not to rob anybody.

Q. Have you ever shot a gun, Dexter?

A. No.

Q. Did you shoot the victim, Cora Rollison, Dexter?

A. No.

Q. Who shot Cora Rollison, Dexter?

A. The other boy in the car, Joe's friend.

Q. What's his name, Dexter?

A. Mr. E.

Q. What's the name?

A. Mr. E. That's what I call him. I don't know his real name.

> COURT: Ms. Braxton, what exactly is the defendant signing here?
>
> MS. BRAXTON: It's a name sign, apparently of his own invention. He is using finger spelling to sign the written abbreviation *mr* and then the letter *e*.
>
> COURT: Would you ask the defendant if anyone else calls this third person by that name, or is it just him?

MS. BRAXTON: Certainly, your honor.

A. Just me.

Q. Why did you lie in your confession, Dexter?

A. Joe said they would kill me, the Indy Boyz.

Q. Who are the Indy Boyz?

A. Joe's gang.

Q. Is Mr. E in this gang?

A. I don't know.

Q. Didn't you think you'd get in trouble if you said you killed the woman?

A. Joe said nothing would happen to me if I got caught because I was too young to go to jail. Joe said that maybe I'd go to the boys' school for a few years, but that it was better there than at home anyway. And being deaf, they'd have pity on me. Joe said that if he got caught, he'd go to jail for sure, maybe they'd even execute him. So I could not say anything about Joe or Mr. E. Either way Joe or me would get killed.

Q. When did Joe tell you this?

A. Before he left.

Q. When did he leave?

A. A week before the police got me.

Q. Who killed the woman, Dexter?

A. Mr. E.

Q. How did he do that?

A. He was in the front seat with Joe and he leaned back and stuck his hand out and shot through the window.

Q. What were you doing at that moment?

A. I was down on the floor of the backseat.

What did the jury think, I wonder, having heard two versions of the truth, first the confession, then this startling recantation? What would I think, were I a juror, having seen this deaf child first on videotape, then in person, having his words spoken by an adult woman as he sat there moving his hands?

34

Mr. E. It's patently unbelievable, arrogant even, like a child's imaginary friend taking the blame for the spilled milk, the broken window.

Mr. E. For a moment I am ready to chuck the research and follow the judge's instincts.

But big-boned women hate being told what to do.

8

By evening the sky has cleared, leaving a sparkling autumn dusk, unseasonably warm and bright. As I turn into my driveway I see for the first time a figure outside the Hinton home, a gray-haired black man bent over the flower beds at the front of the house, his hands full of what appear to be the dead, dry remains of weeds.

I sit in the cab of my pickup and watch his figure hover over the dirt, his hands snatching at the ground. Every few seconds he stops and crouches, motionless, apparently trying to catch his breath.

Carl Hinton.

I get out of my pickup, leaving my coat and briefcase where they are in the cab, and I cross the front lawns of the two houses between ours.

As I do this I am completely aware of the danger that my actions pose to myself and to the judge. But I am twenty yards from him and closing, and in front of me is the opportunity to get some answers to my questions about Dexter Hinton's treatment by the police.

There is no way, I tell myself, for him to find out that I work for the judge who is deciding his grandson's appeal.

There is no way, I tell myself, for the judge to find out that I am acquainted with Dexter Hinton's grandfather.

If no one knows, what's the danger?

Too-clever-by-half Lumsey.

He senses my approach and turns toward me as he unbends from his stooped position. He looks at me quizzically, then a smile creases his face. He is a tall man with a wide mouth, glasses, and large powerful hands.

I haven't the damnedest idea what I'm going to say.

"We are truly blessed," he says, smiling, as he drops the weeds in a pile at his feet. "God has given us a day to make order out of the chaos. And what a lot of chaos I have in my garden."

He reaches out his hand, which feels like a soft, warm paw when I meet it with my own large hand.

"I'm sorry it's taken so long for us to meet each other," I say, and I introduce myself.

"I'm Carl Hinton," he says plainly, "and it's no wonder because I've been ill and busy. But thank God I'm all right now."

I nod, and I am about to add my thanks for his good health when he squints at me and says, "You're the lawyer, is that right?"

"Yes, I graduated from law school last May."

"Cumberbatch told me so. Well, then. Where was it he said you worked?"

"I work . . . for the state."

"For the state? Uh-huh. Well, you'll forgive me if I haven't a kind word to say about lawyers. My God, I've spoken to enough lawyers in the past two years to last a lifetime, more than a lifetime."

I laugh, as graciously as I can, and say, "That sentiment is all too common."

He ignores me. "For the state? I used to work for the city. Landscaping. You ever see those beautiful gardens down by city hall? You ever go down to the library and look down over the plaza there toward the courthouse and the post office?"

I shake my head.

"Well, if you go there in the spring, you'll see some lovely beds of tulips and irises and the nice pachysandra border, just like I planted it three years ago, before I got on disability. Got problems with my hip. May have to have that hip replacement surgery. Too much of my life spent on my knees in the dirt, bent down digging holes to drop bulbs into, too much up and down and crawlin' around on all fours. Not that I didn't love it. Still do, though I can't do it anymore. You can see here that I try to keep the place up as best I can. You should've seen this place when my wife was here. She was twice the gardener I was—had a rose garden you won't see the likes of in this city. Biggest, brightest blossoms, spreading perfume all over the block. I swear you could step out your front door and the air would smell so sweet you'd stop a while and give thanks to God for the day and for the joy of being alive. That's what flowers do, you know—they're one of God's messengers, and they bring us peace like nothin' else will."

I look at him sympathetically as he rambles on, and I wonder if I dare bring the conversation around to his grandson. There is a long silence. He looks off into the distance patiently, as if knowing that I am floundering for words.

I say, "Perhaps you could give me some advice about my yard. I really don't know the first thing about gardening."

He brightens instantly. "I'm so glad you asked." He grins. "I wasn't gonna say nothin' about it, but you sure do need some help. But don't you feel bad, because that place was never properly gardened. The Johnsons never did the earth around that house justice, I swear."

He falls abruptly to his knees, apparently unable to bend smoothly, and resumes clearing the debris from his flower bed. "I'll be by Saturday," he says. "I'll be by and we'll talk some about your dirt."

For the rest of the week I am a happy idiot, fantasizing about the wonderful garden I'm going to have and wondering what Carl Hinton will tell me about his grandson's arrest.

At lunch on Friday, Haberman and I stroll through the maze of underground and elevated tubes that leads from the State House to the Circle Center Mall, our newly rejuvenated, hermetically sealed downtown shopping center. We do not once have to step out into the open air, or onto the dirty street.

We come here to walk and talk, Haberman and I; it is a place where we can get some exercise while sniping at one another, and when we've worked up an appetite, we graze on mall munchies.

"You've been with the judge for what? Three months now?" Haberman queries, gazing salaciously at a scantily-clad mannequin in the window of Victoria's Secret.

"Thereabouts."

"And so far you've affirmed the conviction in every criminal case you've written, right?" He forces a smile as he says this, and we walk on.

"Yeah."

"And now you think this Hinton case ought to be reversed, right?"

"Yeah, I do. What do you think?"

"I don't know. You could be right."

"The judge practically ordered me to affirm it. What should I do?"

"Do whatever the judge wants."

"But you're the one who says we're accountable to a higher power."

"We are. But our job is to play devil's advocate to the judge, not tell him how to decide a case. And when I say we're accountable to a higher power, I mean in what we present to the judge, not in the opinion the judge issues." Without breaking his stride—or his monologue—he sidles over to the frozen-yogurt stand and orders two no-fat strawberry yogurts, our usual. "Our obligation to God is to do everything we can to ensure that justice is done."

"But that puts you between a rock and a hard place, doesn't it? What if your convictions tell you to do one thing and the judge tells you to do the opposite?"

"When it's in the judge's hands, it's out of our hands. If his decision keeps a teenager in prison for the rest of his life, it's his heart that's going to carry that burden, not yours."

"But what if you know you're right and you think, well, if I don't convince the judge a terrible injustice will result?"

"Do you think he doesn't know the law? Do you think he doesn't read the briefs?"

I let him pay for the frozen yogurt, and we stroll to a bench overlooking the mall's three stories of shopping. "I don't know how you can keep doing this after seven years."

"Why? It's better than being a lawyer. I don't have clients to hassle with, no billable-hour requirement to make, and I don't have to win any cases. All I have to do is research the law and write opinions for the judge. What could be nicer?"

"Yes . . . but it's like . . . never having the responsibility—or the power—to make the decision yourself. To affect someone's life. To do justice. To do *something*. You assist the judge, but you're insulated from the really hard part, which is being accountable."

"But that's bullshit." He stabs his spoon into his yogurt. "My job is to provide the judge with the tools he needs to do his job. There's nothing wrong with that."

I bury my spoon likewise and turn to him. "There's nothing wrong with doing that for a year, but for a guy like you to make a career of kissing the judge's ass is a tragedy. You talk to me about being responsible to a higher power. But you don't mean God, Larry, you mean your paycheck. You say it's our job to play the devil's advocate, but you wouldn't contradict the judge if your life depended on it."

He picks up his spoon and licks it slowly. "That's not true. I present him with my ideas, and if he thinks differently, I don't make a pest of myself."

"In other words, you take the path of least resistance."

"Nonsense."

"You just pucker up and kiss his moldy ass."

He laughs. "I do not."

We are silent for a moment, then he says, "You've got to understand that being a judge means weighing all kinds of competing interests. It's not just a matter of doing what the law requires. It's a political job. The judges on the court of appeals are appointed by the governor, and to get that appointment you've got to be active in the governor's party. In Judge Albertson's case, that means the Republican party, and you can be damn sure the judge had to kiss acres of Republican ass to get his job."

"What a delightful thought."

"And those obligations don't stop once a judge is sworn in. Let's be real. A judge is a politician like any other, and a judge is not going to let the party down."

"What are you saying?"

"I'm saying you, as a clerk, only get to see a small piece of a very big picture. Your job is to do what the judge tells you to do, regardless of whether you think it's right or wrong."

"I don't know if I can do that."

He puts his hand on my shoulder and smiles. "There's an old Yiddish saying, 'If you insist long enough that you're right, you'll be wrong.'"

"What the hell does that mean?"

"It means, there's a point when the insistence itself makes you wrong, whether or not you're right. It has to do with hubris, being too proud to back down."

"That's idiotic. If you're right, you're right."

"And you're so full of yourself you can't imagine that you might be wrong."

"No," I say weakly. "I just want . . . the right ending. I want there to be justice for this defendant."

"To quote another Yiddish proverb, 'In this world, we have the law. If you want justice, you have to wait.'"

I wake up late on Saturday, as I always do, and I stumble naked to the kitchen to start a pot of coffee before showering. I am standing at the coffeemaker, dumping measures of ground coffee into the filter, when I see a gray-haired head bobbing beneath my kitchen window. I jump, startled, and drop the coffee can to the kitchen floor.

Suddenly Carl Hinton looks up through my window, panics at the sight of me, and disappears.

I throw on my robe and peek out the back door, but he is gone. I see that the flower bed under my kitchen window has been cleared of weeds and is covered with mulch.

After showering, I walk over to his place. I find him sitting on his back porch, the *Standard* spread open on the floor in front of him.

"Good morning," I say.

"And good morning to you," he says, his color deepening.

"Thanks for all you did in my back flower beds," I say. "When I asked for your help, I didn't mean for you to go ahead and work on my place."

He glances up at me. "I tell you, I'm happy to do it. I work my own bit of property so much, I do the same things over and over again just to keep busy. I'm happy to have another bit of earth to get my fingers into, and if you wouldn't mind, I'd be happy to work on the place for you."

"That would be wonderful," I say, and I reach out my hand to shake his, as to seal the agreement. "And I'd pay you, of course."

"No, no," he says, shaking my hand. "I could pay you for the pleasure of it."

"No," I say. "I must give you something."

"Well," he says slowly. "There is something you could do. I've got a grandson who's in some trouble, and I sure could use some advice from a lawyer."

9

As he makes coffee, I sit at his kitchen table and stare into its pink Formica top. I have never been in the home of a black person before, and I am ashamed by my sense of wonder at how much it is like the home I grew up in.

It is a home suffused with religiosity. There is a crucifix on the kitchen wall, and through the kitchen door I can see a larger crucifix on the living room wall, above an upright piano. A sampler next to the kitchen telephone reads, THIS IS GOD'S KITCHEN; I JUST COOK HERE. Even the smell of the house, sweet and woody, is churchlike.

He turns from the coffee machine and smiles at me, waiting, again, for me to give speech to my thoughts. I try to improvise an explanation of why I cannot offer him legal advice.

I tell him that because I work for the state, I am bound to provide my services to the state only.

He shrugs. "I'm not looking for a lawyer. I've had enough of those."

And so I ask: "What kind of trouble is your grandson in?"

"He's incarcerated," he says firmly. "The boy is in jail. If you'd been around this city two years ago, you would have heard about it. He was convicted of killing an old woman because she wouldn't give up her money."

He brings two mugs of coffee to the table and proceeds silently to apply butter to a stack of thick pieces of white toast. When he is done he brings the toast to the table with a handful of napkins and he sits down and he tells me his grandson's story.

"His momma and papa separated shortly after he was born. They was never really married anyway. His father is my son John, and he's somewhere in California, or so they say. His mother lived here for a while with Dexter and her other son, Joe, by some other man. Now I'm just waitin' and prayin' for a miracle. It's been two years since he was arrested—and he's spent most of that time in the Boys' School. Can you imagine the horror of that place? You cannot. You have to see it."

He stands, his face tight with worry, then paces the kitchen, pausing to straighten the toaster, the sugar bowl, the blender, and other items on the counter, which is already unnervingly neat.

"Ten years old when he went in there. Just a ten-year-old deaf child. How do you think bein' in that place changes a child? What do you think he's like now? You know how a dog gets when he's been mistreated all his life? What a scroungy, mean thing he be? Well, that's what this boy has become. He wasn't like that before. He was a bright kid, for all his problems. He got deaf when he was just three or so. Some fever, now, I forget the name of it, but he learned sign language and was doin' just fine at the deaf school—you know the place, up on Cambridge Avenue? They are wonderful people up there—they loved Dexter and took good care of the boy."

He stops moving for a moment and looks at me with a terrible sadness in his eyes. "It's here—in this house—that things went wrong. It was that other boy, Joe. He was a wild one. Left school. Didn't work. Stole from me. Was in and out at all hours, like a stray cat. It was him that turned the boy wrong, if it was true, even, that the boy done what they said he done. I don't believe it, frankly, myself, as I say. But the boy made a confession, and how you gonna go up against that? *I* know the boy lied. *I* know he was protecting somebody else. But how you gonna prove that if he insisted he did it?"

"Where's Joe now?"

"I don't know. I haven't seen him, not since before Dexter got arrested."

"Why do you say that Joe turned Dexter wrong?"

"Joe was mixed up in a gang, I know that much. Called themselves the Indy Boyz. What they did and what made them a gang I don't know. Maybe it was because they had nothin' else. All I know is, Dexter wanted nothin' so much as to be one of those Indy Boyz. He'd go on about how 'bad' they was, how 'down.' Now, I don't have cable TV here, I won't pay for what I can pull out of the air, and I don't need the rest of that crap. So for some years now, ever since he was maybe five he'd go with Joe to the homes of Joe's friends to watch TV, 'cause they got cable, and Dex would watch videos with them for hours. Didn't matter that he couldn't hear it. He loved to watch. Then he belonged to them. Like a kind of mascot, a little puppy for them. He dressed differently, all baggy and sloppy. His hair got wild, with the cornrows and braids on half his head and all. And he talked some trash talk that I could not understand. It came from the rap music, of course, and his signing got to be like the way they dance on those videos—all rockin' back and forth and cuttin' the air with their hands. Well, he had that down all right. He raised it to a new height—finger talkin' and rappin' and dancin' all in one."

I ask Carl if he knows sign language.

"Some. About enough for Dexter, most times. He can read lips some, he been doin' that since I can remember, and when it's important I write it down for him. And I can figure out what he's signin' well enough, when he sticks to English."

He rubs his hand over his face and breathes hard. I can see him working hard to keep the corners of his mouth from collapsing.

"When Dex was arrested, I thought I'd go out of my mind. I couldn't believe it. He was a good boy, not like those others. And when he admitted that he'd done it—you could've blown me over. I did not believe it. Still don't. So I got a lawyer for Dex, a man I had a good deal of faith in—before I hired him. This lawyer—his name's Sawhill, Ralph Sawhill—he's a black man with an office in Broadripple. He was an important man in this town back in the sixties. He defended a couple of local Black Panthers who got into trouble, and he filed suit against the city to enforce desegregation. But he's old now, maybe too old to care. I didn't see it then—I was a damn trusting fool—but he thought Dexter was guilty. Always did. And he was just goin' through the motions."

He glares at me. "I hope you never be that kind of lawyer. He didn't even try to get the confession thrown out. So after the jury heard it, that was all she wrote. The trial was over."

I look at him sympathetically. I cannot speak, and he seems to recognize that.

"Now the case is up on appeal. I was so disgusted I didn't want to see any more lawyers. So I did all the work myself. Studied the law, wrote the brief. The librarian at the law school helped me. Praise God for the kindness of people."

He smiles and touches my shoulder. "And I thank God for your kindness too."

"I'm sorry for what's happened to Dexter," I tell him. "But I can't help you with legal advice. It would be against the rules of my job."

He shrugs. "It's okay. I guess maybe I just needed to talk about it."

"I'm happy to listen," I say.

"Well, you could do me one favor," he says. "I don't have a car, so I've been taking the prison shuttle service out to the Boys' School every few days to see Dexter. Their driver quit on 'em and I been hopin' to get out to see Dexter next Saturday."

He grins and he touches my shoulder again. "Now it would do Dexter a world of good to see a new face come to visit him, a woman like yourself; it might give him hope. I'd be most appreciative if you could maybe come with me, drive me."

"Ahh, I don't—"

"And I tell you, I see a very beautiful spring at your house. All kinds of bulbs comin' up, and forsythia, lily of the valley, hostas, ferns . . ."

10

Big-boned women are wise women, having suffered for our size and been branded as outcasts ever since our earliest school days. Bigger than the biggest boy in class, by nature stronger than most men and any woman but a big-boned woman, we do not fit the conventional expectation. We exceed it. And so we know something about suffering.

We are wise fools.

Our knowledge of pain, our big hearts and brains, and our big bodies form a creature that acts despite knowing better and breaks things by using too much force.

So I drive Carl to see Dexter. It is beyond me to say no. And how can I pass up the opportunity to see the defendant himself, to see in the flesh the character whose fate I may hold in my hands? What's the harm?

In-denial Lumsey.

The prison shuttle service is a storefront near the corner of Twenty-ninth Street and Anderson. On windows of opaque milky-white glass are the words USE WHAT GOD GIVES YOU MINISTRIES, INC. hand-stencilled in black.

We drive past it on our way to the far-west side of town.

Carl, sitting in the passenger seat of my pickup, says, "They got to get themselves a driver. Lot of people depend on that service."

As we drive west, the city gives way to mile after mile of new residential development. Indianapolis is a boomtown here, and I recognize the walled enclaves as the place where I might have or should have lived.

Further west the development dries up, and the land looks poorer, the growth sparse, the soil lean. There are signs indicating the approach to our destination, the Indiana Boys' School, a correctional facility for juvenile offenders, and then from behind a tall stand of oak it abruptly emerges, brick walls topped with barbed wire, lookout compartments studding the corners.

The guard at the gatehouse, a powerful-looking, balding young black man, looks across me to Carl and reaches in over my lap to shake Carl's hand.

Carl knows the protocol, so I follow him through the sign-in, the ID check, the metal detectors, the march down gleaming corridors, the lining up with the other visitors—a group of about fifteen of us waiting for our prisoners to be summoned to the various visiting rooms. Because Dexter is one of the youngest prisoners, Carl tells me, we have the privilege of seeing him privately.

The room is clean and spare and small. It is empty but for a rectangular wood veneer table with chrome legs, at which the boy is sitting when we arrive, and there are six chairs. The floor is speckled black linoleum, the walls are beige, the ceiling is acoustic tile. There is no window in the room. The room is cold.

He is a child. He appears older than the photograph impressed upon my mind—there has been a lengthening of his limbs and neck and a thinness to his face, but he has not yet, not by far, broken into adolescence.

As he watches us approach he waits motionlessly—mostly scared, I think, but also angry, defiant, cool. By this time he has been incarcerated for nearly a year and a half. I wonder to what extent he has been socialized into the culture of the reformatory, crushed by it, and the closer I get to him the better I can see in his large eyes the impenetrable look of one who has been damaged.

He stands. He is wearing a dark-blue set of work clothes, which looks like a Cub Scout uniform without badges.

He signs something to Carl, who goes around the table and embraces the boy expansively from behind, hugging him tightly. The boy cringes, but he touches his grandfather's hands wrapped around his chest. His eyes flicker, he glances stealthily at me. When his grandfather releases him, he looks shaky, like a calf, and sits quickly.

"Dexter, this is a friend of mine, Miss Lumsey," Carl says, signing with surprising fluency as he speaks. "She's a neighbor of ours. Lives in the Johnsons' old place."

I lean over the table and extend my hand to him. "Hi, Dexter. I'm glad to meet you."

He accepts my hand, permits me to squeeze his hand once, then pulls his hand away.

"Miss Lumsey is a lawyer," Carl says, adding quickly, "Not our lawyer. But she's been kind enough to help me figure out what to do next if this appeal doesn't work out."

Dexter looks at me and signs laconically, shrugging.

" 'Just what I need, another liar,' " Carl translates. "It's his little joke. He understands the sounds of words, somehow. Always making puns. I think he used to study the dictionary. Lord, I swear it's true. To see how the pronunciations might match the words."

I nod. "Remarkable."

"So how you feelin', Dexter?"

Dexter shrugs.

"We'll be hearing something soon about the appeal. I have hope. And I have faith. The lord forgives many things, but not a lack of faith."

Dexter frowns, then signs. Carl murmurs, " 'Here, hope is only allowed during visitors' hours. And there ain't no faith in nothing.' "

Carl breathes dispiritedly. "So what they got you doin' this week?"

Dexter lifts his hands and signs as if weary of the effort. " 'Just school, Pop'—he calls me Pop—'it's just that them other niggers'— how I hate that word, and now he uses it all the time—'are so damn dumb.'—Dumb, that's another one of his favorite words." Dexter signs again. " 'I want to get the f—' "—Carl shakes his head—"Don't use that word, Dexter. He says he wants to get the you-know-what out of here."

"Dexter," I say firmly, looking squarely at him and trying not to raise my voice, "Would you tell me about that day? About what happened in the car?"

He glares at me. " 'Why should I?' "

"I want to find out if you'd make a good liar."

He smiles, then signs gravely, " 'There are no deaf lawyers.' "

"That's not true," I say. "There are even blind lawyers."

Dexter signs quickly in response, and Carl laughs. " 'And judges,' he says."

"You're right." I laugh. "Tell me what happened."

" 'Joe was driving. Mister E be beside him.' "

"Who is Mr. E, Dexter?"

" 'He's a tall dude. White guy, big shoulders, strong, bald' . . . no, 'shaved.' "

"He was *white?*"

Dexter nods.

"How old?"

" 'Old. Like Joe.' " Carl shakes his head. "That ain't old, Dexter."

"What happened in the car?"

" 'I was in the back. We didn't have no money'—of course—all he had to do was ask me for a few dollars."

Dexter, signing untranslated, hits his grandfather on the forearm like a petulant cat.

"Okay. 'We was looking for . . . a sucker, for something to take— a wallet or a pocketbook. And we see this old lady. Joe turns and I see him say to Mr. E, "Get that old bitch bag." And I didn't do nothin' because I thought he was talkin' to Mr. E. Then he turns all the way around to me and says, again, like he's mad, "Get the bitch's bag." And I stick my head forward, like, who, me? And he nod . . . bug-eyes? . . . then say, "when we stop, just put your hand out and grab the bag." ' "

He stops signing and looks at the table for a moment, as if gathering himself, and Carl echoes the gesture, as if unconsciously translating it for me.

" 'And then,' " they go on, " 'we was there, stopped, before I knew it. I didn't want to do it. So I just sat there. When Joe sees me just sit-tin' there he . . . freaks? Gets real mad. And starts driving again. We go around the block and he says, "You little faggot! You scared? You scared? If you don't do it this time I'm going to beat the—you know what—out of you." Mr. E just sit there. Then we go back. The win-dow was down but it took me too long. I reached out and grabbed the bag and I . . . couldn't help myself . . . I looked up at the lady's face . . . she was scared . . . her mouth was open like she was screaming . . . I pull real hard, then harder because I was scared and I just wanted it to be over. Then I look up at her face again. I look and I see her get shot. One second, she's okay, the next second, she got a hole in her head.' "

Carl edges away from the table and rubs his brow. Dexter glances at him and continues to sign to me while Carl seems to need to calm himself. I cannot understand what Dexter is signing, but he goes on as if I can, making soft mewling and grunting sounds as he does. I watch his fingers and face closely, and fleetingly I believe I understand.

Mostly it is his expression that I am reading—his earnestness. I re-alize at that moment that I believe him. I believe he did not shoot the woman.

I need to know more.

"Dexter," I say, "Who do you think shot the woman? Was it Joe or Mr. E?"

Now, without Carl's translation, I recognize the sign. "Mr. E."

"Why?"

Carl translates, " 'Because if Joe done it, I would have seen his arm come across the front seat.' "

"Did you know that Joe or Mr. E had a gun with him that day?"

He shakes his head and signs emphatically.

"Did you know before you got in the car that you were going to rob someone?"

He shakes his head again, more slowly, and seems to sign "no."

"Are you sure?"

He taps Carl on the arm and signs slowly, " 'We needed some money. I didn't know how we were going to get it. Maybe we were going to go to one of Joe's friends and get some. Maybe Joe took Pop's bank card' "—and here Carl pauses, speaking each word slowly, incredulously—" 'and would try to get some from the bank machine.' Good lord."

Dexter pauses. " 'But after we got to the car, I knew. He said we would steal from somebody. But he didn't say I would be the one had to do it.' "

"When did you know you would be the one?"

" 'When he turned around and told me to grab the lady's bag.' "

I nod.

"That's the truth of it," Carl says. "The boy only gave the confession he did because Joe threatened him."

Dexter taps Carl on the arm and signs excitedly. Carl watches him quizzically for a moment, then shrugs. "He says you should talk to Owedia Braxton. Owedia was Dexter's teacher at the deaf school, and she interpreted at the trial. Dexter speaks with her often. She probably knows more about the case than anyone. And she's a fine young woman."

Dexter signs gracefully, eyes flashing.

" 'And pretty, too,' he says."

We stand, about to leave Dexter, when Carl's hands and arms suddenly break into motion; his hands move, first one and then the other, as if coiling an invisible rope around each wrist, and then the wrists move apart and jerk to a stop, as if pulling that rope tight. As

Carl pretends to strain against the rope I see that it is a chain, and in an instant he has broken it and thrust his hands up, free. Dexter repeats the gesture perfunctorily, discouragement clouding his face. The two embrace quickly, I shake Dexter's hand, and we are gone.

In the cab of my pickup, Carl can't stop talking. He is not talking to me, but to someone who isn't there—I can't tell if it's God or his wife or another spirit—and the words he babbles are curses and prayers and moans of horror. I cannot speak at all. After a time I see that he is crying, quietly at first, but then, seemingly overcome with despair, he buries his face in his hands and sobs outright. I pull over, stop the truck, and put my hand on his shoulder.

"That boy is so good, so good," he says, his voice gaining strength. "And it makes me so damn *angry* to see him locked up there like that, his youth stolen, his God-given potential wasted!" He takes a handkerchief from his pants pocket and wipes his eyes delicately, then blows his nose.

I remove my hand from his shoulder and put the truck in gear.

"And I miss him so much," he goes on. "If you'd only known how different my house was when he was there! Hell, not just my house—the whole neighborhood! Everybody loved that boy; and him being deaf, they showed the kindness of noticing him, watching out for him, being his ears. And he paid them back with his joy! He was an angel for us, that boy."

His use of the word *angel* brings a rush of fear across my skin as an image of that word, written in his brief, flashes in my mind.

As if reading my mind, Carl asks me if I think there is any hope that his appeal will succeed.

"Generally, it depends on two things," I tell him coolly, and I rattle off the standard: "First, whether there were legal mistakes made at trial resulting in it not being fair, and second, whether there was enough evidence presented to support the conviction."

"What happens if we lose?"

"You can apply for transfer to the Indiana Supreme Court. They have the choice whether or not to take the case."

"And if they don't take it?"

"You can appeal to the United States Supreme Court."

"In Washington?"

"Yes."

"Isn't that awfully expensive?"

"Yes, and your chances of getting the case heard are minuscule."

"Then this is our only hope."

"It's your best hope," I tell him.

11

On Monday morning, I return to my desk to find the box containing Dexter's case on a corner of my desk, and I am afraid to touch it.

Suddenly, everything has changed. Now I understand why judges must recuse themselves from cases where they have a personal connection.

I have met the defendant, and I am convinced of his innocence.

Shit.

I remind myself that Dexter's guilt or innocence is irrelevant to the question the judge must decide, which is whether Dexter received a fair trial. The judge thinks he did; I think he did not. Meeting Dexter hasn't changed that. What's changed is—now I *care.*

Judges can't care.

It is not the big-boned way to avoid confrontation, but I'll do it in the interest of a greater goal—in this case, the hope that if I stall long enough I can find a way to change the judge's mind. So I go to the shelf and from the stack of file folders by the Indiana Code I pick up another case—a huge utility regulatory case with a trial record of more than eight thousand pages. It will be distraction enough, and the effort is made entirely worthwhile when Haberman catches sight of me lugging the record to my desk.

"My God," he gasps, "Are you crazy? That'll take you a good month to finish!"

"A chance I'll have to take," I say.

"What about the Hinton case?"

"I need a break."

He smiles. "Having trouble reconciling your sense of justice with the demands of the law?"

"Yeah." I drop the record on the floor next to my desk; it lands with a thud that sets the whole room vibrating. "Tell me, Larry, have you ever reversed a criminal conviction?"

"Yeah, maybe three or four times."

"In seven years?"

"Yes. And it was a fight every time."

"Oh." I feel my whole body start to wilt.

"But don't let that discourage you," he says cheerfully. "It's fun when it happens."

I go on, and I try with some success to avoid thoughts of what I have labelled in my mind "my Dexter problem." I shuttle between the State House and my house, occasionally catching glimpses of Carl working in his yard as I pull into my driveway.

Over the course of a few days, the shrubs and grounds around my little house are transformed while I am at work. Debris is removed, the curved edges of future flower beds now wrap gently around the house, the surface has been mulched, and in some places stems and small bunches of green are visible above the mulch.

Carl is never at my home when I arrive, and I wonder if he knows that I am avoiding him.

I do not know what to do. In between work on the utilities case I continue to research the issue of meaningful consultation, looking for a way either to do in good conscience what the judge has demanded I do or to change his mind. I search all fifty states and the federal circuits for a flexible application of the "meaningful consultation" requirement. What I find only bolsters my sense that we must reverse Dexter Hinton's conviction.

On the Thursday following my visit with Dexter, I see Carl sitting on his front steps leafing through the *Standard*. It is unseasonably warm, a cheerfully sunny afternoon. He waves to me as I drive up my driveway, and I wave back through the window of my pickup.

I park and step out, and I see him fold the paper neatly and bend upward as if to await my strolling toward him across the lawns that separate our homes.

I glance at him for an instant and turn away.

I do not learn that he had something to tell me until later, when the telephone rings, and there is a woman's voice on the other end. It is a young voice, smooth and clean and southern, a voice as rich as heavy cream.

"This is Owedia Braxton," she says, and she tells me before I can respond that Carl had called her and told her that she should meet me to talk about Dexter.

"Yes," I tell her, "I've been giving Carl some informal legal advice."

"Carl needs more than advice," she responds, with an odd emotionality.

"Yes, I know," I say, "but there's little more—"

"All of this . . . is so horrible, and so unjust. I know Dexter is telling the truth. He didn't kill that woman."

I don't know what to say to that.

"If you're a lawyer, why don't you take the case?"

"I can't. I work for the state. It would be a conflict of interest."

"So how can you give Carl advice?"

"I can't. That is, I shouldn't be . . . but—"

"What about the appeal?" she demands. "Do you think there's a chance?"

"I don't know," I tell her. "I mean, of course there's a chance. Carl has raised some good arguments. But . . . the chances for success on appeal are very small, even under the best circumstances."

"Like when you've got a lawyer."

"Right."

In the silence that follows I can hear her breathing loudly, as if she were pulling in air in great draughts, and the sound of her breath is as sonorous and emotion-laden as her voice.

"You were Dexter's teacher," I say.

"Yes," she says, almost sighing.

"Do you still work at the deaf school?"

"Yes." Her voice picks up energy. "The work is rewarding. The children are beautiful, but difficult. Often deafness is not their only trouble. Many have other mental disabilities, learning disorders. And that's only the physical stuff. Some of the kids come from terrible situations."

I hold the phone in silence. She goes on.

"Dex was one of the lucky ones. He has his grandfather."

Again there is silence as she waits for me to speak. She goes on.

"He wasn't so lucky with his brother."

There is something in the dead ends of her speech that forbids me to respond.

"Or his mother or father."

Then I say, "He was lucky with you."

"Maybe. And maybe with you."

"Maybe."

"So when am I going to meet you?"

"How about dinner, say, Friday?"

A silence. Then she says, "How about church, say, Sunday?"

I laugh apprehensively.

"It's the Lord's Light Christian Church at Forty-fourth and University. Ten-thirty A.M. Carl will be there."

"Wonderful," I say.

"Are you a Christian woman?" she says.

"I don't know. I was raised Southern Baptist, but I don't know now."

"Come Sunday," she says. "Hear Rev. Jones. And maybe you'll find out."

It has been seven years since I set foot in a church, since I left Unity for college in nearby New Albany, Indiana. But that voice has gotten under my skin, and church is as good a place as any to meet Owedia Braxton.

I park at the side of the sprawling brick church building. In the narrow asphalt lot, families emerge from their cars, gathering themselves, the men putting on jackets, the women smoothing down the wrinkles in their dresses and turning their attention to the children.

A large woman in an aquamarine dress and fox throw bends uncomfortably to adjust the lace collar on a toddler's white dress.

A gray-haired man in a black suit and an African pillbox-style hat wipes the chrome trim of his Cadillac with his handkerchief as his wife, wearing a similar hat but dressed in a colorful caftan with gold threads running through it, chats with a young woman in a blue blazer and beige pleated skirt.

Everyone is black.

Owedia had told me to look for her in the choir and to meet her in the "fellowship room" after the service. "I'm easy to find," she had said, "I'm the only blonde in the choir. Look for me, and I will look for you."

I had not gotten the joke. It had not occurred to me, even after she had told me that Carl would be here, that she and I would be the only white people attending.

I sit in the last row on the left side of the church's middle aisle.

This is not like the church I was raised in. There is no picture of Jesus, no scenes from the Gospel, no figure of Christ on the crucifix. Hanging vertically along the wall to my right are colorful banners bearing the words FAITH, FIDELITY, RIGHTEOUSNESS, and LONG-SUFFERING. On the left wall is a flag bearing the outline of the continent of Africa within the outline of the state of Indiana.

The room fills slowly. It is a supermarket-sized sanctuary, large enough for thousands. A small army of ushers in white suits and white gloves patrols the aisles, distributes hymnals, officiously crowds people down toward the front of the church.

I see Carl move down the aisle on the right side of the church, carried along by a throng of women in bright shades of pink, salmon, lime, and violet. I wait for him to turn so that I might catch his eye, but he is pressed forward by the crowd.

The five-piece band to the left of the pulpit begins a soft and steady beat, the piano and bass vamping infectiously, and suddenly the air is charged with a joyous spirit. In a moment, the congregation is seated, the ushers have assumed stations at the top of the aisles, and a trio of dark-suited men appear at the pulpit. There is the distant sound of hands clapping, and the floor begins to vibrate under my feet.

A moment later, the doors at the back of the church burst open and the choir—a motley parade of about forty, each dressed differently, some in African-style dress, others in church clothes, but all with banded kente cloths around their shoulders—comes roaring down the right aisle in twos, swaying and smiling as they move swiftly toward the stage.

I scan the choir for the white woman. There is none. But as they move across the stage and distribute themselves in front of two semicircles of chairs, one a step higher than the other, I see her.

Her hair is a short, nappy, neon blond halo around a face that is the color of dry clay soil, a smudging of brown and black. Her nose is broad and African, and there is much strength and grace in her appearance as she sings, her head rocking vigorously. And all of her is utterly beautiful.

I feel my face flush as I watch her. I am embarrassed by my presumption that she had been white; and then I am frightened by the thought that I am the only white in this place.

The choir starts to sing "Jesus Met the Woman at the Well," and the congregation joins in. More men in dark suits appear on stage, busily engaged in mysterious preparations. The music intensifies, and then some. I am clapping and moving now too, moving with her, astonished by the energy in the room.

A large balding black man with gleaming eyeglasses, evidently the Reverend Jones, appears at the left side of the stage and moves slowly toward the pulpit, seemingly isolated, unaffected by the ecstatic rhythm of the band, choir, and congregation.

He takes his time. He stands at the pulpit and looks around him, nods to the other dark-suited men, nods a greeting toward the congregation. He smiles at the choirmaster, a tall, graceful man standing inconspicuously at the edge of the stage. When the preacher smiles, he reveals a keyboard of gold and white teeth, and that smile is evidently a cue for the choirmaster, who raises his hands, fingers spread, and conducts the choir into a long cadenza of cries and devotions.

When it is done we applaud wildly, and already my hands are aching.

Owedia Braxton throws her head back and laughs prettily, her hand grasping the hand of the woman next to her.

Rev. Jones leans forward and slips the cordless microphone from its stand beside the pulpit. Holding it just below his lower lip, he says softly, "Good morning, brothers and sisters."

The voice is a nasal mumble, dusty and wet, like a summer sun shower, and it is soothing beyond belief. It is not the least terrifying, not like the preacher I grew up under, a wild-haired man named Brother Jesse, whose steely voice carried the constant threat of eternal damnation.

Pacing slowly behind the pulpit, Rev. Jones announces upcoming church activities, welcomes new members, offers congratulations on births and marriages and condolences on deaths. Then he says: "And this is the ninety-second week that we have seen our beloved child Dexter Hinton incarcerated for the evil deed of another. We pray with our brother Carl that there may soon be an end to the child's suffering, to Carl's suffering, and to the worry and anxiety we have all felt over Dexter. Amen."

The congregation responds with hushed *amens* and the organist begins softly to play a sustained, shifting, bluesy chord. In a moment the choir is on its feet singing "Home in That Rock" and then we are on our feet too, and I am singing too, this familiar gospel tune from my childhood.

It is only then that I remember the judge mentioning Rev. Jones as one of the activists who had been involved in Dexter's case.

Of course.

And now I see myself standing in Dexter's church, befriending his grandfather and praying for his release. The thought of how much I have betrayed by coming here sickens me, nearly sends me fleeing.

Yet I do not go. I stand trembling and watch *her*. I am feeling set up, used, despite knowing that they have no idea how much I am bound up in Dexter's fate. But I must speak with her, if only to connect that voice with that face, and to be close enough to study her.

"No man can serve two masters," Rev. Jones begins, and there is a palpable settling back in the congregation, a making ready to receive the preacher's words. "For either he will hate the one, and love the other; or else he will hold to the one, and despise the other. Ye cannot serve God and mammon.

"What does it mean that no man can serve two masters? It means you cannot love God and love money. That's what *mammon* means—money, wealth, greed. But mammon is just another word for *sin*. And there are a million words for sin. There's temptation! No one is ever tempted to do good! You are tempted to sin. And what are some sins? We all know the familiar sins—lying, cheating, stealing, murdering, taking drugs, being unfaithful, being unkind—unkindness is a sin!

"Temptation! No one is ever tempted to love Jesus! When you come to Jesus you come because your heart has been opened by God! You come because you have a hunger for wisdom and purity!

"Temptation means you want to do it . . . but you know you shouldn't! Temptation means feeling guilty for wanting something that God has told you is wrong! Temptation means having an angel on one shoulder and a devil on the other!

"Who you gonna listen to? MTV? Or the church?

"Who you gonna obey? Drugs? Or God?

"What path are you going to take? The path of vice? Or the path of righteousness?

"No man can serve two masters. It's as simple as that!

"I'll tell you what you should do. You should serve one master. And that master's name is Jesus.

"Now some of you may have a problem with that! You may have a problem with the very idea of serving any master. Lord, we know what that's about. Like they say on TV—Been there! Done that! But there is a master we all must serve, black and white, old and young, man and woman. And that master's name is Jesus!

"Praise Jesus! Praise Jesus!"

The fellowship room is a wide linoleum-floored church basement, warm and crowded with scents of bodies and perfumes and coffee. I push my way toward the tables bearing coffee and pound cake, apologizing and smiling insipidly. When I reach the table she is there, her back to me; the short hair, brilliantly blond, tapered down the back of her head, is a shocking sight against the skin of her neck and shoulders.

I walk to her side and I gaze at her profile as she pours herself coffee from a silver pot.

When she turns, she is startled by the sight of me and nearly drops her coffee. I reach out to steady the cup as she says, "Hi."

"Hi," I say, "Owedia?"

"Yes," she says slowly, squinting, and hands me the coffee. "Are you Nora?"

"Yes, hello." I smile; she looks distraught.

"Forgive me," she says. "I wasn't expecting someone so young." And, it is clear, someone so white.

"Well . . . I just got out of law school."

She laughs softly and turns to pour herself coffee. "Forgive me again. I have the awful habit of speaking without thinking. Or while I'm thinking. It's a brain-mouth thing."

"No apology needed."

She leads me to the back of the room, where we lean against the stage and sip the coffee.

"Carl told me that he took you to see Dexter."

"Yes. Or I took him."

"Uh-huh. I've taken him a few times. He hates to use the shuttle."

"Ah."

"He's so lonely without Dexter. The church is all he's got now."

"People in the neighborhood seem to care about him."

"Yes, but it's not like family. Or church. Carl is the one who introduced me to this place, you know. Now this is my family, here."

"Where are you from?"

"Terre Haute. Ever been?"

"No."

"It's awful. It's a little town with big-city problems. Lots of crime, drugs, poverty, and everything that goes with it. How about you?"

"I'm from Unity."

"Never heard of it."

"It's in southeastern Indiana. About a half hour north of Louisville. A farm town."

"Uh-huh."

I gaze at her, unable to restrain myself from examining her hair; it is a startlingly fake blond, incredibly at odds with her quiet confidence and intelligence.

"It's the hair, right?" She grimaces. "Last week I made the mistake of having my hair done at the Indianapolis School of Cosmetology. I was bored with the way I looked, right? I wanted to save myself some money, right?" She touches her hair gently. "I guess it wasn't fair of me to tell you to look for the blonde. I'm sorry."

"That's really all right," I say. "Your hair is . . . truly awesome."

"Thanks," she says, looking away. "So why did Carl want me to meet you? Does he think I can tell you something about the case?"

"It was Dexter who suggested it. And Carl says you know more about the case than anyone."

"I know Dexter is innocent." She looks at me frankly. "I know he was in that car tagging along behind his big brother like any kid would. Except that Dexter's brother is evil. Truly. He is everything that is evil. He uses drugs. He commits crimes. And he's fathered and abandoned at least one child I know of."

"Did you know Dexter's parents?"

"I knew Diana Baker when Dexter first started at the school. She was like Joe. Completely irresponsible. There were times when she would pick Dexter up drunk. Other times stinking, unbathed. Other times she wouldn't show up and I'd have to bring Dexter home."

Her dark eyes gleam sadly, and she goes on, her voice breaking, "He had a well-ordered, positive life after Diana left. He had the school. He had this church and all the people here who love him. He had his grandfather, who adores him. And he had me. Now Joe has destroyed all that. And destroyed Dexter."

"Maybe not," I say hopelessly.

"How? What are you going to do about it?"

"I don't know yet," I tell her. "I will do what I can to help Carl."

She looks out toward the crowd standing with coffee cups, chatting in clusters. Children chase each other in the open spaces, breaking the din with their laughter.

"Dexter loved to come to church," she says quietly. "He loves Rev. Jones. We all do. But Dexter liked to sit close. And read Rev. Jones's lips. When he was here I would translate the sermon for him. He's an incredibly bright child. And I think his love of words, of language, comes from this place. You know how a preacher takes a few words from the Bible and holds them up in front of you? And twists them and turns them so you can see them from every angle? And explores the many meanings of those words so you can see how important they are to you?"

"Yes."

"Dexter understood that. And he loved to play with words the way preachers do. He loved the idea of puns, which is rare for a deaf child. He could make puns. He made sign-language puns, but he also made homonym puns. Though he is profoundly deaf, he understands sound. Vestigially, perhaps. But he does."

Abruptly, she takes my right hand and holds the palm upward. "Do this," she says, smiling, and releasing my hand, she moves her own hand under her chin and forward.

I imitate her clumsily.

"Now do this," she says, and she moves her hand in a similar pattern, but more forcefully. "In ASL, the first sign means to sing loud, like an opera singer. The second sign means to throw up." She laughs. "I was watching opera once on TV when Dexter came up with that one. Funny how a kid can hate opera without ever hearing it."

"Who is teaching Dexter now?" I ask. "They don't have deaf education at the boys' school, do they?"

"There's a teacher who comes in three times a week for half a day. Mrs. Martell. She used to be a special-ed teacher in the Indianapolis public schools. She's competent, but she and I don't get along particularly well."

"Why is that?"

She gazes at me sadly and says, "Mrs. Martell doesn't love Dexter. She thinks he's guilty, and it's so obvious in the way she treats him that she regards him as a criminal." Owedia sighs. "I'm sure Dexter realizes this, and it must be so painful for him. It's painful for me even to think about it."

She glances up quickly, and following her gaze I see Carl coming toward us, trailed by the group of women, all in their fifties and sixties, that had surrounded him in the sanctuary. There is an odd look in his eyes: reluctance or embarrassment or fear, I don't know which.

He shakes my hand, exchanges a kiss with Owedia, then sets about introducing me to each of the six women around him. It is clear that these are the women who get things done at this church, who organize the church suppers and teach the Sunday school and put flowers in front of the altar. As I am shaking hands, I hear one of the women whisper, "This is the lawyer who's helping Carl with the appeal."

I smile, heat rising in my face, and I talk about the neighborhood and the stunning quality of our homes. Then one silver-haired woman comes right out and says it: "So what do you think is going to happen with our Dexter?"

All around us, conversation stops. I glance at Carl, who winces, pained, his brow creased with mortification. I am about to mutter, "I don't know," when Carl breaks in. "Now, how do you expect her to answer that, Mary? She can't see the future any better than you can!"

Mary turns to him, unruffled. "I just want to understand what might happen," she says. "She's your lawyer. She should be able to tell me that."

"She's not my lawyer," Carl says evenly. "She works for the state."

A sixtyish woman with light brown hair presses forward and extends her hand to me. "Miss Lumsey, is it?"

"Yes, Nora Lumsey," I say, shaking her hand.

"I'm Barbara Jones," she says, "I'm Rev. Jones's sister."

I tell her how much I enjoyed the service.

"I think I have some information that may help you," she says. "If you're trying to prove that it wasn't Dexter who killed that woman."

At that, the others withdraw, oddly in concert, as if to free the preacher's sister to speak for all.

12

This past Tuesday," she begins, her hands clasped together in front of her, "I attended a workshop on church interventions in the lives of inner-city youth. I met a man from the Indianapolis police department, a Lieutenant Curtis, who spoke about the street gangs that have proliferated in our town. One such gang is the Indy Boyz, whose members have been involved in car theft, drug dealing, and violent crime for several years now. I have heard that Joseph Baker hung around with several members of the Indy Boyz and that he was probably a member himself."

Owedia and I glance at each other. Barbara goes on. "There is another gang, predominantly white kids from the suburbs, who call themselves the Vipers. For some time now the Vipers and the Indy Boyz have been working for organized crime selling drugs and God knows what else. Members of the Vipers wear a distinctive tattoo on their necks, just behind the ear. It's a tiny coiled snake, looping around like that." With her index finger, she describes the shape in the air. "It looks kind of like a cursive *e.*"

Owedia gasps. I say, "Dexter talks about a 'Mr. E' being in the car with him and Joseph. I thought it was something he made up, some kind of joke."

"Yes, I've heard about that," she says, "but I don't know. When I have visited Dexter, he talks about a third person being in the car, but he's reluctant to give details. I think he may know who it is, but he's afraid."

"Afraid of what?"

"The gangs. Of someone hurting his grandfather. Or someone hurting him in prison. I think he's saying as much as he feels he can."

Owedia, clearly distressed, gazes earnestly at Barbara and says, "Dexter never said anything to me about a tattoo."

Barbara shrugs and takes Owedia's hands in hers. "I don't know, darlin'," she says. "I'm just passing along the information." She drops one of Owedia's hands and takes one of mine. "I hope you can do something for Carl. And for Dexter. We despair over the awful wasting of their spirits."

As she moves away into the crowd, I see Rev. Jones, standing alone on the other side of the room, watching us, a peculiar consternation clouding his face. Barbara acknowledges him with a tilt of the head, but she does not go to him.

As the fellowship room empties, Owedia suggests to me that we go together to see Dexter. "He may be more forthcoming if we're both there," she says.

"I don't know," I mutter, feeling my face grow warm with a rush of guilt. "Next Saturday looks busy for me."

"See what you can do," she says cheerily, offering me her hand to shake. "Let's go Saturday to see Dexter, and maybe I'll see you here on Sunday."

I admit it, I'm scared. Even big-boned women have their limits, and finding myself so swiftly recruited to Dexter's cause by Owedia and these church women has pushed me to mine. For me to join their investigation of Dexter's case would be beyond foolishness. It would be career suicide.

If I am to do anything for Dexter, I promise myself, it must be through the law.

———

"Meeting you has given me more hope than anything that's happened since Dexter's trial. Meeting you makes me believe that God had a purpose in bringing us together."

It is Owedia's voice on the phone that very evening, sliding around my mind like a drug, soothing and irritating at once.

She is thanking me for something, but I don't know what I've done.

I tell her, for the sake of politeness, "I enjoyed meeting you. And I thought the service and your singing were absolutely beautiful."

"And the sermon. Did you like the sermon?" She asks this like we're kids who've just seen a play together.

"Yes." It's all I can say.

"Rev. Jones is really a very shy man, but he loves Dexter and he's working to set Dexter free."

"Yes."

"I wanted to take you over to meet him, but I . . . I know how uncomfortable that makes him."

"Oh, that's all—"

"His sister does the talking for him."

"Oh."

"Can I ask you a question about the law?"

And now I see her laying in a bed, her legs crossed, the phone cradled between her ear and a pillow, with all the time in the world for chatting. I am standing in my kitchen, leaning on the counter with no place to sit. It is 10:22 P.M. and I am ready for bed.

But it's been a long time since I've been on the phone with another woman and just talked. And talked. So I slip down to the floor and get comfortable.

"Sure. Though I have to tell you that I'm not offering you legal advice in any professional capacity. You must not act on anything I say."

She laughs at that. "You sound like a lawyer commercial."

"I'm not kidding." I know I sound annoyed, but I can't help it.

"If I think that Dexter is in prison because his lawyer at trial did a bad job, can I do anything about it?"

"Generally, you can do two things. That is, Dexter can. He can appeal the conviction on the grounds of ineffective assistance of counsel. Which means that he was denied his constitutional right to a fair trial because his lawyer was incompetent. It's too late for him to do that now, however, because that argument had to be raised in the initial appeal. The other thing he can do is file a civil action against his lawyer for legal malpractice. But that won't get Dexter out of prison. All it might do is get him some money. But both of those things require Dexter to show that if not for the incompetence of his attorney, he would not have been convicted. If the court finds that there was enough evidence to convict anyway, Dexter loses."

"If it wasn't for his confession, there wouldn't be any evidence."

"Yes . . . that's what Carl told me."

"Wasn't there any way for Dexter's lawyer to keep the jury from hearing it?"

"I don't know. I just don't know enough about it."

We hold our phones silently; Owedia breathes so deeply that I fear for a moment that she's fallen asleep.

"I know Dexter did not get a fair trial," she says finally. "I was there. I saw it all. It was so one-sided, it was like . . ." Her voice trails off morosely.

"Like shooting ducks in a barrel." I finish it for her.

"Yes. Just like that."

Her voice stays with me long after I hang up the phone, its timbre rattling my nerves. I have known her only a day, yet she has invaded my consciousness.

And Christ, I am so in need of a friend, so fucking lonely, to tell the truth, that I won't let myself cut her off. I don't know a soul in this town outside of work and outside of my neighbors; those few friends I made in law school were smart or lucky or adventurous enough to leave the Hoosier heartland for places like Chicago, Albuquerque, San Francisco, New York.

I came here, not because I had to but because it was the place my imagination took me as a child, a fantastic metropolitan place planted in 1821 in the middle of my state, a capitol in the making where there'd been no city before.

But there's no one here for me, not a soul. I had thought for a time that I might live here with Paul, briefly and tempestuously my lover during my second year of law school. But Paul graduated a year before I did and moved to Chicago that June—just for a year, he said, to make some big bucks and pay off his student loans while I finished up.

His calls stopped coming by the time September rolled around.

And it has not hit me, not until now, not until this moment in the silence after putting down the phone, how much I crave a friend.

And I like Owedia, despite the evangelical streak. There is something in the bigness of her voice and the grossness of her blond hair that makes me think that inside her slender body she is a big-boned woman.

She carries, at least, a recessive gene for big-bonedness.

Big-boned women stick their noses where they shouldn't, are curious about everything, aren't afraid to get dirty, like to get dirty. We try too hard, hold too tight, talk too loud.

We are fighters. And I know that if I let her, Owedia will drag me body and soul into her crusade for Dexter Hinton.

On Tuesday night, Owedia calls to tell me that she has made an appointment for tomorrow evening for us to meet with Ralph Sawhill.

"You have to speak with this man if you're going to understand why things went so wrong for Dexter," she implores. "If not for this man's incompetence, Dexter wouldn't be where he is now. You're a lawyer, you'll understand it far better than I can."

I tell her—or try to tell her—that it's impossible, that I can't get that involved.

"Just talk to the man. And then you can tell me what you think and maybe *I* can do something about it."

"I can't. Really. I shouldn't."

"Nora, please. I need you to do this."

Shit.

At six o'clock the next evening, Owedia pulls into my driveway.

"I've never heard of an attorney with evening office hours," I tell her as I fold my body into the tiny passenger side of her Toyota.

"A lot of this guy's clients can't come out during the day," she says. "All he does is defend criminals." A pause, then, "And the falsely accused. He represents a lot of gang members. He's famous for it. When these kids get into trouble their mommas drag them to see lawyer Sawhill."

"Carl said he used to be politically powerful."

"Yes, he used to be. Back when there was political power to be had by a black man."

"What do you mean?"

"Did you ever hear of something called 'Unigov'?"

"That's something to do with the city government, right?"

"Yes, basically." Owedia takes a deep breath. "Back in the sixties, before Unigov, Indianapolis was about half its present size. It was what we now call Center Township, and it had a powerful black political organization. There was talk of a black mayor in those days, and Sawhill would certainly have been a contender.

"But after the election of 1968, the Republicans not only had the mayor's office, they had the majority of the city council, the county council, both houses of the state assembly, and the governor's office, and so the conditions were perfect to do something to put Indianapolis politics into the Republicans' pockets for a long time. The mayor came up with a plan called Unigov to make the entirety of Marion County—meaning Center Township and the white suburbs that surround it like a doughnut—into one political entity. The Unigov plan was passed into law in 1969, and the city council was replaced by a city-county council. And since nearly all the black folks in the county are in Center Township, Unigov added two hundred and fifty thousand white people from the suburbs to the city's population, ending the possibility of a black mayor for this city and ensuring that the city government will forever be dominated by white Republicans."

I have heard this history before, in a dimly-remembered high school Hoosier history class, but Unigov was taught as a model of urban inclusiveness, an efficiency-enhancing allocation of resources, not as a tool of racism.

"And to seal the deal," Owedia continues, "the Unigov plan specifically excluded the public schools from countywide consolidation. That way, the rich white townships of Marion County got to keep their rich white schools, and poor black Center Township . . . it's criminal what they've done."

"I never knew that side of it," I say weakly.

"Well, now you know," Owedia says without bitterness. "Men like Ralph Sawhill fought Unigov, of course, but there was no way to stop it. He still makes his voice heard on community issues, but the wind was taken out of his sails long ago."

"Carl says he's not much of a lawyer."

"He isn't. Unless you're guilty. Because if you're guilty he's got enough connections in the prosecutor's office to get you the best possible plea bargain. Very few of his clients serve time. He plea-bargains ninety-nine percent of his cases, and that's because he hates to go to trial. It's too much work."

"But Carl refused to plea-bargain."

"You got it. It infuriated Sawhill that Dexter insisted on his innocence. Up until the day of the trial Sawhill kept after Carl and Dexter to plea. I think he was so sure they would give in that he went to trial unprepared."

"And what is it exactly you hope to accomplish tonight?"

"I want to ask him about the trial, about why he did certain things. So in case we lose this appeal, we can have something new to say when we take it to the Supreme Court. And having you there, maybe you can translate for me."

Uh-huh.

Sawhill's office is in a run-down strip of stores, a minimall of fifties vintage, north of Broadripple, our town's Left Bank, or so they say. It is nothing like the pictures I've seen of Paris or of Greenwich Village, but it has its coffee bars and pretentious restaurants, jazz clubs, and a gallery or two.

Sandwiched between a barber shop and a Laundromat, Sawhill's office is a storefront with his name in chipped gold lettering on the plate-glass window. Inside, in the dimly-lit waiting room, there is a leather couch and chairs and ashtrays on pedestals. Behind a partition, a light glows brightly.

Owedia raps sharply on the door, disturbing a brass bell hanging on the other side of the glass. A moment later he appears, a stooped man in his seventies—at least—with thick, nearly opaque, glasses.

Yet when he speaks, his voice is vigorous, startlingly clean and crisp.

"Come in," he says, holding the door open for us. "Quickly! It's cold out there."

Owedia and I scurry in and smile at each other at the lawyer's scolding tone.

He leads us back toward the glow behind the partition to where his desk sits swarming with papers. In the center of it an unlit cigar stub rests in a metal ashtray about a foot in diameter. He motions to two molded plastic swivel chairs opposite his desk.

"This is Nora Lumsey," Owedia says as we sit, and I reach out my hand. "She's a friend of mine and Carl's."

Without a word he shakes my hand, then picks up the cigar end and lights it.

"How's Carl?" he says, smiling. "He owes me some money."

"He's not well," Owedia replies. "He had bursitis for a few weeks this fall and couldn't do any yard work."

"That's too bad," he says.

"And of course he's heartbroken over Dexter."

75

"I know." He nods and says, without emotion, "It's a heartbreaking thing." He sucks the cigar hard, then tilts his head back and carefully blows smoke into the air above him. "So what can I do for you, Owedia?"

"I just need some friendly help, Mr. Sawhill, on what to do if Dexter loses the appeal."

"Are you Dexter's lawyer?" he asks, deadpan.

"No."

He turns to me. "Are you Dexter's lawyer?"

"Ahh, no."

"Then you've no business representing Dexter."

Owedia moves forward in her chair and leans toward him. "We just want to help him with the next appeal if we lose. Carl is too stubborn to come here on his own. You know that. And you're more familiar with the case than anyone. If you could just give me some ideas, I'd be grateful."

He examines his cigar, seeming to ponder this for a moment.

"For Dexter's sake," Owedia implores.

"For Dexter's sake!" he explodes, and he pushes himself up out of his chair. "For Dexter's sake! That is a shameful thing to say! Shameful!" He jabs the air with his cigar. "Do you know that if Carl had accepted the plea bargain I'd arranged for that boy, he'd be out of prison by the time he finished high school? Did you know that?"

Owedia replies softly, "No."

"Carl is stubborn, you got that right. He tells me Dexter is innocent when the boy's own story, as credible as could be, is that he shot the woman. Now Carl wanted me to argue about the confession, and I did that. But when a jury hears that a boy gave one story before his grandfather showed up, and another story after, they're gonna think that the boy told the truth to the cops and then lied to his grandpa to save face. How's a boy gonna tell his grandpa he killed some old woman?"

"I believe Dexter did not kill that woman," Owedia says, seething.

"Well, all right. Believe that. The only witness who knows for sure is Joe Baker, and he's not here to help us, is he?"

Owedia is silent.

"I deal with these gang boys and girls every day, child. I stand by them in the police station, and I stand by them in court, and I stand by them in prison, and when they get out I work with 'em to get 'em back into school. It's not much but it's what I do. Yes, I plea a lot of these kids, but I do it only when it's clear it's the best thing for them."

I look at Owedia, whose eyes are fixed on Sawhill's desk, and then I look at him and I watch him talk at her, pacing behind his desk like a preacher:

"And then you get men like Carl, so trapped and so blinded by their belief that God or Jesus or some such is going to come down and save them and put it all right. It's sickening to me, it's so wrong. That man came here and told me there were angels helping his grandson. I laughed at him. I did, I could not help myself, though I can tell you it's no joke.

"What the hell did he need me for if he had angels? Could the angels represent that boy in court?

"And where were these angels when that woman got shot? In the car? In the gun?

"And why didn't that woman have angels looking out for her? Was she bad? Was she a bad woman?

"I've been a lawyer for forty-six years. That's right. And I've seen it all. I defended a mother accused of drowning her own child in the bathtub. Had she done it? Yes. She was deranged, but in ways so cold-blooded it couldn't be seen. The prosecutor was ready to execute her, but no, we arranged for her to be institutionalized for life.

"I was the fourth black lawyer to practice in this town. Do you have any idea how hard that was? Goin' up against racist judges, prosecutors, cops. And not finding it easy to get clients, even among my own people. And who can blame them? If you're going up against the system, you want a lawyer who's a member of the same club the judge goes to. That's the simple truth!"

He sits, puffs once on the cigar, and yawns. "You wanted to talk about Dexter. All right. Carl was upset with me for losing the case and decided to do the appeal himself. I haven't read Carl's brief, so I don't know what he raised. It's a shame he didn't ask me to do it. I've got a law student workin' for me who could've done a wonderful job, cheap."

Owedia lifts her gaze to meet his and says quietly, "Can you think of anything that happened that should have been raised on appeal?"

He shakes his head. "No. No, it's been too long now. I don't remember. And there's no point in torturing yourself over it. If an error at trial is not raised in the initial appeal, you lose it. You can't raise it later. The only thing you can ask the supreme court to look at is whether the court of appeals made a mistake in addressing the errors raised. So you'd best hope Carl did a good job."

Owedia glances at me, despairing.

I ask, "But isn't there any way a new issue can be raised?"

"Well, you can assert ineffective assistance of appellate counsel, but where it's *pro se,* you're gonna have a hard time selling that—you can't ask for reversal on the grounds of your own mistakes. The other way is if you've got fundamental error—that is, if Dexter's constitutional rights were violated. But that's a hard row to hoe, and sad as it is, I do not recall anything in Dexter's case that meets the standard for fundamental error."

Sawhill leans back in his chair and relights his cigar. Owedia and I watch the cigar end glow and fade as he draws on it. I am waiting for Owedia to speak, for someone, even myself, to speak, but I cannot say a word.

Sawhill looks down now at a document on his desk, a pleading of some sort; it is as if he is a doctor who, having delivered bad news, withdraws for a moment to give the family time to absorb the shock.

It is just like that for Owedia. She breathes deeply and resumes her blank stare at the front of Sawhill's desk. I can feel her depression—it radiates from her body like an aura—and I must touch her shoulder and tell her that it's late and we must go.

Driving me home, she says, "I think Carl was wrong about him."

My days consist of combing the record for errors Carl should have raised.

I know I should not do this; my job, the judge has repeatedly told me, is to address the arguments of the parties' counsel. If the case is well briefed, he says, I should not even have to look at the record.

But Dexter's case is not well briefed. The record—and what it may reveal—is the only hope he's got.

I look at the photo lineup, and I read and reread the search warrants and supporting affidavits. So much of the evidence that brought the police to Carl Hinton's home points to Joseph Baker. It is as if, being unable to capture Baker, the cops took Dexter, the next best thing, and built their case around him.

The affidavit supporting the search warrant of Carl's home, sworn to by an Officer Oldham of the IPD, states that Joseph Baker's fingerprints were found throughout the car, along with fingerprints matching those of the car's owner—a man who lives just blocks from Carl's home—and other unidentified prints. It states that a positive match was found in the IPD's computerized fingerprint bank, and that Baker has a string of drug offenses beginning at age twelve.

But Baker's connection to the case ends there. When the search of the home is executed and Dexter is found, from then on it's Dexter Hinton's arrest, Dexter Hinton's trial, Dexter Hinton's conviction and imprisonment, not Joe Baker's, and without the murder weapon, without an eyewitness close enough to see the shooter, and most of all without Joe Baker or this Mr. E, there was no probative evidence for the jury to consider but Dexter's confession and the testimony of the police investigators.

For all the paper in the record, the case against Dexter is sparse, and the confession absolutely crucial to the prosecution.

Sawhill must have realized this. Maybe he did realize it, yet saw no way of getting it excluded. Realizing that Dexter was likely to lose at trial, he had good reason to push for a favorable plea bargain.

Or had he just grown too tired to believe that this boy might truly be innocent?

On Friday evening, Owedia calls to ask me to come with her tomorrow to see Dexter. I lie and tell her I can't, that I have to work.

I do work, though at home. I spend Saturday eating egg salad sand-wiches in my old rocking chair in my living room with the record in my utilities case in my lap. At noon, while gazing through my win-dows out on a rainy day on Rutherford Avenue, I see Owedia drive by with Carl in the front seat next to her, on their way, no doubt, to the Boys' School.

At 6:15 that evening I am there again, same spot, in this peculiar solitary life I lead; the same rain is still falling, and I am eating a bowl of pasta and watching the news on TV when Owedia calls.

"Dexter was fine and hopeful," she says cheerily, "and he told me he really enjoyed meeting you last week. He said you're the nicest person he's met since he's been in prison. Some compliment, huh?"

"I should say he's the nicest prisoner I ever met," I say.

"Did you get done the work you wanted to get done today?"

"Yes," I say, and then I realize that she might have seen my car in the driveway at noon. "I've had my head in law books all day."

"Why not give yourself a break and come to church tomorrow?"

"Maybe," I tell her, and for an instant I actually mean it.

Sunday at noon the sun has emerged and I am raking the thousands of leaves that have blown onto my front lawn and are stuck there, still wet from yesterday's rain. As I stop to pay attention to the squirrel perched on my gutter chattering at me—annoyed that I have not filled the bird feeder—I see a car slow in front of Carl's house. The back door swings open and he steps out dressed for church, a crisp new hat, a gray felt fedora, snug on his head.

"I like that hat!" I yell to him when he waves.

He steps warily toward me through the leaves covering the side-walk, careful not to dirty his shoes, and he holds out his hand for me to shake.

"Well, thank you. I see you're doing what I should be doing."

"I'd be happy to help you with your leaves," I tell him.

He hesitates a moment, then says, "Well, all right. I could use the help. Pulling a rake is an activity that seems to use all the wrong muscles and bones in this old body, and I do suffer after a few hours of raking. If you'd lend me a hand I'd be grateful."

He stays and watches as I finish raking the last few unraked places on my lawn.

"We missed you at church this morning," he says after a time.

I laugh. "I'd only gone once!"

He laughs. "Yes, but . . . well, I suppose what I want to say is we're happy to have you join us. Owedia thinks very highly of you."

"Well, I think highly of her. I'm glad to have met her."

"She told me that you went to see Sawhill. I hadn't known beforehand. I want you to know that—I wouldn't have imposed on you like that. Particularly with you workin' for the state and all."

I lean on the rake and regard him. "Well, yes, it likely was pretty foolish of me to go see Sawhill. But there's no harm done. I'll do what I can to help you and Owedia help Dexter."

"You don't have to," he says sweetly.

I shrug. "I don't know. Maybe I do," I say, suddenly heartsick.

"That Sawhill is full of excuses," he says. "Did he tell you there was no way to keep the jury from hearing the confession?"

"We didn't get that far. He doesn't remember much about the trial."

"He knows. He remembers. He denies it, but a man I know who's Sawhill's client told me that Sawhill once said that he could have won Dexter's trial if he'd only figured a way to keep that confession out. And the librarian down at the law school says that old criminal lawyers like Sawhill don't ever do a lick of research—they just cut their deals with the prosecutor and if that doesn't work out, they go in and try their cases by the seat of their pants. That's what he did, you know. And if there was a way to keep that confession out, he wouldn't have found it because he didn't look."

When my leaves have been raked and bagged, Carl goes to change his clothes. He'll meet me in his yard in ten minutes, he says, and when he's gone I sit on my front step and take off my gloves and put my head in my sweaty hands.

Shit, once Dexter was in custody, it was inevitable that he would be convicted. To his lawyer, he was presumed guilty, and so not worth fighting for. To the judge he was one in a long day of black kids who'd come before him. To the jury he was a threat to be locked away for as long as the law allows.

And to the court of appeals, he is presumed to have gotten a fair trial.

It's almost funny.

Carl emerges in flannel and overalls, and I want to grab his shoulders and tell him everything, tell him how his Dexter was screwed from the get-go, how he hadn't a chance, hasn't a chance, and that maybe the only thing to do is to put our money together and arrange for a prison break.

But I don't. I rake with him, me silent, him jawing away about the weather and me not listening but thinking with each stroke of the rake that this is the moment, now, for something to be done.

13

When Carl and I finish raking his lawn, the afternoon has turned to dusk. Without changing, I climb into my pickup and drive across town to Meridian Street, Indianapolis's central north-south artery, and turn south, toward the State House. I want to look again at the transcript of Dexter's trial. I want to find *a way.*

One can drive down Meridian Street to the center of town without ever seeing a white person on the street. It is like that today. There are white people in cars travelling between downtown and the neighborhoods north of Kessler Avenue, which bisects the city going east to west at Fifty-seventh Street, but there are no white people walking. The people walking, many still coming from their churches in their Sunday clothes, are all black. There are black kids on bicycles, black men clustered in the parking lot of a boarded-up gas station, black women carrying bags of groceries. At the corner of Twenty-eighth Street, a black woman standing at a bus stop reads a paperback book. Two black boys are fighting in front of a hair salon at Nineteenth Street, one punching the other while trying to pull the other's shirt off. At Twelfth Street, a legless black man in his twenties sits in a wheelchair and stares.

It's a sad fucking city.

Alone in the office, I remove everything from the surface of my desk and lay the seven volumes of the transcript of Dexter's trial across the desktop.

Under federal precedent, the constitutional issue of whether Dexter's Fifth Amendment rights were violated when he was denied his right to a "meaningful consultation" is enough for a reversal. But I know the judge won't buy that, just as he nixed the argument that the search warrant had been stale.

I need something else, an error the court can raise *sua sponte*—on its own authority.

I need a procedural error that renders a crucial piece of evidence inadmissible; under the law, Dexter's conviction can only be reversed if, in the absence of that piece of evidence, the reasonable juror would have voted to acquit.

The prosecution's case began with the testimony of the good citizen. Then there was testimony from the woman who witnessed the aftermath of the crime, followed by testimony from the police officers who examined the crime scene, gathered the evidence, found the stolen car, performed the fingerprint analysis, traced the leads to Joseph Baker, secured the search warrant, executed the search warrant, arrested Dexter and questioned him.

It is, by all appearances, a clean case, but for the impatience of the officers who questioned Dexter too soon. Sawhill seems hardly a presence. His cross-examination of the state's witnesses was perfunctory, and he allowed numerous opportunities for objection to slip by until the final state's witness introduced the videotaped confession.

In the table of contents to the transcript, I see that the defense case consisted of the testimony of Carl, of Dexter, of the Rev. Jones, and, oddly, of an Officer Wheeler, a state's witness who had been recalled.

I turn to the pages containing Wheeler's testimony, in volume five of the transcript. A glance at the defense attorney's opening question indicates that Wheeler had been the officer who picked up Carl and transported him to the police station after Dexter had been arrested. Evidently he had been recalled based upon something in Carl's testimony.

I turn back to Carl's testimony, and as I read his words I can hear him, see him, there on the stand, weary, shy, forthright.

A. I was watching the store for my friend Charles down at 38th and Illinois. He own a place called Fins and Gills, sells tropical fish. I was there by myself. When they come and took me away I had to lock the place up.

Q. What time did they come?

A. About four-thirty.

Q. And who came?

A. That man, Officer Wheeler. [Witness indicates.] And another man, but he didn't say anything.

Q. And what did they say to you when they came in?

A. The one said who they was. Then he said that Dexter had been taken to the police station and he was being questioned about a robbery and a murder. I could not believe it. I said, you talking about Dexter Hinton? My grandchild? Deaf boy? He said, yes, that's him, and so I got into the police car.

Q. Did Officer Wheeler say anything to you on the way to the station?

A. He told me about the murder. And then he told me about finding the car and the purse and the fingerprints. And how they traced the stolen car to Joe.

Q. Did you ask Officer Wheeler any questions?

A. I asked him if Dexter was all right. And he said, he's fine, don't worry. And then I ask him if Dexter had said anything about the crime, said that he hadn't done it. And he said that Dexter had admitted to it.

MR. SAMUELS: Your honor, I must object. The witness's comment about the comments of Officer Wheeler as to the Defendant's admissions is clearly hearsay upon hearsay.

COURT: Response?

MR. SAWHILL: Your honor, none of these comments is being admitted for the truth of the assertions contained therein. It's Mr. Hinton's recitation of the circumstances of the arrest that we're trying to get at.

COURT: Overruled. Continue.

Q. Please go on, Mr. Hinton.

A. Well, I felt like my chest had been sliced open. I was in shock. I said, he admitted it? He said he killed that woman? And the policeman said, yes, he said so, but you have to be there for him to give an official confession.

Q. Did Officer Wheeler say anything else?

A. I said, what's going to happen to him? And he didn't say anything. And so I said, is he going to face death? Would they put him to death for this? Or is he too young for that?

Q. What did Officer Wheeler reply?

A. He said, the death penalty has been given in cases like this. But that maybe a deal could be struck if Dexter confessed.

Q. Did he say what kind of a deal?

A. I asked him what I needed to do to keep Dexter alive, and he said that he didn't know, it was up to the prosecutor and that it all might depend on whether Dexter's case was handled in juvenile court or adult court. I said, how will they decide that? He said, I can't say. I said, I got to get a lawyer. He said, that's up to you.

I play these moments in my head like a film; first I see Carl speaking on the witness stand, the focus of scrutiny of the judge, the lawyers, and the jury, and then I see the events he describes, Carl in the backseat of the police car, leaning forward, terrified, speaking his questions through the Plexiglas partition.

I turn forward to the testimony of Officer Wheeler, who denies telling Carl that a deal could be struck if Dexter confessed. But then:

Q. But you tried to impress upon Mr. Hinton the seriousness of the charges, didn't you?

A. Yes, I did.

Q. What did you say?

A. I said what he was accused of doing. And I said it was very serious.

Q. Did you say anything to the effect that it might be a capital case?

A. Um, maybe. I might have said that cases like this have been capital cases.

I realize with a sinking feeling that this is the error Carl should have raised, that here, in these two bits of testimony, is the evidence of coercion needed to reverse. A halfway competent appellate lawyer would have caught it. There is no way Carl could have.

He and I had been making the same mistake—focusing on the police conduct toward *Dexter* as spoiling the voluntariness of Dexter's confession. But the police conduct toward *Carl* was just as important because Carl, as the boy's guardian, had the power to make decisions regarding his defense.

Coercing Carl to convince Dexter to confess was as good as coercing Dexter.

And threatening the death penalty for failure to confess or plea bargain is prima facie coercion.

It's reversible error. And one we can raise *sua sponte.*

I switch on my computer and close my eyes as I wait for it to boot up, imagining how pissed off the judge will be.

But if I do it right, he won't stay pissed for long, and to do it right I need the right case to support my position.

From the computer's main menu I choose Westlaw, an on-line legal research service, and when I am connected and signed in, I request a search of all Indiana cases for the words *parent* or *guardian* and *admissibility* and *confession* and *voluntary* and *coercion* or *influence.* The machine thinks for a moment, then informs me that no matches were found. I try the same search in the database of federal cases, and a moment later, success—nineteen cases. I skim through the first three, none of which have anything to do with the coercion of a parent affecting the voluntariness of a juvenile's confession, but on the fourth, I hit gold.

The case is *Illinois v. Harvey,* decided recently by the Seventh Circuit Court of Appeals, and it deals with the blatant browbeating of a juvenile defendant's parents who had been confined in a separate interview room in a Chicago precinct house for six hours in order to convince them to apply pressure to their fifteen-year-old son to confess. That child too had been accused of murder in a bungled robbery, and the parents were told in no uncertain terms that he faced the death penalty if he did not confess. The court wrote:

> The admissibility of a confession is determined from the totality of the circumstances and whether the confession was given voluntarily and not through inducement, violence, threats, or other improper influences which would have overcome the free will of the accused. Such tactics are particularly egregious when used to exploit the intimacy of the parental relationship.

If Sawhill had read this case, he wouldn't have thought so little of Dexter's chances. If Sawhill had read this case, he would have filed a motion *in limine* to declare the confession inadmissible before the trial, and maybe even gotten the case dismissed.

I print the case, exit from Westlaw, then switch to my word processing program. And I begin to write.

I sit at my desk far into the evening, intent on having a draft of the opinion to show Haberman the next morning before I submit it to the judge.

As I write I am calmed by the sense that I have made the right decision, despite the judge's instructions. Looking at the "totality of the circumstances," as the law requires, encompasses not only the suggestion to Carl that Dexter faced the death penalty, but the interrogation and taking of a statement from Dexter before his opportunity for "meaningful consultation" with his grandfather.

The work goes easily, as it always seems to go when the law is on my side.

I finish the opinion at 11:30 P.M. I print it and put a copy on Haberman's desk, along with the briefs and a Post-it begging "ASAP, please."

When I return home that night there is a message on my answering machine from Owedia. "Please call me tonight," she says. "Anytime before one-thirty."

A glance at my watch tells me it is twelve-fifteen. She answers on the second ring, a thick "hi."

"Hi. This is Nora Lumsey."

"I know," she says with a small laugh.

"You stay up awfully late."

"I don't sleep much. Maybe five hours. I do most of my reading late at night."

"What are you reading?"

"At the moment it's a book called *Out of the Ashes*. It's a collection of sermons delivered in Los Angeles following the 1993 riots."

"Oh."

"It talks a lot about how to have hope when things look hopeless, when people let you down."

"Oh."

"I wanted to tell you I'm sorry if I keep pushing you to come to church and to come with me to see Dexter."

"No. You're not—"

"I have this habit of roping people into doing things they don't want to do. It's the irresistible force of my personality, I guess."

"Uh-huh."

"I'm glad you want to come. It's all so discouraging. I need to be around people who believe we can fight this thing and win."

There is a lump in my throat; I am afraid to speak.

She says, her tone childlike, compelling, "Do you believe we can win?"

"There is hope," I whisper, my voice breaking. "At the very least."

"I will speak with you later this week," she says. "We'll make plans."

"All right."

"Call me."

As I enter the office the next morning Haberman is whistling merrily at his desk; when he sees me he manages to grin and whistle at the same time.

The opinion and brief are already back on my desk. Haberman has scribbled a note across the top of the opinion:

Nice going, Farm Girl. I didn't think you had the balls.

When I look up at him, he says, "You have the balls."

"I have the ovaries," I reply.

I make a few minor corrections, print the opinion, then place it and the briefs on top of the box containing the transcript. With a glance at Tammy, who smiles her approval at seeing the case finished, I balance the box on my left forearm and knock on the judge's door.

"Come in." As I push the door open, he stares my way, registers that it's me, and turns back to the pile of correspondence in front of him.

"I've finished a draft of the Hinton opinion." I slide the box onto the battered conference-room table at the back of his office where we place our opinions upon completion.

"I was under the impression you'd be a while with that."

When I turn to him I see that he is gazing at me amiably, an uncommon look of pleasure on his face.

"I . . . had a revelation . . . of sorts," I murmur.

"I hoped you would," he says, returning his attention to the work in front of him.

All that day I wait for the explosion. It does not come. He goes about his business, his meetings, his lunch, the long stretches when his door is shut and there is silence within his office. At 3:00 there is an oral argument that keeps him out of the office for the rest of the afternoon.

When I arrive the next morning the atmosphere in the office is so altered it is indeed as if an explosion has occurred. The judge's door is wide open. Tammy looks at me slowly, edgily, rabbitlike, and her "good morning" is morose.

When Haberman sees me he blushes. "Once you get settled the judge would like to have a word with you," he says.

I put down my briefcase, pour a cup of coffee, straighten my skirt, and walk into the judge's office.

He does not look up.

"Close the door and sit down," he says.

I do as he says. Approaching his desk, I see the opinion in front of him.

"I am appalled," he begins. "And I am angry. You had your viewpoint. You expressed it to me. I gave you my viewpoint. I told you how I wanted you to write the opinion. End of story."

"I'm sorry, Judge," I stammer, "I thought—"

"I don't raise issues *sua sponte,*" he snaps. "I don't do the advocates' work for them. If you had asked me first, you would know that."

Blood rushes to my face, and I open my mouth to speak, hoping something good will come out, but he speaks first.

"You have wasted the taxpayers' money in the time you wasted writing this nonsense. If there is one thing I want you to learn from me it is that justice is not a result. It is not a product. It is a process. Justice is not the decision. Justice is a fair trial and a fair review. The adversary system provides justice by creating a forum in which opposing viewpoints are heard. We are not a third advocate. We are not a party to the dispute. We do not raise issues *sua sponte!*"

He rises from his chair, pushes the chair back noisily, and walks around to where I am seated.

"I am going to offer you the opportunity to rewrite this opinion as I directed you to write it, or, if you feel incapable of doing that, you may demur and I will ask Mr. Haberman to write it."

"I will write it," I say weakly.

"Good," he says. "That's the right answer. Go to it."

I place the opinion on top of the box, which sits on the floor next to his desk, and lift it. My fingers are clammy and slippery against the smooth cardboard; it takes me a moment to balance the box, and when I glance again at the judge, he has turned away from me.

In the outer office, Haberman is staring at his computer, his lips trembling.

"You son of a bitch," I mutter, dropping the box on my desk.

"Ovaries," he laughs.

14

I write it, chastened, while the sting of the judge's rebuke is still fresh.

I know what he wants, and so the writing is not difficult.

What is difficult is to ignore the glaring injustice, the willful neglect by the police of their constitutional responsibilities, the judge's disregard for precedent and common sense.

To refuse to raise an issue *sua sponte* in the name of an abstract notion of justice as process! What incredible arrogance! It is to elevate procedure over substance, form over content, theory over reality!

The notion of justice as process assumes what the lawyers' rules of professional conduct require, but which is rarely the case—that an attorney will be a tireless advocate for his client's position. But what happens when an individual chooses to represent himself? Is he entitled to less justice because he isn't a lawyer?

I understand the judge's view that the justice system is just a system; it's a referee, not God. And I understand that the appeals process only reviews whether the rules of the game have been followed.

But the boy is innocent.

I work until 3:00 affirming the conviction, then I deliver the draft to Haberman, who accepts it contritely.

"That was shitty of me," he says. "I should have told you the judge has a thing about *sua sponte.*"

"I should have known."

"If it's any consolation, I thought you did a damn good job. And you were right to reverse it."

"That's no consolation, Larry," I say. "To the contrary, you asshole."

Forty minutes later, Haberman hands the draft back to me with the notation:

You have the ovaries, Farm Girl. But ovaries aren't the only thing.

By the time I get through correcting and proofreading the draft, the judge, Tammy, and Larry have gone for the day. I slide the box, briefs, and draft onto the judge's table, dead to the enormity of what I've done.

I cruise up Illinois Street from the center of town to my neighborhood, enclosed in the cab of my pickup, slipping past the activity at curbside and on the sidewalks and stoops. After a time, I think of Dexter's incarceration and the dashed hopes of his grandfather, his friends, his church, and I wish I'd let Haberman write the damn thing.

But big-boned women don't abdicate. We swallow our pride, take our medicine, and slowly corrode from the inside out.

Carl is outside his home when I pull into my driveway. He waves happily and I wave back, my heart sinking.

I do not see the judge again until late the next morning, when he emerges from his office on his way out to lunch. He whispers something to Tammy, then turns to me.

"That Hinton opinion will do nicely, Nora," he says, addressing me by my first name for the first time in a long while.

I know he expects me to say, "Thank you, sir," but I cannot say it.

I smile tightly, nod once, and silently wish the old fart would drop dead.

When he is out the door, Tammy looks hard at me, her eyes saying, "you pathetic soul," her voice saying, "Buy you lunch?"

As soon as we step out the front door of the State House, Tammy stops to light a cigarette.

I watch her fiddle with the lighter and the pack and the cigarette, and once the cigarette is lit we descend the thirty or so steps down to the pretty paths that lead from the State House through immaculately landscaped grounds down to Washington Street.

As we walk the cigarette stays in her mouth; her hands are stuffed into the pockets of her fuzzy blue wool jacket. Suddenly she is not the small-boned woman kowtowing to the judge; she is a tough old bird, and I am startled by the tubercular laugh that issues unprompted from her throat as she tells me she's about to divorce her second husband.

"He's such a lump," she says. "Does not do squat to keep up the house, and he acts like I'm lucky he's got a job! As if I didn't make more money than he does to begin with!"

She takes me to a place directly across Washington Street, a bar called the Caucus Room, a place too shiny and bright to be called a bar, but there are drinks here to go with your burger and fries and that's just what Tammy has in mind.

"I'm planning a mellow afternoon," she tells me after ordering a margarita. "God knows I need it."

"No thanks to me, I suppose."

"I should say not." She lights a fresh cigarette on the one burning into its filter, then tilts her head to one side and says, her words emerging in little puffs of smoke, "The judge is a good guy, but he's a cowboy, like all the judges. It's his show. His court."

"But you manage to get along with him all right."

"Sure I do. Thanks to technology, I've got him over a barrel. He doesn't know squat about computers."

Our drinks arrive—mine an iced tea—and we order our burgers. Tammy tells the waiter to bring her the check.

"I should be taking you out to lunch," I tell her. "I really appreciate all your work for me—"

"It's the judge's tab, honey."

"Oh."

"I've been working for the judge for twenty-nine years. When I got out of high school I went right to work for him in private practice down in Salem before he was appointed to the bench. Hard to believe how fast the time has gone by."

"I imagine he's changed a lot in that time."

"Not one iota. He always was overbearing. But he's been grand to me. When my first husband left me, he had me and my kids over for dinner, often, him and his wife Pat, before she died."

I did not know the judge's wife's name, not until that moment, and I feel myself flush with embarrassment at not having had the courtesy to ask.

"How long ago did that happen?"

"Oh, it's at least six or seven years." She takes a sip of her drink. "It's twelve years."

"Does the judge have children?"

"He has two girls. One's here in town. A veterinarian. The other's down in Louisville. He doesn't talk to her."

"Oh."

"She was the older one, and he broke her with criticism. She's a lawyer down there, and the damn shame of it is how much alike they are."

The burgers come, but by this time my stomach is knotted with the horrible sense of having understood nothing.

"I'm afraid he doesn't like me," I say, nearly weeping.

"He doesn't like you much at the moment."

"He thinks I'm too idealistic."

"He thinks you're naive. But he likes naive. So long as you're willing to learn."

I sip my iced tea, wishing I'd had the courage to order a beer.

"Let me tell you a story," she says. There is a lit cigarette in each of her hands, and for an instant I think she's going to smoke them both. She stubs the short one out, takes a long drag on the other, then exhales, coughs, and speaks. "I had only been working for the judge a few months when this happened—it was back in the late sixties. He was hired to defend a lawyer in Hayes County, in the town of Newkirk, who'd been accused of rape. When it happened, this lawyer had been away on a fishing trip with three other men—two attorneys and a magistrate from the Hayes County Superior Court. The police investigation brought to light that these four may have been doing some fishin', but they weren't sleepin' out in the woods—they were stayin' at a motel in Newkirk not too far from where this lawyer lived with his wife and children. The rape took place in a field in back of a highway bar where this lawyer and his three companions had been seen earlier that night.

"Of course at the trial the magistrate and the two other lawyers said this son of a bitch had not been out of their sight all night, despite the victim's testimony that she had run into this man in the parking lot of the bar and that he had taken her by the hand and drug her out into the field and raped her. At the same time, there was no physical evidence linking this lawyer to the crime, and this woman was too drunk to make a positive identification. So it was not a difficult case from Judge Albertson's point of view, and with the testimony of these men, all respected members of the bar, the jury was convinced that this lawyer had been mistakenly identified as the rapist.

"About six months after the acquittal, the judge was at a judicial conference down in French Lick when he ran into the magistrate who'd accompanied the lawyer on the fishing trip. They were drinking together along with a number of other men from that part of the state, and the subject of the trial came up. Some of the other men suggested—and they were laughing about it—that the magistrate had covered up for his fishin' buddy. The magistrate denied it, but he didn't deny it strongly or seriously. In fact, as he denied it, there was a smile on his face, as plain as day, and there was no mistaking, it was obvious he'd lied to Judge Albertson and to the court—that he had perjured himself to protect his friend."

"Shit."

"The judge was devastated. Not that he was naive about the lies criminal defendants tell, you know? He sure wasn't. But he struggled for a long time to understand what it meant that these four men, all officers of the court, would defy justice, and he felt he had defrauded the court in arguing the case based upon his client's lies. He had always thought himself a good judge of character, and he believed he usually knew when his clients were lying or telling the truth. At trial, he would tailor his arguments accordingly, so as to advocate his client's position with integrity—straightforwardly and based on the evidence.

"When he found out that these four men had lied to him, he said to me—and I'll never forget this—he said, 'Men like that don't deserve our system of justice. It's too good for them, too fair and too forgiving. But if there's a better way to get to the truth of a matter, I don't know what it is. And I would rather see four guilty men go free than to lock up a single innocent man.'"

As she says those words my hands begin to tremble, my right hand holding the fork rattling against the plate as I struggle to maintain my composure. It seems such a lie, such an impossible lie that he should so value justice, yet ignore the truth of Dexter's innocence.

"I feel . . ." I take a deep breath and try to find the words. "I feel . . . so utterly sure in my heart and in my mind that the judge's decision is wrong . . . and that this boy is going to spend—at minimum—the next twenty-seven years of his life in prison because of the judge's mistake. I'm finding it very hard to deal with that."

She frowns and lights another cigarette, taking her time. "You know," she says, after a moment, "if you told the judge what you just told me, he'd ask for your resignation. Effective immediately. If I told him what you just told me, you'd be fired." She takes another puff. "But I won't do that. Because I think you're real good and real smart and I think your passion for this job is good for him. But you gotta understand something, and it's real easy: He's the judge."

I swallow hard, and I want to reach for her drink and her cigarette.

"Right," I say, and I clear my throat. "He's the judge."

With the judge's approval in hand, Tammy sends copies of the opinion to the other two judges on the panel; the judge must have the concurrence of at least one other judge before the opinion can be handed down. If both of the other judges were to be troubled by an issue in the opinion, the process of negotiation over the final decision could take weeks or months. Most often, in criminal cases like this one, the other judges take a cursory look at the case and concur.

The Hinton opinion is circulated to Judges Waldron and Johnson on Wednesday afternoon. By Monday morning their copies have been returned to Tammy with their notes of concurrence.

Tammy makes a phone call to the office of the clerk of the court of appeals, informs the clerk that a decision has been reached, and asks the clerk to schedule a hand-down date—the date the decision will be announced to the public and to the parties.

The clerk schedules a hand-down date of Wednesday, November 27, nine days away, the day before Thanksgiving.

Occasionally during the next several days I see Carl outside his home, often in the company of Mr. Williams, with whom Carl takes evening strolls for exercise.

I cannot bring myself to speak with him.

On Thursday evening, I return from the State House to find Carl working in the far corner of my backyard, installing some sort of enclosure.

"Here's your compost heap," he tells me, leaning a roll of chicken wire against a tree. "Just throw your vegetable peelings and any leaves you rake into this bin, turn it over once in a while, and by summer you'll have yourself a beautiful mulch to put on your flower beds. It'll do wonders for the soil around this place."

I thank him, promise to follow his instructions, and then I tell him that it would be best if he didn't do any more work around my grounds.

He looks at me quizzically, hurt.

I tell him, "You've done too much. I don't feel right having you do all this work and not paying you for it."

He looks relieved. "Well, that's nonsense," he says. "You took me to the boys' school. You talked to me about Dexter's case. You came to my church. We're neighbors, and I hope we're friends. We do for each other."

"It's not that simple." I look away, the words coming out tentatively, and I don't know where they're going.

"What do you mean?"

"I would just rather . . . you didn't."

"I don't understand," he says, a look of genuine concern on his face.

"Please," I say, "I can't have . . . the obligation."

"The obligation," he repeats, breathing hard. He picks up a wire cutter from the ground and tucks the roll of chicken wire under his arm.

He looks me over once, angrily, and leaves.

Later that evening, I call Owedia and tell her that I won't be able to go with her to see Dexter that weekend.

"I'm not feeling well," I tell her, not realizing until the words are out of my mouth that it is true. "So I'm heading home for a few days to see my father."

"Oh." Her voice is softer than before. "I'm sorry."

"It's a bug of some kind," I lie. "Nothing serious. I hope."

"Some home cookin' make you feel better, right?"

"Yes."

"I suppose I won't see you Sunday, then, either."

"No."

"I hope you feel better soon."

"Thanks."

"I will say hello to Dexter for you."

"Yes, do that, please."
"Call me when you get back."
"Okay."

I *am* ill—dizzy, nauseated, feverish. I know this illness has to do with this horror I've done, but the grinding in my stomach is real, as is the sweat on my forehead, the crazed confusion of my mind.

I have not felt this bad since my first semester of law school, when my near-constant anxiety fueled a full-scale bodily rebellion.

I want desperately to go home.

The drive from Indianapolis to Unity takes about three hours, first going south on Route 37, a four-lane road connecting the capital to the towns of Martinsville, Bloomington, Bedford, and Oolitic, and then eastward on two-lane Route 19 through the succession of small towns that leads to Unity. As I drive southward I feel physically better with each passing mile. I am struck by the sense of expansiveness I feel, and I realize how claustrophobic my life has become.

The dormant fields splay out around me, immense carpets of bare soil, some stubbled with the remains of the year's corn crop. I feel an intense relief, a palpable relaxation. This is my landscape, my home, and I wonder at the phenomenon of Indianapolis, a busy, built-up place stuck smack in the middle of a thousand farms.

Outside the city, one can throw a seed at the ground anywhere and it will germinate and grow, and it is easy to feel the presence of God here, in the beauty of the open skies and the damned miraculous fecundity of the soil. It's no wonder ours is a state steeped in agriculture and dedicated, in its politics and its beliefs, to the individual on earth serving God in heaven.

On this trip I notice for the first time how the world whitens outside the city. The further I go from Indianapolis, the fewer blacks I see, and by the time I get to Bedford it is as if I have crossed a border into another country. Everyone is white here. It hits me hard when I stop at a McDonald's on the highway. Everyone working behind the counter is white. One would be hard-pressed to find a white person working at McDonald's in Indianapolis. In the city, one becomes used to seeing blacks in menial positions; it would be odd to see a white janitor or dishwasher. Here, whites do every kind of job, and it is as if the job itself is elevated by the fact that a white is doing it.

I slip into my racism like a frayed pair of overalls, and it feels good to wear, a comfort for my doubts, a balm for my aching conscience.

I remind myself that the boy had a record. He was a thief, he was a vandal. He had come from a broken home, a home without marriage, like so many blacks. He had known that they were going to steal from the woman. Even if he had been egged-on into it, he had done it, he was a willing participant. Even if he had not pulled the trigger, he was an accomplice to murder.

All that nonsense about due process, about a "meaningful consultation," about constitutional rights, could not obscure the truth. The boy had been there. He had done the crime, or had as good as done the crime. The rest is just window dressing. What had I been thinking?

Out here, commonsense truths are apparent.

And God didn't make little green apples.

I know I am home when I see the sign on our neighbor's silo, brightly lit by a spotlight from the field below: JESUS IS LORD.

It is after eight when I ring the doorbell on the white Victorian farmhouse I grew up in. Through the window I can see the television and my father planted in front of it.

He lumbers to the door. He is a beefy barrel-chested man—there's about one chromosome's difference between us—and as I glide into his waiting arms I am acutely aware of the awful reek of him, the tobacco and alcohol and sweat, and the bristly unshaven scrape of his face against my cheek as he kisses me.

15

B ig-boned women can't keep their hands off; they've got to touch everything, fix it, make it right.

From my littlest years, my mother was often gone. I don't know where she went—she never held a job—but when she was gone my siblings and I were placed in the care of my paternal grandmother, Molly, who was so wracked with ills that she was, for me, just another child to look after.

Molly was a large woman, big-boned like me but also a fat woman, truly fat, nearly as wide as she was tall. And when I think of her I think of the taste of the peaches I'd put up as she sat at the kitchen table giving orders.

But here's the thing—and this is the damn scary thing, and I hate to be such a goddamn cliché—but my grandmother was also my great-aunt. That is, my mother and father were first cousins.

Of all the hilljack shit to be saddled with, that is the worst, worse than big-bonedness, my paleness, my plainness. I am genetically trash, fucked from the start, branded worse than illegitimacy, worse than a nigger in the woodpile, worse than poverty.

My mother hated the farm, hated the life she married into, hated the kids for keeping her there. My father had been a good-looking boy, and she could not have helped but love him.

I remember him with a bushy moustache when I was a child, so soft like a tiny paintbrush against my cheek. When things were good between them she would sit in his lap and kiss the moustache and smooth it nice and even with her fingers.

He tried. He would take her into New Albany or Louisville for a movie while Molly watched us, and once they even spent some money and got a hotel room for a week on the gulf coast of Alabama, the white-trash Riviera.

It was not long after they returned that she left.

We woke up together on a Saturday morning in October, me and Luke and Naomi and Royce, and when we went downstairs there was Daddy making breakfast.

He looked at us, face tight as a pig's skin, and said, "Dress up now. Look nice. We'll have something and then we're going to fetch your momma."

We put on our church clothes without fussing, knowing that something was terribly wrong. I put on a navy-blue velour dress with long sleeves and lace around the cuffs and collar; I remember the starched lace cutting into the skin under my chin; the boys wore blazers, and Naomi put on a white summer dress, too thin for the weather that day, which was sunny and blustery, but she insisted—it was the prettiest thing she owned.

He quietly put on his suit too, a brown double-breasted suit, as ugly a piece of cloth as you could imagine, but he looked strong in it, like a beast barely contained.

We choked down some biscuits with jam and cold milk and piled into the back of Daddy's truck, sitting carefully on a blanket so as not to get dirty.

Then we rode to a place in the next county, a town called White's Mill. I remember the sign at the side of the road.

We drove through a neighborhood of houses, not farmhouses, but suburban houses, one after the other like in a city—pretty, clean, and new, with lawns as bright green as new carpet.

We stopped in front of a white house with blue shutters. My father got out and left the motor running and told us to get into the cab and wait.

He went to the door and knocked.

She came to the door and let him in.

He was gone a half hour. We sat silently in the shuddering cab, the heat turned up to suffocating. Then he came out, smiling—grinning really—irrepressibly, like a corner had been turned and it would all be okay.

"She'll be just a few minutes," he said, slipping into the driver's seat. "Now you kids hop in back and be little angels when she gets in, you hear?"

So we got out and climbed into the back of the truck. As I pulled the gate shut I was desperately thankful that she was coming home. But as I joined my sister and brothers on the blanket, I hated the woman in a thousand ways, one for every psychological horror she'd done to us.

When she came out, she was all dolled up in a pretty dress and her hair was pulled tight up around her head like we were going to a wedding. We all were dressed for a wedding.

She stepped out of the house, pulled the door closed behind her, took three strides toward the car, and stopped.

The four of us kids were lined up in the back of the truck, leaning over the side, staring at her, real quiet now.

She stood there. Looked at us for a moment. Then turned around and walked back into the house.

And that was it. I didn't see her again for three years, and then she was back for a week, gone for six months, back for a month, gone for two years.

To this day my father won't hear a word said against her. Disparaging remarks are dismissed with a wave and the words, "She's family."

Excruciating. Pitiful.

My father and I sit at the kitchen table, him with his cigarette and his decaf coffee, me with tea and pound cake. Stone Baptist that he is, he drinks alcohol, but not in front of me.

Each time I see my father, I am amazed that standing eye to eye, he is the same height I am, and he has become so unlike the powerful figure of my imagination. I tell him about my work. He listens, pleased at the fine young woman I have become, pleased that I am on my own at last.

I tell him nothing about my neighborhood or Dexter Hinton. I know that he would disapprove strongly that I had purchased a home in a "colored" neighborhood, as he would put it. He would be shocked at my stupidity, would worry about my safety.

My father supported George Wallace, loved the man, and still keeps a Confederate-flag license plate on the front of his truck.

Saturday morning I walk around the farm with my father, both of us carrying rifles. He'd feel naked walking his land without a firearm, as would I, though I wouldn't dream of having one in the city.

He takes me to the new barn he put up to shelter my sister Naomi's ponies. She, four years younger than I, lives just over the border in Kentucky and comes home three times a year to ride. Yet he keeps the ponies for her, maybe somehow expecting that in time she will return for good.

My father shows me the pieces of an old bulldozer he bought, a monster of a machine with huge tread belts like a tank. The thing is in pieces in the old barn, and he smokes his unfiltered cigarettes as he tells me his plans for repairing the machine. I watch his puckered, weathered face, not hearing him, not really, but feeling soothed by his smoke-damaged voice.

I am home.

Maybe it's here I should make my practice of law, in this verdant place, here among my people. I know that I belong here, not there, and racism be damned, it is another world there in that black town, another society, another culture.

In back of the barn are stacked crates of empty beer bottles, hundreds of them. He and I haul a couple of crates out to the far side of the paddock and set up ten at a time on the fence posts, then come back to the barn, a good sixty yards away, and take aim.

I am a damned good shot, better than he is, and he claps me on the back every time I explode one of the glass soldiers on the fence. He knows too that I am a damned sight tougher than either of his boys, both of whom inherited their mother's flightiness and ended up in opposite corners of the country, one in Miami, the other in Seattle.

The jolt of the rifle butt against my shoulder, ringing through all my bones, is the most satisfying physical sensation I've felt in ages—better than sex, better than drink, better than food. Together we shoot five dozen bottles, and by the last of them we are laughing at the tinkling sound of glass raining upon the scattering of broken glass behind the fence.

On Sunday morning my father and I go to the First Baptist Church, where the announcement board outside informs us that Brother Jesse will be preaching on "the Reality of Jesus." I have heard this sermon before, but it is an old song that will still give me pleasure to hear.

This church is a spare, small room, the pews hard and close together, as if to maximize the discomfort of the parishioners. There is an organist, no band, and the walls are barren but for the shiny wooden crucifixes, as elegant as fine furniture, and the portrait of Jesus behind the pulpit. The choir, a dozen or so women of my mother's generation, sits in a place like a jury box to the side, behind the organist. All thirty-eight of us who congregate there that morning come tired; we are farmers with winter eyes, loving Christ, believing in salvation.

"And who is it in this universe who is worthy of your faith? Who stands tall as a mountain, hard and everlasting as granite, against whose steadfast presence the rest of our reality is but a mist, a vapor, an intangible nothingness? You know his name! What is his name?"

This is not a rhetorical question. So we answer, all of us murmuring.

"In Hebrews it is written, 'Jesus Christ the same, yesterday, today, and forever!' There is no greater reality for you in this world than Jesus Christ! All your concerns vanish into insignificance! In the light of

Jesus! Your problems, desires, needs, dilemmas! They will pass, just as surely as you and I will pass from this earth! Only one thing remains the same, yesterday, today, and forever, and that is the reality of the Son of God who for a brief time walked and suffered and preached among us. Hold on to Him! Hold on to that rock in your time of crisis! Hold on to Jesus! And in His love you too will be everlasting! Yesterday, today, and forever!"

16

I return to Rutherford Avenue as much a foreigner as when I moved here, renewed in my isolation, as though the scales had fallen from my eyes.

I am embarrassed at having involved myself in Dexter's case and I am acutely aware that I have violated my duty of impartiality. I was wrong. I was arrogant and presumptuous to have written the opinion contrary to the judge's wishes.

It is not yet Thanksgiving, but the Indiana winter, a parade of cold gray days, has begun, and so thankfully Carl is not to be seen.

At 6:30 P.M. on Monday evening, the telephone rings. I know that it is Owedia, and so I let the answering machine pick it up.

She says, "Hello, Nora, this is Owedia. I hope you're feeling better. I saw Dexter on Saturday. He'd really like to see you again, and he said he thinks you're good luck for us. I think so too. We've been praying a long time for some luck, and like it or not, you may be it. Call me, okay?"

Tuesday morning I find the final draft of the opinion on my desk when I arrive at work. It is neatly printed, the caption on the front page setting out starkly the matter to be determined: *Dexter Hinton v. State of Indiana.*

The opinion opens with the usual matter-of-fact statement of the case and the result: "Dexter Hinton appeals his conviction for murder. We affirm."

I read through the opinion, which seems to me now to be cogent and concise, then I check the citations to be sure that the cases cited remain good law. It is a workmanlike job. No one who did not take the time to read the record would suspect it was wrong.

I hand it to Tammy, who is to prepare the opinion for distribution the next morning.

When I return home from work that evening there is a message on my answering machine from Barbara Jones. "There is someone you should meet," she says, "someone with information about Joseph Baker." She pauses for a long time, and I think for a moment that the call has been broken off. But then her voice returns. "We invite you to join us on Sunday," she says. "Pray with us. God bless you."

It is done without drama. At 10:00 A.M. on Wednesday, a secretary in the office of the clerk of the court of appeals telephones the attorneys of record in the case and informs them of the result. In this case, the clerk would have informed the attorney general's office, representing the state, and Carl Hinton as next friend of Dexter Hinton. The opinion is then mailed to the parties and transmitted electronically to West Publishing for inclusion in the case reporters.

I sit at my desk, two floors above the clerk's office, as 10:00 passes. The chambers are quiet. I am surrounded by stacks of the black-bound record of the utilities case. With each moment, I slip deeper into miserable imaginings of Carl's pain at the failure of the appeal. I see him sitting in the wide, fat chair in his living room, paralyzed with agony, contemplating the child's bleak future. I want to tell him that we tried our damnedest, he and I, but that it could not have been enough.

That evening, I see several cars parked in Carl's driveway and along the street in front of his house. Through his living-room windows I can see silhouettes move, but the house is quiet; all I hear is the sound of cars whizzing by on Meridian Street to the east, and the faint drumbeat of a marching band rehearsing at Butler University to our west.

I park in my driveway and lock the car, leaving my briefcase inside. I know that I must go there, if only because I live in this place, and maybe as a final act to the secret drama I have been living.

Through the screen door I see that his front door is ajar. Without knocking I push it slowly open and enter Carl's living room.

A wake is in progress. Carl is seated as I had imagined him, but he is surrounded by a dozen or so of our neighbors and people from the church. Owedia is there, as is Barbara Jones. Carl's table has been pushed against the living-room wall, and it is laden with plates of food and a percolator.

When I enter the room is quiet. No one is eating. The women are seated in clusters of chairs pushed together, the men stand and smoke. Owedia is sitting on the arm of Carl's fat chair, and they are looking at a copy of the opinion as they notice me walk in.

All eyes turn toward me. Owedia stands and says softly, "Did you hear?"

I shake my head.

"We lost the appeal," she says, touching Carl's shoulder.

I swallow hard and nod. Owedia takes the opinion from Carl and holds it out to me, her hand shaking with fury. "Look at this!" Her eyes shine with tears. "It's a joke to them! After everything we've been through! And . . . Dexter!"

A couple of the women murmur their agreement. I take the opinion from her and look at my words, my heart racing.

"You take it. Read it!" she commands. "You tell me if that makes any sense!"

I do not reply. I go to Carl, who holds his hand up awkwardly. I grab it, squeeze it, and he squeezes back.

"Look what I did," he rasps, his voice thick with emotion. "I was angry with all the lawyers so I took it into my own hands and look what I did. If I had more money, I said, I would have got a real lawyer,

111

a good one. But I didn't. I should have done whatever it took to hire one. I should have sold this house if need be."

A gray-haired woman turns abruptly to Carl and says, "Don't you talk that way. No goddamn lawyer could have done what you done."

"Miss Lumsey's a lawyer," Carl says, gesturing toward me. "Not all lawyers are evil. I wish Miss Lumsey could have been our lawyer."

The woman looks hard at me.

"But she can't," Carl goes on. "She works for the state."

I roll the opinion in my hands and crouch by Carl's chair. "It's not over yet," I tell him. "There's the state supreme court. You've got to appeal this ruling."

He frowns. "You told me yourself that it wouldn't do a damn bit of good."

"It's a slim chance. But it's a chance. And you can't not try."

He looks away. Then I remember how I had hurt him, and I stand and move toward the coffee.

Barbara Jones moves with me. She hands me coffee in a china cup and saucer and asks if I had gotten her message.

"I spoke to a woman who has seen Joseph Baker," she whispers, glancing at Carl. "The niece of a woman who comes to our church. Her name is JeTaun. J-e-capital-T-a-u-n. JeTaun Holley. Works in a beauty shop at Ohio and St. Clair. She told me that she had seen Joe in a car on West Thirty-eighth Street and Joe stopped the car and talked to her."

I nodded, but I didn't get it. "What did he say?"

"He didn't say anything much, except that he wanted to see her. So she told him where she works."

"Uh-huh."

"Don't you understand? If we can talk to him, we can find out who the third man in the car was! And if we could find that man, they'd have to let Dexter go!"

I feel a hand slip around my upper arm. It is Owedia, having come up behind me. "How are you feeling?" she says sweetly.

"I'm okay."

"Did Barbara tell you about JeTaun?"

I am about to answer her when the door swings open silently, allowing a gust of chill air into the room. A tall black teenager enters with forceful strides, his feet clad in heavy black work boots. The rest of him is dressed in dark green trousers and matching shirt and jacket, military-style. His expression is nervous but determined. The gasps around me tell me that this young man is Joseph Baker.

17

He looks me over appraisingly, the x-ray look I have endured a million times, his eyes cool with the arrogance of the assumption that I am attracted to him. I am not, though I have been foolish enough to mistake the sensation of annoyance creeping over my skin for something resembling lust.

In the next second, all hell threatens to break loose; he subjects Owedia to the same meat inspection, all the while standing frozen before us, threatening, an action figure from a Schwarzenegger movie.

I want to leap on him, drag him to the floor with these other women, and hold him down until the police come.

But we just stand there, rigid with fear, weak, and too stunned to move.

He glances around him, sheepishly almost, apparently embarrassed at having made too strong an entrance.

"Grandpa," he says hoarsely, and he stumbles toward Carl, falls to his knees, and places his head in Carl's lap. Suddenly he looks ten years old.

Carl touches Joe's head tenderly.

"I saw it on the news," Joe says. "I feel bad for you, Grandpa, and for Dex."

"That is strange," Carl says. "He wouldn't be there at all if not for you."

"There was nothin' I could have done."

"You got him in that car."

"He begged me to come."

"You made him steal from that woman."

"He wanted to do it."

"You hung around with that trash, that Mr. E, or whoever."

"No such brother I know."

"The white boy who did the shooting."

Joe stands and backs away. "There wasn't any white boy in that car. Dexter shot that woman."

Carl pushes himself up from the chair and moves stiffly toward Joe. "Still you lie!"

Joe shakes his head slowly. "No."

Owedia steps toward him, the skin of her face trembling, her voice a study in control. "Why are you here?"

"To see my grandfather. I didn't know *you'd* be here."

Owedia steps toward him, closer than I would have dared, and grasps his upper arms. "You've got to turn yourself in to the police, Joe, and tell them what happened, the truth. If you won't say that this white boy did it, then tell them you did it. It doesn't matter, so long as Dexter gets out."

"Owedia," he says, taking her hands away, "forget it. I ain't gonna do that. Dexter shot the woman. If I give myself up, then they've got both of us. And they ain't gonna let him out on my say-so."

"Who are you protecting?"

"Nobody."

"Who are you protecting, Joe?"

"Nobody. What's the matter with you? You think Dexter's some kind of good little boy who wouldn't do nothin'? Hey, he is one crazy fool. You wouldn't believe some of the shit he pulled! We used to go stealin' all the time, trollin' for bikes, messin' people up—"

Owedia slaps him hard across the cheek. Instantly, his hand is up, and he returns the blow with such force that Owedia is knocked sideways to the floor.

My anger sends me at him, but Mr. Cumberbatch moves swiftly

between Joe and Owedia, and then Mr. Williams and Barbara Jones confront him.

"You are a coward," Williams says. "You're no man. May Christ have mercy on your soul."

Joe hangs his head, but his eyes stare up defiantly at Williams.

A couple of the women and I help Owedia to her feet. The right side of her jaw and her right ear have already begun to swell, and she is close to tears.

"You sold your brother, Joe," she tells him, her voice tremulous. "And for what? For cocaine? For money? To keep you out of prison?"

"I didn't do nothin'," Joe murmurs. "He killed that woman. That's all. I ain't goin' down for it."

All of us become aware, seemingly simultaneously, of Carl shifting in his chair behind us. "Somebody . . . help me up, please," he implores.

I have not seen him look so weak. One of the other women and I help him out of the deep chair and to his feet, and once he is standing his back straightens and he moves firmly toward Joe.

His hand comes up, swifter than Joe can move to block it, and he hits Joe hard across the side of the head.

Joe utters a strangled cry as his head snaps back. His hand reaches up to rub his ear.

"Don't you *ever* hit a woman!"

Joe glares at Carl, and for an instant I'm afraid he's going to deck him.

Carl goes on, "I don't know why you're here, and I don't know why I don't just call the police now. But you came with good intentions, I think, so I'm gonna give you the benefit of the doubt on that. And I'm gonna give you the chance to do the right thing and turn yourself in and come clean. For the good of your own soul."

Barbara murmurs, "Amen to that," and her words are echoed by others around the room.

Joe glances up quickly at Carl, then at Owedia and me, as though afraid to meet our eyes, and wrenches his body away from Cumberbatch and Williams, though neither of the men are touching him. Once free, he rushes to the door and is gone.

The others in the room stand paralyzed. I hurry to the door, open it, and watch Joe run down Carl's driveway to a big shiny boat of a car that has apparently been waiting for him. There are at least two other men in the car; the one on the passenger side is black, and I cannot see the other.

He opens the rear passenger-side door, looks back at the house, and is startled to see me. His movement halts for just an instant, then he slams the door and the car takes off.

In Joe's wake, the pall in the room is worse than before. Carl is seated again. He stares forward as if turning to stone before our eyes.

The other men lumber around each other, wordlessly sharing their worry.

Barbara Jones says, "You shouldn't've let him go, Carl."

Carl's voice is like the rumble of an old dog. "I couldn't stand to have him in this house another minute."

"He's Dexter's last hope."

"No," Carl says, "he was right."

"Right? What do you mean, right?"

"About Dexter. Having shot that woman."

Barbara dismisses him with a cluck of her tongue. "What?! You're crazy! You'd believe that liar?"

"He's right." Carl looks at her, then at the rest of us. "No use in us denyin' it. It just makes sense. Dex was good, he had the love of God in him, but in his heart he was as wild as any of them boys. He wanted guns and drugs and all of that. And most of all he wanted to be one of the big boys—the gang boys."

Owedia crouches by Carl and takes his hands in hers. "No. That's not right. Joe's wrong, I know he is. I know when Dex is telling the truth; I can read it in his hands and in his eyes. He can't lie to me, because when he lies I can feel it inside—there's a hesitancy in his signing that makes my heart ache." She lays her head on Carl's hands. "He did not shoot that woman. We have to find who did."

Carl touches her cheek, still flushed, with his big fingers. "I love you, honey," he says. "You're a daughter to me, and I love you. But I can feel the truth too. And I feel it now."

It's then that I leave, slipping out of there as silently as I can.

I cannot feel the truth; I cannot feel my way anywhere near it, not with all my senses, not with the strength of my long arms.

18

I spend Thanksgiving alone, ignoring phone calls from Owedia and from my father, feeling intensely lonely and stupid and wondering why I am in this city.

The Thanksgiving edition of the *Indianapolis Standard* is thick, stuffed with advertisements, and the bottom panel of the front page is devoted to news of HINTON CONVICTION UPHELD ON APPEAL. There is a picture of Dexter—the same one printed more than a year before—and the story briefly recounts the murder and trial before starkly noting that Judge Carter Albertson, writing for a unanimous panel, held that no coercion was employed in soliciting Hinton's confession and that Hinton's constitutional rights against illegal search and seizure were not violated in the search that led to his arrest. And the story goes on:

> Governor Donald Doyle released a statement applauding the decision as an important precedent upholding the rights of police officers to perform their duties without interference from the courts.
>
> Governor Doyle's likely opponent in next year's gubernatorial election, Attorney General Emmett Furness, also applauded the court's decision, but ridiculed what he called the governor's "recent conversion" to a tough law-

and-order stance. In a State House news conference, Furness reminded the governor of his support for Dexter Hinton and reminded voters that during Doyle's two terms as mayor of Indianapolis violent crime rose sharply to make the Circle City one of the most dangerous cities in America.

Furness, who made his reputation as a law-and-order Democrat in two terms as Lake County Prosecutor, hopes to capitalize on a coalition of traditionally Democratic black votes and conservative Republican defectors who perceive Doyle as soft on crime. Doyle, who has relied upon a coalition of religious moderates in the black community and white religious conservatives, has found himself floundering for support in the wake of Democratic inroads into the traditional Republican power base. Republican insiders also acknowledge that Doyle's presidential ambitions hang in the balance. Doyle's reelection as governor is a prerequisite to a presidential run, and Doyle's margin of victory must be substantial for him to mount a credible challenge to the nationally established Republican front-runners.

Democrats, Republicans, coalitions, and elections. How odd that next to Dexter's face and under that headline the *Standard* should say so little about the boy and his fate.

I am coming to understand that Dexter isn't what counts.

On Friday I cruise the malls for Thanksgiving sales. It's the first time I've had real money since beginning law school, and I buy seashell-shaped soap, a glass cow to put in my china cabinet, a stone angel for my garden, a set of pretty wicker baskets, scented candles, two pairs of low-heeled pumps, and a big wool sweater, all at a third to half off.

On Saturday I find places for all my useless purchases.

Sunday morning, my cool sheets tangled around me after a restless night, I decide to go to church.

The parking lot of the Lord's Light Christian Church is even more crowded than usual, and as I am inching my way toward the back of the lot I see why—there are television trucks lined up all around the church and a stretch limousine idling at the side door.

As I crawl past, trapped in traffic, I see him, at long last, as handsome as his photographs, as distinguished as he should look.

Our governor.

He emerges from the limousine, then reaches in and takes his lovely wife's hand and helps her out. The pretty blond woman smiles and waves and he waves, wincing, and I wave at them both as they scurry into the church.

From my seat on the aisle in the back I watch the governor's head as he prays and sings like he's been going to gospel churches all his life. No doubt he has, and it's clear in the familiarity and warmth with which he is greeted that he has been here before, and often.

And then he takes the pulpit.

He begins with a quote we all know—"Whosoever believeth in Him should not perish, but have eternal life"—and he prattles on about faith in ways that seem to ignore the tragedy of Dexter's case, yet when he gets around to Dexter, what he says is startling.

"How odd that when a conviction is upheld on appeal, it is called an affirmation. Yes, it is a way of saying that the trial court's decision was consistent with our laws, but when people of faith think of an affirmation, we think of a renewal of the spirit, a rededication of our commitment to God, a rebirth of faith. Faith is itself an affirmation, a daily affirmation of our trust in God.

"I know that today it is difficult for many of you to have faith, for you are suffering the affirmation of Dexter Hinton's conviction. Some of you are angry, and I know that many of you are disheartened. I too am disheartened, and I have no relief to bring, only a word of caution. In a few weeks we will be entering an election year, a year in which I will be seeking a second term as your governor."

121

There is a brief confetti of applause and a single "amen."

"There are those who would seek to make Dexter Hinton into our Willie Horton, who would use him as a political football, as a symbol of leniency. Even in the wake of the affirmation of Dexter Hinton's conviction, those voices continue to seek to divide our community and distract us from our common goals.

"Dexter Hinton is not a symbol. He is a young man whose life has taken a tragic turn. I am not here to discuss or debate or preach about the guilt or innocence of Dexter Hinton. He was convicted of the crime, that conviction was upheld, and he will continue to serve his time.

"But let us take from one tragic affirmation, an affirmation of the other kind—an affirmation of faith, and let us rededicate ourselves to improving the lives and minds of our youth."

The governor finishes, the organist plays a cool riff as the governor shakes hands with Reverend Jones and others at the podium, then he descends the steps and joins his wife, who is waiting at the side door.

The Reverend Jones leans into the microphone and intones, "We thank Governor Doyle for sharing his thoughts with us this morning. The governor is moving on to speak to another congregation, and we wish him Godspeed."

For the rest of the service, I find myself watching her—Owedia singing joyously, passionately, Owedia swaying devoutly.

I feel the music shake my skin but I don't hear it. And I don't hear the Reverend Jones's words. It's just a mime show there now, meaningless, wrong.

I don't even know why I am here.

In the fellowship room I wait for her by the coffee. Carl is there, across the room, the center of a crowd of women, as always, and he and I exchange glances.

I do not see Barbara Jones or Rev. Jones.

Then Owedia is there walking toward me, her expression as remote as I had expected it to be, a long vertical bruise showing at the side of her right eye.

"Hi," she says, turning to the coffee.

"Hi."

"Why did you leave so suddenly the other night? I wanted to talk to you."

"I'm sorry. I guess it got a little intense for me."

"For me too."

"That's a nasty-looking bruise."

"It feels just as nasty."

She sips at her coffee and turns her eyes on me.

"How strange to see the governor here," I say, hoping to lighten the mood.

"He and Rev. Jones go way back," she says. "In the mideighties, when Doyle was mayor, Reverend Jones supported him over the Democratic candidate. When Doyle ran for reelection as mayor, Reverend Jones even formed a group called Preachers for Doyle that bought radio time to promote Doyle. That was a chancy thing for Reverend Jones to do—it cost him a lot of friends—but it paid off."

"What do you mean?"

Owedia gestures as if displaying the room. "It got us this place, this church. Before this the Lord's Light was a storefront on Central. The land where this church now stands was the city's land. Mayor Doyle wanted to sell us this land, and he pushed it through the city-county council. They say we got it for peanuts."

I search her face for signs of shame; I see none.

"So Reverend Jones owes the governor this church."

"They owe each other."

I smile; of course she's right.

"I saw Dexter yesterday," Owedia says sadly. "He's angry about losing the appeal. I think Carl had done too much to raise his hopes."

"I think so too."

"I challenged Dexter with Joe's version of the way it happened," she says. "It made him sad. It really hurt him to think that I didn't believe him."

I look away, not wanting to hear this.

"He has insisted all along that a third person was in the car. His Mr. E. I believe him, and I think it's time we took it upon ourselves to find this person."

I shrug a little, unable to speak, my heart high in my throat.

"I can't do it alone. I need you to help me."

With those words, my heart drops back to where it belongs; it is as if my body has made up my mind for me. That's it. Enough.

"I can't, Owedia," I say, more firmly than I could have hoped. "I'm sorry, but Carl is right. Joe is probably telling the truth. And I just can't do any more."

Her face reddens. "What do you mean, do any more? What have you done?"

I cannot answer.

"Who are you? Why are you here, if not to *do more?*"

I stammer, "I-I'm a neighbor. That's all."

"A neighbor?! Uh-uh. Let me tell you who you are. You're a white woman. From southern Indiana. A Christian. A serious, tough, stubborn, kind person. And you got a chip on your shoulder a mile wide. I don't know where it comes from, but it's why you're here. You don't have a choice. You have to *do more.*"

Around us, conversation has stopped, and big-boned fool that I am, I can't take the scolding and let it go at that. Not when there's an audience. Without shifting my gaze, I mutter, "And what about you, Owedia? Why must you do more?"

"Look at me! Do you have to ask? I am black and I am a woman and I am hearing, but I work in the deaf world. I am Christian and I am hated by many of those who call themselves Christians." She swallows hard. "I don't belong anywhere, and I don't have nothin'. That's why I have to do more. Because the only way I can feel like I exist is to do something."

She is so strong, so clearheaded and sure. Yet her tone strikes me as false and self-bolstering—that the truth of Dexter's innocence is of less consequence to her than her belief in it. It's like Haberman's Yiddish proverb about insistence, but I don't dare quote it to her.

I try looking at her with tenderness. "I admire the courage it takes to be who you are," I say. "You—"

"Don't," she says. "That's patronizing. And unfair."

"I'm sorry. I just don't have your faith."

"No, you don't."

She puts down her coffee cup, throws me a sad, guilt-provoking smile, and turns and walks away.

I am unburdened. It is a wonderful relief to admit that there are some things that must remain out of one's power, no matter how tragic.

I'm so damned proud of myself. Saying no was the sanest thing I've done in weeks.

I tell myself I gave it my best shot, jeopardizing my career for the sake of a principle.

I can't save Dexter from the courts, from the gangs, from society.

Even big-boned women have to know when to put down the sledgehammer and accept that the rock won't crack.

On Monday morning Haberman brings me coffee and a pecan pastry, and he presents these to me in the gentlest, most solicitous manner. For the rest of the morning there's no badgering about justice, God, or playing devil's advocate.

At lunch time, Haberman and I head to the mall. A crush of early Christmas shoppers bears us along as we make our way to the food court, but Haberman slips adroitly out of the crowd when we pass the newsstand. I follow and see what caught his eye; there, on the front page of the *Standard,* is a color photograph of the governor addressing Rev. Jones's congregation.

Haberman skims the story and chuckles softly.

"Doyle is so thrilled with the Hinton decision he doesn't know what to do with himself. He'll talk about it to anyone who'll listen."

We get plates of greasy Chinese food and take seats beneath one of the huge video monitors that tower over the food court.

Nonchalantly, I ask, "What do you know about Doyle's connection to this Rev. Jones?"

"When Doyle was first elected mayor, there was a series of police 'mistakes' that always ended up with a black man getting killed. There was a guy named Richard French who was mistakenly killed in a bank parking lot. There was a guy named Joseph Griffin who was mistakenly killed in front of his wife and child when a cop was giving him a ticket. There was a guy named Clarence Barnett who was mistakenly shot five times when he got out of his car after a high-speed chase. And then there was Michael Taylor, a fourteen-year-old who got picked up for questioning. He was handcuffed and put in the back of a police car. And somehow he managed to get hold of a gun and shoot himself. While handcuffed.

"Mayor Doyle took a lot of heat for those things, but Rev. Jones stood by him. There were marches on City Hall and people demanded the resignations of the mayor and the police chief, but Rev. Jones stayed home and said, 'Let us work together.' Jones supported Doyle when he ran for reelection and was beside him when Doyle announced his candidacy for governor. He even stumped for Doyle in churches throughout the state, saying 'Here is a Republican candidate we can trust.' Doyle got more black votes than any Republican ever has, and plenty of people think it made the difference in the election."

"So why is it so good for Doyle that Hinton's conviction was affirmed?"

"Doyle's trying to walk a fine line. He wants to keep the support of black clergymen like Jones, so he can't appear to lean too far to the right, and he can't afford to lose the support of his beloved white conservatives, so he can't look like he's in bed with the blacks. The affirmation of Hinton's conviction enables Doyle to look compassionate to the blacks and tough to the whites. And it spares him a potential Willie Horton when he runs for president."

"Do you really think he has a shot at the presidency?"

"A damn good one. He's like a Republican Clinton, only better. He's smart, good-looking, and clean. And he's got the pretty wife and three young kids."

"Doesn't it matter to anyone that he hasn't an ounce of integrity?"

He puts his arm on my shoulder. "There's an old Yiddish saying, 'Those who live near a waterfall do not hear its roar.' "

"What the hell do you mean by that?"

"I mean that the atmosphere of influence and patronage is so pervasive in this town, it isn't even noticed."

For the rest of the afternoon, I bury myself in my utilities case, the acres of transcript piled high around me, the books of Indiana statutes, cases, and the administrative code laid open and stacked, covering every inch of my desk.

I've had enough of Dexter Hinton, of hurt, of grief, of politics.

It's not my problem.

That evening I see Carl and Mr. Williams standing at the curb beside Carl's garbage cans, put out for collection.

I wave and they wave. After Mr. Williams has lowered his arm, Carl keeps waving and smiling, oddly, as I coast up my driveway.

Early the next morning, there is a hard knock at my door. I hear it from my bed, where a glance at my clock tells me it's 5:35 A.M., not a time when I expect company.

I throw on my robe, and as I hurry to the door I see in the pale light that it is snowing, a steady shower of fat, wet flakes.

Before opening my front door, I glance through the window to see who is there.

It is Paul, dressed now as he would be, without a thought for the cold or the snow in jeans and a tweed jacket, collar turned up, and no scarf, no gloves, no hat on his rapidly balding head.

Somehow I am not the least bit amazed to see him, and my reaction is embarrassingly physical. I unlock the door and pull him in. Across the shoulder of his jacket he is carrying a garment bag—stuffed, if I know him, with every bit of clothing he owns.

His mouth lengthens slightly, somewhere between a pout and a smile, and he is about to apologize when I take the garment bag from him, hang it on the coatrack behind the door, and put my arms around him.

I kiss him hard, hoping he won't try to talk. He tastes good, like coffee, and his skin, wet with snow, warms quickly. I let the robe fall open, and the cold droplets on his clothes sting my skin.

He slips his hands under my robe, catching a nipple with his thumb. I let him kiss me a moment as he sheds his wet clothes in the hall, then I lead him to bed.

I don't often pull a man out of the air on a Tuesday morning, but I'll be damned if the timing could have been better.

He is tender and energetic, just as I remember him, though I feel with some chagrin the weight he's put on since we last made love.

No doubt it's the result of the high living he's been doing in Chicago, where he's been practicing corporate law with the world's largest law firm for the past year and a half. It is a far cry from the work he used to profess to want to do. He was the student liaison with the local ACLU chapter, an active participant in the free law clinic for indigent defendants, and the only male member of the women's law caucus—where I met him, of course, clever man that he is.

Now he earns three times what I earn, and it's starting to show in his love handles.

We go at each other like grave diggers in the dark, quite joyfully from my point of view, having not had a lover for nearly a year. He feels good, his body warm and alive with movement, and I am following the urge to come, pressing hard against his thrusts, when I entwine my fingers with his and squeeze tight.

And that's when I feel it.

It is odd, my not having noticed it before, but, as I say, I could not have waited for us to catch up over breakfast.

There is no mistaking it, the plain smooth round ring.

The impulse toward orgasm fades like a decrescendo, and there is silence, coldness, and my detached awareness of his breathing, his lips on my shoulder, his movement inside me.

I am angry at first, but then I look at his face as he kisses me and I decide I don't mind.

I really don't. Not now.

"So when did you get married?"

It is the appropriate first thing to say, I think, as I curl against him.

"July," he says.

"Do I know her?"

"No. Her name is Linda. I met her at the firm."

"A lawyer?"

"Secretary."

"Ahh."

"We're expecting."

Expecting what? I think for an instant, not attuned to marital jargon.

"Congratulations."

"Thanks."

"When's it due?"

"Next month."

"Ahh. So is this your prefatherhood fling?"

"I didn't plan it that way," he says timidly. "I really hadn't expected such a warm reception."

He is here, he tells me, because he hates his job, hates Chicago, hates himself for what he has become, and he has an interview this morning at 9:00 with the Marion County public defender. It is his dream job, he says, a chance to earn a quarter of his current salary in the service of his ideals.

He claims not to have realized it was so early. He claims to have stopped by to say hello, hoping I'd provide a place for him to change into his suit before the interview. And he claims to have intended to take me out to breakfast.

Instead, I make him breakfast. Somewhere on one of my chromosomes there is a gene that compels me to reward a man with food after sex. Rich, replenishing food, hot hearty stuff that goes right to the balls. And so I do it, even under these ludicrous circumstances.

"I don't give a shit about the money," he says, digging into the biscuits and gravy I've whipped up for him. "If I get this job it'll be an opportunity to provide justice to those to whom justice is too often denied."

The words come out cartoonishly. I smile and try not to pity him.

He goes on. "It appalls me that we imprison a higher percentage of our population than any country on earth. More than even the most repressive regimes, the poorest countries, the ones with terrible ethnic and political conflicts! And consider that a third of black men live within the criminal justice system at any given time! Why?"

"Maybe we do that to preserve the freedoms the rest of us enjoy." I say this half believing it, half to play the devil's advocate; in law school, his sixties-throwback liberalism had seemed charmingly recherché, particularly since he was heavily recruited by all the most politically incorrect megafirms. Now, he seems merely spoiled and irresponsibly romantic.

"That isn't my idea of a free society," he says.

"You really want to defend rapists, cocaine dealers, murderers, and child molesters?"

"We're all entitled to a defense."

"But are you prepared to do everything in your power to help a guilty man go free?"

"A vigorous prosecution should be met by a vigorous defense."

"I've worked on a few appeals handled by the public defender's office," I tell him, "and I've read hundreds of others. Can I tell you a secret? The defendants are always guilty. Every one of them. By the time they get to trial you can be damn sure they did it. Whatever race they are. And that's because the prosecutor's office doesn't go to trial without strong evidence. They don't have the money to prosecute losing cases."

"Then there's something wrong with a society that produces so many people who can't survive within the law," he says. "Theft is an economic crime. So is selling cocaine."

"So do something useful," I say, surprised at the bitterness staining my voice. "Become a teacher."

"I can't afford to do that," he protests. "I've got nine more years of student loans to pay for my law degree. And who can live on what teachers earn?"

"Yeah. Or public defenders, for that matter."

"Mmm. Maybe."

"Especially with a family to support."

He smiles softly. "No kidding."

We dress together. He changes into his suit, a charcoal Brooks Brothers number that looks way too Wall Street for the public defender, but I don't tell him that. I slip on a tent from Laura Ashley, something I can be free in, my skin feeling pleasantly raw, my muscles tenderized from the morning's workout.

I tell him to call me when it's over, and we part without touching one another.

At 2:00 P.M. Paul calls to tell me that the interview went wonderfully, and that the public defender is eager to employ his litigation skills "in the service of good instead of evil," as he puts it.

"Unfortunately, they can't make me an offer until the codirector meets me, and he was in court all day," he goes on. "But he can see me tomorrow."

"Oh."

"I'm thinking about staying in town tonight."

"Uh-huh."

"I'd really like to stay with you," he says, the words well rehearsed. "How do you feel about that?"

"How would Linda feel about that?"

"I'll tell her I'm staying with a friend from law school. That's all."

"Uh-huh."

131

"I would love to spend some more time with you."

"Uh-huh."

"There's so much I want to talk with you about. I feel like . . . you know . . . we really only scratched the surface this morning."

"Uh-huh."

On the way home from work I stop for a fifth of Jack Daniel's, a necessary ingredient for the night's lunacy.

I also stop and get a bagful of groceries, wondering what does one cook for one's married lover? Something carnal, redolent of illicit sex?

I buy him beef liver—organ meat—and potatoes and onions and garlic and peppers, good strong stinky food, delicious and vile.

I cook waiting for him in a sweaty heat of anticipation, the garlic, onions, peppers, and slabs of liver frying noisily in my big cast-iron skillet.

When he arrives he brings a fifth of Jack Daniel's, and I wonder for an instant how he knew to buy it. Then I remember a dissolute night after final exams that second year, a night I have no right to remember.

I open his bottle, pour us fistfuls, and we drink the glasses straight down.

Then I drag him to bed to make love while dinner simmers.

I have decided that I will use him as best I can this night, to have him without giving a shit that he's married.

And why the hell not? I need a lover.

And a slice off a cut loaf isn't missed.

Over dinner, loosened by the whiskey, I tell him about Dexter. I watch him watching me as I tell him; he is intrigued at first, then his face clouds with anger.

"Are you out of your fucking mind?" he says finally. "Do you realize that you could be disbarred for what you've done? That the judge's decision could be vacated? That you could be subject to criminal charges for tampering with the judicial process?"

I start to cry, my fork in my hand, a curl of onion quivering on a slice of potato about to enter my mouth.

It is not the danger to my career, so bluntly spelled out by Paul, that troubles me, but the awful bungling I've done, the hideous mess I've made of Dexter's chances.

Paul gazes at me piteously, guiltily.

"I'm sorry," he says. "I know you tried to do the right thing. I don't know what I would have done."

"You would have waved to the man three doors up the street, and no more. You would've known better."

We look at each other, shame coloring both our faces.

"But it's over now," he says quickly.

"Yes."

"So you'd better hope nobody finds out what you did."

"Yeah."

"Has the case gone up on transfer to the supreme court?"

"Not yet."

"You're not planning to help the grandfather with that, are you?"

"No, I've pretty much washed my hands of it all."

"You're better off staying as far away from those people as you can. Unless you want to commit career suicide."

I shrug, melancholy washing over me.

He says, "I can't believe you're living in this neighborhood."

"Why?"

"The obvious reason. Don't you feel uncomfortable here?"

I shrug again.

"I don't think it's racist to feel uncomfortable being the only white person for blocks."

"I don't pay much attention to race," I lie.

"There's a lot of crime here. Drug dealing. Crack houses. Don't you worry about your safety? Especially being a white woman living alone."

"What do you mean?" As if I don't know.

"That you might be a target for rape."

"Do you think black men are more inclined toward rape than white men?"

"I don't know," he says.

We finish his bottle and make a start on mine as we sit opposite one another at my small dining-room table, the dirty dishes pushed aside to make room for the drunken slouch of our heads in our hands.

Sodden and stupid, I ask him, "Why are you here?"

"Because I've made the biggest mistake of my life," he moans.

For an instant I think he's talking about me—about having made love with me.

He says, "I got caught. It's that fucking simple. I was so hot for this girl . . . and she is a girl, really, she's only nineteen . . . that I didn't think. And then, it was, like, one, two, three. One, 'I'm pregnant.' Two, 'I don't believe in abortion.' Three, 'We're getting married.' "

"You don't love her."

He shakes his head slowly.

"What an ass you are."

"Yes, I'm an idiot."

We drink more, then we leave the dishes and stagger dizzily to the bed, where we have a sloppy, ugly fuck and neither of us comes. We roll apart, my head spinning as painfully as I deserve. Somehow the light is shut off.

Nauseated and sweating feverishly, I find oblivion.

I awaken at 4:43 the next morning, the red numbers on my digital clock goring into the darkness, and I am dreadfully ill.

I push myself out of bed gingerly. My hand touches Paul's thigh. It feels cold and wooden to my touch, like dead flesh, and I feel something sharp and nasty kick at my heart.

On my knees I hug the bowl and heave, and as all that stinking

134

meat and whiskey comes up I start to cry, overcome by my stupidity, my grief, my weakness.

That's when I lose it.

I go back to the bedroom and shake his shoulder hard.

"Paul, wake up! You've got to wake up! Come on!"

His eyes flutter open and he asks me if he overslept.

"Get up," I tell him.

"What's wrong?"

"I don't want you here. Get out of bed. Now. Get dressed and get the fuck out of here."

"What's the matter with you?" Awake and sitting up now.

"Nothing's the matter with me!" Now I'm shouting. "I just don't want you here, okay? Go stay at a motel!"

"Nora . . ."

"Get *up!*"

He gets up and moves naked toward the bathroom. When his back is to me I shove hard at his shoulder blades and he trips forward a step.

He glares back at me, fearful.

19

I am a big-boned woman, and there is little I am physically afraid to do. As a child of thirteen I was so strong and immovable that I once dared my siblings, all three of them, to hang from my shoulders and limbs and try to pull me down.

Of course they couldn't do it. And by the time they got old enough to win that dare, I'd gotten over wanting to be the strongest thing on earth.

In my last existence I was a cow—a beautiful brown Jersey with passionate flaring nostrils, a broad proud face, and soulful eyes. I lived from feed to feed, shortsighted, unhurried. All my muscles were sturdy and stiff, and I passed my days in obliging stupid bliss, giving milk and manure and calves, asking nothing but peace, the blessed peace of the field.

My father always kept a bull and six or seven or eight cows, and it was I alone among my siblings who helped him care for them. I fed them, milked them, stroked their heads and necks when the inseminator came and did his business, tended them when they calved, and all this bonded us, truly; we came to love each other, and I came to feel myself one of them.

Cows, big-boned females, strong and beautiful, placid; but don't make a cow mad. Handle a teat too roughly and get the shit kicked out of you.

Big-bonedness is genetically linked, I think, to outsized emotions. I get overwrought. I cry. I yell. When my mother left, shortly after my eleventh birthday, I had to be strong for all of us kids and for my father, and I developed a severe intolerance for messes. As my family's substitute mother, I insisted upon order, and I attempted to impose that order with the strength in my arms and the power of my voice.

To little avail. We are all a mess, all four of us Lumsey children and my father too, and the messes I make for myself just get bigger and messier and harder to clean up.

When Paul is gone I crawl back to bed, furious with myself for being lonely enough to want him and mean enough to throw him out. The room spins, and my mind skitters woozily to thoughts of my judge. For a moment, half dreaming, I imagine he is there with me, standing at the foot of my bed, scowling his disapproval.

I arrive at my desk an hour late, still vaguely drunk. There, waiting for me, is a new pleading filed in the case of *Hinton v. State of Indiana*. It is a petition for rehearing asking the appeals court to reexamine its decision to make sure no mistake was made. Petitions for rehearing almost never succeed—maybe one in a thousand convinces the court that it was wrong—and this one, typed out on Carl's old typewriter, is a foregone conclusion. It hasn't a snowball's chance in hell.

> I beg the court reconsider the tragedy of my grandson and the lies that put him in jail. Yes, he is not a perfect boy, but he is not evil, he would no sooner hurt that old lady than he would hurt me, his loving grandfather. If he gets out he will have a real home to come to, not like so many of those teenagers in jail. He has been my guardian angel and I can be his angel and we all know that angels should not be locked up where they can't do anybody any good. Why don't you look for the one who really did it, the one Dexter calls Mr. E?

Angels again. Mr. E. The thought of Carl's wasted effort and wasted hopes sends my heart plummeting.

I look up to see Haberman watching me as I read. He smiles, comes over to my desk, and leans casually against it.

"It's too bad about Hinton," he says. "I hope you don't mind, I saw the petition on your desk and took a look at it."

"No, I don't mind."

"Rather a shame that the boy's family doesn't get themselves a lawyer. If they'd done that, the kid would be free by now."

"Maybe."

"Hell, yes. A decent lawyer would have raised the issue you raised *sua sponte*. The judge would have had to consider it."

"If you're trying to make me feel better, you're doing a great job."

"What Hinton needs to do," he says—and I don't know if he's sincerely trying to help or just showing off—"is to file a petition for postconviction relief. I don't know why they haven't done that already."

Postconviction relief. The concept rings a bell, but I haven't heard about it since the first year of law school.

"Refresh my memory," I ask him. "How does postconviction relief work?"

"Well," he intones, drawing me in, "it's what you do if new evidence comes to light that may exonerate the defendant. You have to file a petition for postconviction relief setting forth the new evidence."

"Oh."

"It's the fail-safe system. It's the last chance, but there's no time limit and you can petition as many times as you want as long as you have something new to say each time."

"But we don't have anything new to say, no new evidence."

He looks at me oddly. "We?"

A wave of panic rushes over me. "I—"

"You're taking this case a little too personally, aren't you?" He laughs, at first a snicker, and then a full roar.

"I can't believe I said that." I laugh.

"Postconviction relief," he repeats. "It's the way to go."

"Where do I find the rules?"

"In your rules volume. I can't believe you've never read them."

"Thanks, Larry."

"You're welcome, Nora."

We.

There's no avoiding it, not now that I understand the procedure of it, that there is hope continuing on indefinitely into the future. Yet it is dreadful. Without finality there can be no rest, no repose, no end to it until the truth is known.

The postconviction rules provide that

> Any person who has been convicted of or sentenced for a crime by a court of this state, and who claims . . . That there exists evidence of material facts, not previously heard, that requires vacation of the conviction or sentence in the interest of justice . . . may institute at any time a proceeding under this rule to secure relief.

And the cases interpreting this rule are clear as day:

> The fact that there is newly-discovered evidence in a case after the appellate decision has been handed down may be raised under this rule. *Ayad v. State,* 263 N.E.2d 150 (Ind.Ct.App. 1970).

So it doesn't matter what the appeals court says. If new evidence comes to light, the conviction can be overturned.

Later that morning I telephone the Indiana School for the Deaf and ask for Owedia. If I do nothing else, I must tell her about postconviction relief and urge her to press forward to try to find new evidence. I am put through to her voice mail and without thinking I almost leave my telephone number at the chambers. I call again and ask the receptionist when I might reach Owedia in person.

"School lets out at three-fifteen," she says.

At 11:30, the judge emerges from his office, smiling determinedly, and approaches my desk. It is such an extraordinarily personal thing for him to do that I feel a momentary adrenaline rush of terror, and I gaze up at him fearfully as he says, "Are you available for lunch?"

He takes me to a restaurant in the atrium of a nearby hotel. We sit oddly exposed on a balcony, enveloped in silence with twenty stories of air above us.

He orders the luncheon buffet and I do the same. Once we have stood on line and filled our plates with salad, he looks at me shyly and watches me eat.

"I feel rather badly about the Hinton situation," he says after a time. "But what you did was inexcusable."

I swallow hard, wondering if somehow he knows.

"I understand that you did what you thought was right. You went out on a limb for your convictions. I admire the courage it took to do that."

I tell him that I only did what I thought the law required.

His expression turns stern. "You don't know enough to make that determination. Your input is welcome. But you deliberately disobeyed my instructions." On his last words he thumps the table with the tips of his fingers, and the silverware jumps and clatters.

"There I go again," he says. "I had hoped to make it up to you, but I am still perhaps somewhat overwrought."

He orders a scotch for himself without asking if I want a drink.

When the drink comes he takes a quick sip of it and suddenly smiles at me. "You are naive and you are headstrong. You're a headstrong woman," he says, repeating that word *headstrong* like it gives him pleasure to say. "You are full of ideals, but you don't seem to grasp that we are all human beings here. We all put on our trousers one leg at a time."

"I try to understand that," I say, "but I don't understand what that has to do with the correctness of a decision of the court."

He takes a longer sip, and then another, and drains his glass. "You don't understand the difference between truth and justice," he says. "Truth can never be achieved absolutely in the courts because truth is retrospective—we are always looking backward trying to find out what happened in a case and why. The truth is by nature an illusion. It is a matter of testimony, of clues, of evidence. We can only hope we have found the truth. We can never *know.*" He pauses for a smile. "Justice, on the other hand, is prospective. It is a decision for the future that attempts to remedy what we believe to have occurred in the past . . . and to make amends for it. Justice is necessarily imperfect because it is made by human beings."

He stops abruptly, then says, "Have you ever thought about becoming a judge?"

"I don't know," I say, flattered. "Not really."

"You seem to think you're qualified to do my job."

I feel myself blush. "No, I don't. Really, I don't." He smiles. It was a joke, it's okay. So I go on, "Well, maybe I would enjoy being a judge."

"Well, I'm going to tell you how to do it." He pauses and takes a long drink. "There are fifteen judges elected to four-year terms in Marion County. Whenever there's an election, the parties each put up eight candidates for judge in a process called *slating.* That way, you have sixteen candidates on the ballot for fifteen positions and only one loser. Thus, being slated is virtually an appointment as a judge. So, you might ask, what do you have to do to be slated? You have to contribute money to the county party. You have to show up at the two-hundred-dollar-a-napkin cocktail party. You have to cultivate the right people."

He drains his glass and orders another scotch. "The goddamn surprising thing is how little it has to do with merit—I mean, with scholarship, wisdom, integrity, talent—that is, with any of the things we would hope to associate with a judge. In fact, it virtually assures that judges will be manipulators, backstabbers, money-grubbers, glad-handers, brownnosing toadies!"

I laugh tentatively, hoping it's what he's after. After a pause, he goes on, softening, "It's a miracle we have as many good judges as we do." He seems angry, though, and I am fearful of offending him. Of course, the next words that come out of my mouth are: "But it's equally political to become a judge on the court of appeals, isn't it?"

His mouth drops open. I have taken him by surprise, complete surprise, and I have never seen his face so animated. Then he starts to laugh, thank God, and I laugh too. It was a joke, and a good one.

"Miss Lumsey," he says when he recovers, "You are a scholar and a fine writer, but you serve at my pleasure. Don't forget that."

Big-boned women are stubborn women, and we are irrationally stubborn. We spite ourselves to spite others, and we do not capitulate or change our minds unless it is in defiance of someone's expectations. If anything were to convince me to disobey the judge, it would be his insistence on obedience. I can't stand doing anything anyone asks me to do, even if I want to do it. Or even if I know it's right.

So I could not say yes when Owedia asked me to help her. But if it means disobeying the judge and possibly ending my career, I can do it.

I call Owedia at 3:30 and tell her that I need to see her to talk about Dexter.

"Wonderful," she says. "What about tonight? Can you make it to Sugar Street by seven-thirty?"

"Sugar Street? Isn't that a bar? I thought you didn't drink."

"I don't. But I'm meeting someone there."

"I'm intrigued."

"Please come. It's at Twenty-sixth and Evanston."

Sugar Street is a corner tavern on a busy avenue of boarded-up fast-food joints, broken streetlights, and abandoned cars. The air is damp, the street is shiny with melted snow. The seediness of the area makes me nervous, but I cannot imagine being afraid in a place Owedia would dare to go.

Of course it is a black bar. Smoke hangs heavily over the dozen or so men clustered around the bar. There is football on the television. Owedia sits alone in a booth along the wall opposite the bar, the light above her table forming a bright cylinder in which she sits, her hands wrapped around a glass, looking lonely and untouchable.

She watches me approach, her big eyes following me slowly, and then she reaches out a hand to me. I grasp it and lean down and we kiss each other's cheeks.

"Hi," she says. "I didn't think you'd come."

"I'm glad I did. For your sake. I sure wouldn't come alone to a place like this."

"You wouldn't come to a place like this at all."

"No. You wouldn't either."

"No."

She looks at her drink, unsmiling.

"So why are we here?"

"You'll find out soon."

"What are you drinking?"

"Diet Coke."

At the bar, I get a beer for myself and a refill for Owedia. The men at the bar, all of them in late middle age, glance at me one after the other, then focus their attention back on the game.

I feel my skin tighten with fear. There is a palpable threat in the air, and though I would not suspect any particular one of these men of bad intentions, there is something wrong with this picture, and it is that Owedia and I should not be here.

As I return to the table, the door creaks open and a woman—at least I think it is a woman—scurries in on a blast of frigid air.

She is a tiny thing, skinny and short, her straightened hair parted in the middle and curled stiffly down to her neck. She is wearing a short red skirt and shiny black-leather car coat, with much dangling jewelry and makeup. My first thought is that she looks like a transvestite, and a well-dressed transvestite.

143

The woman scrunches her arms to her chest and shivers comically. "Oooh! Damn, it's cold," she says to the room, and a couple of the men turn long enough to grunt their agreement. The bartender nods at her and murmurs indecipherably, and she waves back with a weary "hey, darlin'."

Owedia holds up one hand and looks at the woman with that calm, smiling intensity of hers. The woman raises her chin, acknowledging Owedia, and with a trembling walk on her stick-figure legs she arrives at our table as I put down the drinks.

"JeTaun? I'm Owedia Braxton." Owedia holds out her hand to the woman, who shakes it in a businesslike fashion, at the same time tilting her head and looking askance at Owedia's hair.

"Hi," she says.

"JeTaun, this is Nora, a friend of mine."

I shake her hand and introduce myself.

"JeTaun Holley," she responds.

"JeTaun is a friend of Joseph Baker's."

"Well, I used to be," JeTaun says, "till he fucked up."

I glance at Owedia, who continues to smile radiantly at JeTaun.

JeTaun, seeming suddenly embarrassed, says, "Excuse me, ladies, while I get myself a drink. God knows I need it."

JeTaun returns with a tall glass of a slushy pink liquid, and she takes a long, thirsty mouthful as she sits.

"I used to hang with them, the Indy Boyz," she begins. "They been around for a long time. Fifteen years maybe. And they do business with gangs in other cities. It's just like the Mafia, no shit. 'Cept that we the brothers and sisters. We look out for one another, like family. It *is* family. And I'm only talking to you about Joe because he fucked his little brother, fucked him bad, and you can't do that. Maybe some of the brothers will let that go, but I can't. I got four kids of my own now. When I think about that boy Dexter, I know it ain't right for him to be in jail for what a grown man done."

Owedia nods. "You're right. And we thank you for it."

"Well, look, I'm no kid anymore. I'm twenty-six, a grown woman, and I only hope my life has made me wiser than I was."

"Amen," says Owedia, and I can only look at JeTaun and think, shit, I'm twenty-six, and my life hasn't even begun yet.

Owedia asks, "Did Joe tell you the real story of what happened?"

"No, I heard it right from Speed."

"Who's Speed?"

"He's a white kid from Noblesville," she says, glancing at me. "He runs with the Vipers, a white gang that does business with the Indy Boyz."

"Does he have a tattoo on the back of his neck?" Owedia asks quickly.

"Yeah, they all do. A snake. Typical chickenshit thing to do, put it back there where they can let their hair grow and hide it." She glances at me.

"So you know this guy Speed," I say.

"Yeah. I knew lots of Vipers. But I know Speed because he'd hang with Joe."

"What do you know about the murder of that woman?"

"I know everything you want to know."

Owedia and I exchange looks. "Wonderful," I say.

Then she looks hard at me and says, "I need some money first."

"Oh."

I peek at Owedia, who looks down at the table and grimaces, then says, "I had prayed that you would do this for Dexter's sake, not for money. I don't have any money."

"I told you I had to have money," she says.

"How much?" I say.

"Five hundred," she says somberly.

I look at Owedia, who seems about to cry. "We can't do that," I tell her. "Maybe two hundred."

She shakes her head. "I'm risking my ass here. And fucking somebody bad. I'm breaking the code. That's wrong, and it's worth something."

"Three hundred," I say. Owedia looks at me as if I'm mad.

JeTaun shakes her head. "I got kids to feed. I do all right now. I'm a cosmetologist, and I still sell some on the side, but I need some money. Bad. I got to get paid for this."

"Three-fifty," I say. "We're not rich people."

JeTaun nods her agreement.

"Of course I don't have it with me," I say, "but I'll take you to a cash machine when we're done here, and you'll get paid." She looks blankly at me. "You do trust me to do that, don't you?"

"I do because I know what will happen to you if you screw me."

Owedia takes my hand and draws close, engaging me in an anxious sidebar.

"Are you sure you want to do this?" she whispers.

"Can you pay half?"

She nods.

"Then we're in this together."

Owedia squeezes my hand.

"Okay," I say. "What happened?"

JeTaun sips her drink, then slowly rotates the cup to set the ice in motion.

"The Vipers and the Indy Boyz sell drugs. A lot of drugs. Mostly reefer but coke too; crack, crank, PCP, acid. Joe's been with the Indy Boyz a long time, since he was maybe thirteen. About four months before that lady got shot, Joe killed a man, a piece of shit who was working as a confidential informant for the police. He was making a controlled buy from some Vipers up in Carmel, and it was Joe who noticed the guy was wearing a wire. They say he shot the guy on the spot. Right here." She points to the middle of her forehead. "Killed the shit instantly. Of course they knew the cops was listening, so they got the fuck out fast. But before they did Joe grabbed the buy money the shit had brought, and got his ass out before the cops showed up."

JeTaun curls her nose and sniffles, unmistakably expressing a kind of machismo, a facial hitching up of the pants.

"Joe got respect with that move, and with killing the piece of shit, but he also fucked himself up because the Vipers owned him then. They had power over him and he knew it. All they had to do was make one phone call and say who killed the C.I. and that was it. Not that Joe didn't have shit on them too. But that was nothin' like killin' a C.I. It's not as bad as killin' a cop but they treat it like it was. It's like spittin' in a cop's face."

Owedia asks, "Was this C.I. a gang member?"

"No, he was just some poor shit trying to make some money." She sits silently for a moment, glances toward the bar, then glares at Owedia and me. "I know what you're thinkin' and maybe it's true. But I *need* the money."

"I know," Owedia says. "And we are all here for Dexter."

"That's right," she says, then straightens up, physically shifting gears. "You know what a viper is, right?"

"What do you mean?" I say.

"It's what they used to call a marijuana smoker. A long time ago. But it's a good name for that gang. They're mean, like snakes. And sneaky."

Owedia asks, "What do you know about the day Cora Rollison got shot?"

"Nothin'." A pause. " 'Cept that if you hear there was somebody else in that car besides Joe and Dexter, you can believe it. And if you hear that it was Joe who shot that woman, you can believe that too."

"Do you know something about what happened that day that you can't tell us?"

"I don't know nothin' about it 'cept what I heard. I wasn't there."

"What did you hear?"

"Just what I told you, if you was listenin'. There was a Viper in the car. Can I make it clearer?"

"Which Viper?"

"I don't know."

"But you heard about the killing from Speed."

"Yeah."

"Can we talk to Speed?"

147

"If you can find him. It's been a year since I've seen him."

JeTaun hunches her shoulders over her drink, as if hunkering down, closing up.

Owedia reaches across her table and puts her hands around Je-Taun's hands holding the drink.

"You've told us a great deal, and for that we thank you. But we need to know, is there a particular Viper that you think it might have been?"

JeTaun stares into the speckled surface of the table. Owedia slowly withdraws her hands.

"We need names of Vipers, JeTaun," I chime in, the price tag on this information flashing in my brain like neon. "Do you know any names of Vipers?"

She shakes her head. "No. I know some street names. If you're trying to find them, maybe that'll help."

"Go."

"There's one tall, big guy, big shoulders, they call him Samurai. He's very quiet. Then there's Carlos, a blond kid who sure ain't Spanish. And there's a guy called Freeze, a guy Sack, a guy Popeye, a guy T-Bone, a guy they call Slick, a guy Buffalo . . . and there's Speed."

Owedia and I glance at each other, amazed.

"You know these guys pretty well," I say.

"We'd hang. Freeze got a big old place in Carmel, belongs to his old man. We usta' hang there and party."

"But not any more?"

"Shit, no. I been out of that scene for two years. It's okay when you're a kid, but, you know, I got responsibilities. I got a real life now." She looks at Owedia, who is about to reach over again to give the woman's hands a squeeze when JeTaun puts her hands in her lap and moves away. "I don't know what you ladies want to do about all this," she says, "but you better watch your backs. If you haven't figured it out, these people will fuck up your shit without blinkin'."

She opens the collar of her shirt and pulls the fabric down to expose her right upper chest, where there is a thin whitish line, about three-quarters of an inch in length. "Okay? You know what that is?" Then she opens the shirt buttons at her waist and pulls the shirt apart to reveal a larger scar, perhaps an inch-and-a-half in length, enclosed between two sets of dots, a quarter-inch between each. The scar looks hard next to the soft skin of her belly.

She closes the buttons, then pulls up the sleeves of her jacket. Both forearms are speckled with dots and lines, the leavings of knives and stitches.

Owedia murmurs, "Why?"

"Fights mostly. Seemed like for a while there I couldn't turn around without some woman wanting to mess with me. There was a man I was with, called himself Africa; he's the father of my second son, James—that was Africa's name too, his real name. There was always some bitch after Africa. I didn't know he was after them too." She laughs. "I still keep a knife on me. Force of habit, you know."

She reaches into her pocketbook and takes out what looks to me like a Boy Scout knife about four inches long. "It's a flick knife," she says, and with a snap of her wrist the blade swings out and clicks into position. "Can't carry no switchblade no more. It's illegal."

Owedia and I drive JeTaun to the nearest ATM, where I withdraw the cash to pay her. She takes the money without a thank-you and tucks it into her jacket pocket.

Owedia glances at me, frowning, and I return the look. It has occurred to us both that we've been ripped off, that JeTaun has told us little we did not know.

All the time I am with JeTaun in Owedia's car I am aware of the knife she carries, and of the overwhelming odor of cosmetics and hairspray.

As Owedia drives JeTaun to her house, just two blocks from the bar, I watch her huddled in the center of the backseat, trying to look small, yet glancing furtively around her.

"You all right, JeTaun?" I say.

"I just been thinkin' I should'a met you someplace else, in some other part of town."

149

Owedia and I exchange worried glances.

"I'm just used to thinkin' I'm safe here. These are my streets. Now I don't know who's seen me with you."

Owedia says, "But if somebody did see you, what of it? How would they know it had anything to do with the Indy Boyz?"

"They'd know," she says, "They know already."

Before she gets out of the car, JeTaun gestures with her chin toward Owedia's hair and says, "Who did that to you?"

Owedia shifts uncomfortably. "I had it done at a beauty school."

JeTaun shakes her head slowly. "D-minus," she says.

"I know."

"You come see me," she says, "I'll fix it for you."

"I don't think I can afford you," Owedia says bitterly.

"Maybe not." JeTaun slams the door shut and hurries toward her building.

20

When Owedia and I part, we embrace and make plans to see Dexter on Saturday. She promises to give me a check for her half of the money I paid JeTaun.

"Thank you," she says, her voice assuming an unaccustomed girlishness. "I can't tell you how happy I am not to have to do this alone. I'm not good at this kind of thing. I'm easily frightened. I'm not strong."

"I find that hard to believe," I say. "And doesn't your faith give you strength?"

"Yes," she says. "But it's the strength of having the wind at your back. It's the strength to go forward and do what you must. It's not like your strength, which comes so naturally."

I smile and hug her again, but I feel as if I've been kicked in the gut. I'm so damn tired of being expected to be strong.

On Friday, two days later, I come home to find a message from Owedia on my answering machine.

> "JeTaun Holley has been hurt. Badly, I'm afraid. She's at Presbyterian. I'm going to see her tonight. . . . Umm . . . I'll call you. Please be careful, Nora."

I pour myself two fingers of Jack Daniel's. In the glass it looks like too little to give me the will to go back out into the cold, so I pour in as much again and drink a mouthful fast.

I had not believed JeTaun when she said she was in danger. I did not believe that someone would do violence to her merely for speaking with Owedia and me. Now I wonder if we are not closer to the truth than I could have imagined, and if Owedia and I are in serious danger as well.

The taste of the Jack Daniel's is an unsettling reminder of Paul, but I'll be damned if I'm going to throw good whiskey away.

I end up pouring half the glass into the sink.

Presbyterian Hospital is an old hospital, not a bad hospital, but it has old and new wings and if you're rich or well-insured you get into the bright new wing.

JeTaun is in the old wing, where the rooms are small and dim and the air is sodden with a century of illness and death. In JeTaun's room I find Owedia and two other women who Owedia introduces as JeTaun's mother and JeTaun's boss from the salon. They greet me tensely, appraisingly, and I try not to respond in kind.

The mother tells me that JeTaun is sleeping, and when she moves aside, my heart sinks hard at the sight of JeTaun's battered face. One eye is bandaged over, and the exposed eye is bruised black all around it. Her lips are swollen, one nostril is split open, and her skin is peppered with cuts, as if her face had been smashed against a rough surface.

Owedia steps behind me and takes my arm. "The doctor says it looks worse than it is," she says. "But it looks so bad."

"Let's go outside," I say, and with a nod to the two women we go into the hall.

I ask Owedia how long JeTaun has been sleeping.

"A half hour," she says. "I've been here since four o'clock. JeTaun had her mother call me at school."

"Did she tell you what happened?"

"It happened last night after work," Owedia says. "JeTaun had worked late, and didn't get out until after ten. Two guys jumped her outside the salon. At least she thinks it was two guys. She never saw it coming. She heard footsteps behind her and suddenly she felt a coat, a big old wool coat, go over her head. They pushed her to the ground, punched her repeatedly, kicked at her head under the coat, then fled."

"How bad is she?"

"She has broken ribs, a concussion, and some really nasty bruises all over her face." She pauses a moment. "She may lose an eye."

"Ohh, God."

Owedia sighs. "I feel responsible," she says, her voice breaking.

"Have the police been here?"

"Yes, they questioned JeTaun last night and this morning. And they have the coat."

"Did she say anything to the police about why she got beat up?"

"I don't think so. She didn't want to talk about it with me, either. She's scared. I think she's worried that if she tells the police, they'll come after her again. She's certain it's a warning."

"But who does she think it is? The Indy Boyz? The Vipers? Joe Baker?"

"She doesn't know. Or that's what she said."

I put my hand on Owedia's upper arm. "Do you feel safe in your apartment?"

"Safe? Not particularly. But I am praying a lot. And I keep my doors and windows locked."

In the visitors' meeting room the next morning, Dexter does not wait for Owedia to approach, as he had his grandfather; when the door opens he is out of his seat and running toward her. He hugs her close, then they sign to each other animatedly, fingers close, as if to compensate for the long week spent apart.

Then, prompted by something Owedia signs, Dexter looks intently at me and holds out his hand for me to shake.

"Hello again," I say, and he grips my hand firmly.

Owedia sits with Dexter on one side of the table, chairs turned so that they face each other. I sit opposite them. As Owedia signs to him, she speaks her words and his in response.

"Tell me what you know about the Indy Boyz," she asks.

Dexter's eyes are still for a moment, then he signs, " 'That's Joe's gang.' "

"Did you ever hang with them?"

" 'Hang? No . . . but . . . maybe. I hung with Joe and his friends sometimes.' "

"What would you do with them?"

" 'Drive around. They drank and smoked and sometimes they would meet other people and I would wait in the car.' "

"Where would you go?"

" 'I don't know.' "

"Did you ever go into any strange houses with Joe?"

Dexter shakes his head.

"Did you ever meet white guys with Joe?"

Dexter glances quickly at me.

" 'Just Mr. E,' " he signs.

"Had you ever seen him before that day?"

Owedia looks determinedly, sternly, into Dexter's eyes. Then she signs, stiffly, and speaks the words emphatically. "I want you to think carefully back to that day, Dexter. Try to remember if you saw Joe call Mr. E by some other name."

Dexter shakes his head.

I touch Dexter's arm and say, as Owedia translates, "What happened when you got into the car? Did Joe say something like, 'Dexter, I'd like you to meet my friend . . .'?"

Dexter looks at me like I'm from another planet.

"Did this white guy turn around and shake your hand?"

" 'No.' "

"Did he say anything to you?"

" 'No.' " Dexter's face takes on a weary, unhappy expression. " 'He looked at me like I was a freak, like maybe I scared him, and then he acted like I wasn't even there.' "

"Did Joe tell him you were deaf?"

" 'I don't know.' "

Owedia rests her chin on her palm and gazes resignedly at Dexter.

"Have you ever heard of the Vipers?" I ask him.

He squints at Owedia, then at me.

"The Vipers," I say, enunciating strenuously.

Dexter shakes his head, then signs, making a back-and-forth motion with his index fingers. " 'You mean like window wipers.' "

Owedia smiles and touches his cheek. Dexter signs, " 'No, what are they?' "

"They're a gang, like the Indy Boyz."

Dexter looks blankly at me.

"They're mostly white kids."

Dexter does not seem to register this. I go on, "They have a tattoo on the back of their heads. It's a snake but it looks like an *E.*"

Suddenly Dexter's eyes come to life, and he beams at me, smiling broadly.

" 'I saw a guy here who had an *E* on his head, like Mr. E.' "

"When?"

" 'A while ago.' "

"How long?"

Dexter shrugs. " 'Two or three months.' "

"Where did you see him?"

" 'Here, in the yard.' "

"How old?"

Dexter shrugs and signs, " 'Sixteen, seventeen.' "

"Did you talk to him?"

" 'No.' "

"Did you only see him that once?"

" 'Yes.' "

"Why didn't you tell anybody?"

" 'Why should I?' "

Owedia plays the dialogue straight, without excitement, and it

155

occurs to me with a jolt of fear that at the end of this process we will have to find these people, these Vipers, and confront them—something my gut tells me I do not want to do.

"And he's the only other guy with that tattoo that you've seen?"

Dexter nods.

Owedia asks, "Do you see guys from other gangs here?"

" 'Sure. They're everywhere.' "

"Other gangs in Indianapolis?"

" 'Yeah.' "

"Do they have tattoos?"

" 'Yeah.' "

"Are there gangs here in the boys' school?"

" 'Yeah.' "

"Do they give each other tattoos? Here?"

" 'Yeah.' "

"Did someone ask you to join a gang?"

" 'Yeah.' "

I had not noticed it before, but I see now that Dexter's signing is stilted and restrained, the movement of his arms graceless. The cuffs of his shirt are pulled down to his palms, and now, as Owedia takes his hand in hers, he resists halfheartedly, then permits her to push back the sleeve to reveal a crude tattoo on the inside of his wrist.

It appears to be an X in a circle, but the ink has blotched under the skin and the skin is raised and tinged with red. It looks very painful.

Owedia takes his hand, kisses the palm, and holds it to her cheek.

"Oh, dear Lord, don't do this, Dexter."

Dexter lets her hold his hand, and he looks at her timidly.

"What's your grandfather going to say when he sees this?"

Dexter is motionless.

"Why?"

" 'Nothin' else to do.' "

"Dexter, there is everything else to do. You have your schoolwork. You have your Bible. You have to have the discipline and the brains to stay away from those people."

Dexter signs furiously. " 'You don't understand what it's like . . .

to live in this place. You don't know what happens to you if they think you're different. Or if they think you think you're better than they are.' "

"You have to make the decision not to care about that, Dexter. You have to decide that you're going to be good no matter what. You have to set an example. And how could you let somebody stick you with a needle and draw on you?"

Dexter shrugs.

"That's crazy. You could catch AIDS or other diseases doing that, you know?"

Dexter looks away.

Owedia asks, "Did you pray today, honey?"

" 'Yes.' "

"Good. Did you go to chapel last Sunday?"

" 'Yes.' "

"And did you talk to Rev. Davis after?"

" 'No.' "

"Why not?"

" 'He was busy.' "

"You have to go to him."

Dexter stares glumly at the floor.

Owedia says, "Your grandfather will be here this afternoon."

Dexter looks at me.

"I want you to show him your tattoo."

Dexter will not look at Owedia. She touches the side of his face. He turns slowly to her, she kisses him, and we go.

Outside the visitors' room, Owedia leans against the wall and closes her eyes.

After a moment she whispers, "I can't believe he would do that to himself."

"He has to live in this world."

"We've got to pull him out of here."

"Yes."

"We're going to find that Viper." She pushes herself from the wall.

"He may still be in this place, or they may know his name. He may know something about who killed that woman."

Owedia hikes the strap of her bag up onto her shoulder and starts swiftly for the lobby. I follow, a good two strides behind her.

"We've got to be careful!" I yell to her. "What happened to JeTaun could easily happen to us."

"I know. But Dexter is worth the risk, isn't he?"

Catching up, I take her arm and stop her. "I wonder if this might not be a good time for you to go to the police with what you know."

"What do you mean, *you?* Not you too?"

"You've got to remember that I'm not even supposed to be here. I shouldn't be involved in this or any other case. I—"

"—work for the state, I know." Owedia moves toward the metal detector at the end of the hall. "Just what do you do for the state, anyhow?"

Owedia smiles as we pass through the metal detector and into the front lobby, and she doesn't wait for me to answer. She goes directly to the information desk, where she asks a uniformed woman where she might find the principal's office.

"You found it," the woman says.

"I need to speak with the principal about a student."

"What's the student's name?"

"Dexter Hinton."

"And who are you?"

"A friend of his grandfather's."

The woman takes our names, then pronounces them into a telephone.

"The principal, Dr. Franke, is unavailable, but his assistant, Mr. Coleman, can speak with you if you like."

Owedia agrees, and we are invited back through the metal detector, buzzed through the inner door, and ushered through a large room crowded with uniformed correction officers into a small office. There, behind a neat metal desk, stands a frowning black man with an odd, unstylish mini-Afro, an ill-made brown suit—puckered at every seam—and his hands in his pockets.

Owedia steps boldly toward him and thrusts out her hand.

Coleman's hand is momentarily stuck in his pocket, but after an awkward instant he manages to pull it out to shake Owedia's hand suspended in front of him.

I shake his hand too, though he can hardly take his eyes from Owedia.

Owedia tells him about Dexter's spotting the student with the Viper tattoo.

"I know about the Vipers," he says, his voice measured and crisp, in contrast to his rumpled appearance, "but I haven't seen any boys recently with that tattoo. When did Dexter see it?"

"He says two or three months ago. In the yard."

Coleman sighs. "It might have been one of those kids who only stay a night or two. We often get juveniles in their midteens, and the system just doesn't know where they belong."

"Why not?"

"It depends on the nature of the offense and the offender and how overcrowded we are at the time. We're not going to put a violent kid or a kid with a history of abuse in with younger kids."

"Do you keep any sort of record of the gang members that pass through the school?"

"No, unfortunately."

"Would anyone have that kind of information?"

He shakes his head. "There isn't money for that. Not by far."

"Have you ever seen the Viper tattoo?"

"No, not personally, though I have heard about it. To tell you the truth, we don't see many white gang members in here." A glance in my direction. "Occasionally the older ones, in their late teens, after they've been disowned by their parents. Then, of course, they go to adult prison."

"Why don't you see many white gang members?" I ask.

He pauses to pat the top of his hair. "The white gangs, like the

Vipers, are mostly middle-class kids into drugs and hate. They tend to deal in angel dust, pot, and crank, and they hate the government, Jews, blacks, and foreigners. Of course, when they get into trouble, their parents get them out on bail—the first time and maybe the second time. And hating blacks doesn't stop them from doing a regular trade with black gangs in town. In transporting drugs, the white kids have a definite advantage—they hardly ever get pulled over."

"We need to find the Viper who was here," Owedia says. "Or any Viper, for that matter." She pauses and looks at him, a bit too earnestly. "The Vipers were involved in the murder that Dexter was convicted of. The boy who was here may know something about it."

Coleman nods noncommittally, his face clearly conveying that he's heard this line before. "I will check into it for you," he says.

Coleman hands Owedia a Post-it pad, and she writes her name and telephone number on the little yellow square. As she hands it back to him, she says, haltingly, "Dexter has a fresh tattoo."

He does not register. "I'm sorry—?"

"Dexter has a fresh tattoo," she repeats, "on his wrist. It was done sometime in the last few weeks, I'm sure."

His expression tenses. "I'm sorry. We work hard to keep that kind of thing out of here."

"You've got to take better care of him," Owedia says. "It's your responsibility to see that no harm comes to him."

"Did he tell you why he got the tattoo?"

"No. But I can't see that it matters."

"We work hard to prevent the students from tattooing each other. But all you need is a pin and a ballpoint pen. Those items are hard to control."

"Perhaps you need to keep a closer watch on them."

Coleman sighs. "This institution already holds more than twice the number it was intended to hold. And our staff has been cut by thirty percent in the past two years. We're trying hard to do our job with what we've got." He sits. "I'm sorry about Dexter, I really am. I like him. But you know that he gets a much higher proportion of the resources of this place already because he's deaf."

Owedia swallows hard. "It's not enough. He doesn't belong here in the first place. He's innocent."

"That may be. But I don't even begin to get into questions like that. I just can't. To me, they're all innocent and they're all guilty. I'm just here to see that they get an education. Or the chance to get one."

On our way back into town, Owedia asks me if I will come to church with her tomorrow.

"I want to thank God for showing us a ray of hope, even if it is a slender one," she says. "If we pray together, our thanks will be multiplied and our faith all the more powerful."

I stare forward, feeling the heat of her gaze. She goes on, "I know you've been losing heart. But with God's help we're going to find that Viper. Come pray with me."

I decline with a lame joke about not being able to afford the collection plate. What I cannot tell her is that I see her faith and mine being tested in ways far more painful than what we have so far endured. That, and the fact that I would rather spend the morning curled up in bed, alone, than suffer another of Rev. Jones's sermons.

21

My utilities case occupies the entirety of the next three days, and my contact with the judge has diminished to not even a good morning. Since our lunch together, he seems even less happy with me than before, and I am sure now that he is biding his time, waiting for my year of service to be over.

The résumés arrive every day, sometimes three or four of them, a testament to the difficult legal job market and for me a bitter reminder that I need to get my résumé circulating as well.

Tammy files the résumés, dutifully acknowledges each one with a letter, and passes the most promising to the judge. Interviews will begin in January, she tells me, and the judge expects to name my replacement by March 15.

My last day on the job is to be my year anniversary, August 9.

Haberman has grown ever more smug of late. He knows that my chances of usurping his favored position were irretrievably lost in the Hinton debacle, and now his behavior toward me alternates between a patronizing solicitousness and a patronizing disdain.

On the Wednesday following our visit to the boys' school, I pick up a message from Owedia on my daily 2:00 call into my answering machine. The Viper Dexter had seen at the boys' school has been located.

"His name is Roger Swango," she tells me over the phone that evening, "and having passed his eighteenth birthday not long ago, he's now in the state's custody at the Pendleton Correctional Facility."

"What's he in for?"

"Coleman said he's got a string of drug offenses, break-ins, and robberies. Now he's in for attempted rape. Coleman didn't think there was much chance that Roger would talk about the Vipers. Snitching is about the worst violation of the prisoner code. Coleman says Roger has a reputation for being stupider and stubborner than most gang members, and they tend to be pretty stupid and stubborn."

"But will he talk to us?"

"Coleman says he'll talk to us if it means earning brownie points with the warden. Coleman's got a call into him, and I'm supposed to follow-up tomorrow. I'm hoping that we could go out there Friday afternoon. It's a half day for me and I'd rather not wait for Saturday. Do you think you could leave work early and meet me at school? We could drive out there together."

I realize with a sinking feeling that, on top of all my other sins against the court and the profession, I am now considering taking time off from work to investigate one of the judge's cases. In my mind, I see myself testifying about this latest infraction before the disciplinary commission of the Indiana bar, as Judge Albertson shakes his head in disbelief.

"I'll be there," I tell Owedia.

At the corner of Fortieth Street and Gibbs Avenue, a sign, DEAF CHILD AREA, seems to warn that I need to pay better attention to my own senses.

Two blocks east of that sign, past a mower-repair shop, a paint store, a machine shop, and a stonecutting business with a lot full of headstones, the green-lawned campus of the Indiana School for the Deaf suddenly appears. It is a big place, bigger than I could have imagined, a turn-of-the-century brick and masonry structure, ivy-covered, spreading fortresslike from a center entrance at the top of a long flight of steps.

I walk through the halls—brightly lit, carpeted, lined with lockers and papered with the children's artwork—to the classroom, Room 124, where Owedia teaches. Through the classroom door I see her patrolling a classroom in which children of a range of ages are working huddled over books and calculators.

Next to the classroom door is a door labeled OBSERVATION, and I enter the door into a small dark room with a large two-way mirror.

Owedia is gathering the children together as I watch. She signs to each child, touching those kids who need to have their attention redirected toward her, and she herds them into a semicircle on the floor. The children slip into their places, signing furiously to each other as they go.

I wonder if in a silent world there is such a thing as noise. Are the movements of the hundreds of fingers of these children jabbering to each other noise?

She does shush them, I notice, with a fanning movement of her hands, and in response their signing trails off into stillness.

Dexter's world. It is so obvious that he should be here, among these children, so obvious that my brain can't stop from materializing him in the space between two boys his age.

Owedia sits on a tiny chair in front of them, signing with great grace and smoothness—an end-of-the-day ritual, I imagine, with three minutes left before this half day of school is over.

She succeeds in calming them for a moment, but when the buzzer sounds—and it is a loud, vibrating buzzer—the children erupt from the floor and with a clamor of books and bodies in motion, squeeze out the classroom door.

I watch Owedia watch them leave, an odd letdown look on her face. I step out into the hall, now crowded with children.

I am amazed at how noisy it is; even in the lack of voices, there is sound, communication, bit of words and yells. I stand in the hallway and watch them put on their coats and fill their knapsacks, feeling like Gulliver among the Lilliputs.

In her classroom, I find Owedia sitting at her desk with her head in her hands.

"Hard day?"

"Yes," she says, reaching to take my hand.

I take her hand and hold it gently and wait for her to speak.

She says, "I'm afraid of this boy. I'm afraid of what he's going to tell us."

"So am I," I tell her.

In the prison lobby we wait for nearly a half hour. Owedia twirls a tiny curl around her index finger and stares absently; I watch her do this. There are magazines, titles like *Corrections Today* and *State Trooper,* but my mind cannot sit still long enough to read.

In time, a heavy white man in a gray checked suit comes out, introduces himself as the assistant warden, and leads us to the reception room, a long wide room like a cafeteria, where scattered among the rectangular tables are half a dozen prisoners and wives, children, mothers, lawyers.

The assistant warden sits us at a table, then disappears through a heavy steel door. A moment later he reappears with a guard and a young man in an orange prison jumpsuit. The warden points to us and withdraws as the guard delivers the young man to our table.

Owedia and I stand. The guard says nothing. Owedia thrusts her hand out and pronounces her name. The boy smiles broadly at her but does not take her hand.

"Roger, I'm Nora Lumsey," I say. "Thank you for agreeing to speak with us."

"Well, I sure hate to take the time out of my busy day, but for two lovely ladies, why not?" He says this parody of gentlemanly charm with astounding ease, his mouth stretching into a toothy grin. He is an immensely good-looking young man, tall with fine light brown hair cut short and even around his head. The skin of his face and ears and neck is fair and speckled with tiny cuts, bruises, nicks and welts.

With a start I realize that he looks much like a boy I went out with in high school. There is the same country-boy innocence in his expression, and his features, like those of that distant love, seem made for a life of the soil—the eyes set deep for surveying the fields, strong cheekbones for braving the wind, the weak chin—because one does not need a strong chin to be a farmer—the pale lips, barely lips at all, for the spareness of that life.

I remember that boy with a sad ping in my heart, and I see in Roger Swango's face a world where I do belong, abhorrent as it is to me now.

From where I stand I can see the lower curl of the snake tattoo on his neck, and the rest of the *E* is faintly visible through the downy hair of his neck.

"Please sit down," I say, and we position ourselves in the metal folding chairs, Owedia and I opposite him. I glance at Owedia, and with a look she tells me that she knows I can talk to this man, that I speak his language.

"Roger, I see by your tattoo that you run with the Vipers."

"I don't run with 'em anymore, ma'am. I'm done with that life."

"Why do you say that?"

" 'Cause I'm tired of being in trouble. I want to make somethin' of my life. It was one thing to be in the Boys' School, but this place is hell. When I get out'a here, that's it. I ain't comin' back."

"I think that's great. I hope you make it."

"I'm gonna make it. I'm gonna make it or they're gonna fuckin' carry me out."

"Roger, I need to talk to you about the Vipers. How long were you with them?"

He closes his eyes for a moment and leans his head back as if summoning up the patience to speak. Around the base of his neck I can see the beginnings or ends of other tattoos.

He opens his eyes and says sweetly, "You don't want to know my whole fuckin' life history, do you?"

"But I do, Roger. You interest me."

He smiles tolerantly. "Why do I interest you?"

"I'm not sure yet. But you do."

"Well, I was born in Arcadia"—a farm town north of Indianapolis—"and I raised rabbits as a kid. When I was ten I fucked my ma and killed my pa."

He says this with a silly smile, as though he understands that the joke isn't funny.

"That's very interesting, Roger," I say. "Have you fucked any other family members? Sisters? Brothers? The dog?"

He runs a hand over his scalp and breathes loudly.

Time to play the schoolmarm. "I'm here to talk to you about the Vipers, Roger. We can talk about all kinds of shit if you want to, but we're going to come back to it."

He shrugs and looks at Owedia, who returns his gaze.

"So you were born in Arcadia. When did you move down to Indy?"

"When I was twelve."

"Where did you go to school?"

"Lincoln Middle School."

"On the northside?"

"Yes."

"Who did you live with?"

"My mother."

"Where did you go after Lincoln?"

"North Central."

"Is that where you started running with gangs?"

"Hell, no. We had gangs at Lincoln."

"What did you do in these gangs?"

"Steal things. Party. Meet girls. Do drugs."

"Like what drugs?"

"Pot, coke, speed."

"When did you make your first trip to the boys' school?"

"When I was fifteen."

"What for?"

"I stabbed a guy. I asked him for money and he got mad and shoved me." He gets an exasperated look on his face, an apology of sorts. "I hate that. I can't stand to be shoved, and I got a bad temper."

I sit back. "What are you in for now?"

He looks away.

"The warden told me. It's funny, you don't seem the type. I'd think you wouldn't have a problem getting girls."

167

He stares into the middle distance, eyes fixed like a mannequin's, his expression like that of a dog in repose.

"I'm here about a murder, Roger. A woman was killed on the northside about a year-and-a-half ago and we think a Viper might have been involved."

"I don't know nothin' about it."

"How can you be sure? I haven't told you anything."

He turns and looks at me, all smiles again. "Honey, what do you expect me to say? People get killed every day."

"When you were with the Vipers, did you sell drugs?"

"Hell, yes."

"Did you ever deal with the Indy Boyz?"

His face clouds. "Hell, yes." A glance at Owedia.

"You sold them drugs?"

"Yeah, and they sold us drugs. They had the connections for coke and weed, and we knew where to get the speed, the acid, and a lot of other shit."

"Do you know Joseph Baker?"

He shakes his head.

"How about a kid named Dexter Hinton? A deaf black kid."

A glance at Owedia. "No, ma'am."

"Roger, we believe that Dexter Hinton was wrongly convicted of this murder. And the only way we're going to prove that is to find the guy who did it. Do the Vipers have a place where they meet or hang out?"

"Sure. Lots of places."

"Tell me some of them."

"You know I can't tell you that."

"Why not?"

" 'Cause it would get me killed."

"How would anyone know you told us?"

"They'll know."

"Who's in charge of the Vipers? Who's the leader?"

"Freeze," he says matter-of-factly. "And I can tell you that because everybody knows it."

"What's his real name?"

"I don't know."

"Where can I find him?"

"I can't tell you that."

"Do you have a street name, Roger?"

"No."

"I think you do. It's 'Slick,' isn't it?"

Roger's face falls. "You are good," he murmurs. "I think you know a lot more, honey, than you're lettin' on."

"Roger, we're trying to clear an innocent kid, and you're our last hope. You've got to give us some information."

"I'll tell you what I can. That's what I promised the warden."

"I'm going to ask you again, Roger, have you ever heard of Joe Baker? One of the Indy Boyz?"

A shrug. "Maybe."

"Baker killed a confidential informant during a drug buy. You weren't involved in that, were you?"

Roger answers quickly. "No. I heard about it, though. Yeah."

"What did you hear?"

"That it happened."

"Do you know who was there?"

"I can't tell you that."

"Roger, do you know JeTaun Holley?"

"Who's that?"

"JeTaun Holley."

"Uh-uh." He smiles. "But I knowed lots of women."

"JeTaun Holley is a black woman who hangs with the Indy Boyz. She says she knows you."

"Maybe she does. But as a rule I don't fuck black women."

He looks past me at Owedia as he says this. Owedia says nothing, and I cannot bring myself to turn to see her reaction.

"Do you have a problem with black people, Roger?"

He shrugs. "Sure I do. All white people do. But most don't have the guts to admit it."

"Are you a skinhead, Roger?"

"I was."

"Are the Vipers into white power?"

"Yeah. It's one thing."

"But you hang out with the Indy Boyz."

"That's business, honey. If the niggers are buyin', we're sellin'. If the niggers want to spend their money on coke and live in shitholes, that's fine by me."

There is nothing I can say to this.

He seems to take my silence as an acknowledgement that there is truth in what he has said, and he smiles and tilts his head as if to say, "so there."

I notice a blue stain at his throat. "I see you've got some other tattoos on your chest, Roger," I say. "Would you show them to us?"

He is momentarily taken aback, but then he replies, "Sure," and he begins to unbutton his top. "I usually charge for this, you know," he says with a grin.

He unbuttons his shirt to the navel and pulls it open and off his shoulders, revealing his torso all at once. It is a dazzling, shocking sight, and yes, he could charge for it.

His body is a vision of hell; as a sideshow, he could be the star of any low-rent carnival. He could be billed as "the Living Museum of Hate," and as I watch, appalled, he gives us the guided tour.

Beginning under his left shoulder, he points to a swastika in a crude circle. "This here's the swastika, symbol of the Third Reich. This is one of my first tattoos, got it when I was ten. My cousin Ray put that on."

Moving down to his right breast, where there is a mountain and the numbers 4-19-94, he says, "This one's in honor of those Americans who gave their lives at Ruby Ridge, victims of the federal government." Then:

"This KKK here is self-explanatory . . .

"This here's my tribute to those who gave their lives at Waco, Texas . . .

"Here I got a bleeding cross I got done at the Boys' School . . .

"Here's Thor's hammer. Thor is a Norse god. Norse means from Norway, one of the places Aryan people come from . . .

"This *eighty-three* stands for the Eighty-third Street Killers, a gang I was in for a time before the Vipers . . ."

There is also a skull, the words *SIEG HEIL,* a dragon snaked up one arm, a zipper from his sternum to his navel, and logos of rock bands I never heard of. Glaringly absent are names of girls, nudes, or any reference to sex.

Roger shows me these symbols—for he is ignoring Owedia completely—without a trace of shame, his pretty face beaming, his eyes bright. I am struck by the strange authority his single-minded stupidity gives him; like a pure belief, it is something against which one cannot argue.

As he speaks, I feel my eyebrows scrunching closer and closer together in perplexed amazement; after a while, they start to hurt because there's nowhere left to go.

"I'd show you somethin' below my waist that you'd never forget," he smirks, "but if the guards saw me pullin' down my drawers they'd beat the shit out of me."

"That's just as well, Roger," I say as he buttons his shirt.

As I get up to leave, I turn to Owedia next to me, daring to look at her for the first time since we sat down. Her expression is stern and miserable, and set tight on Roger. She has not said a word since uttering her name.

"I'm done, Owedia," I say gently. "Let's go."

She glances at me, closes her eyes a moment, then licks her lips and says, "Roger, I see who you are and where you come from as clear as day. You come from a place where suffering has turned to hate, and that hatred has become so much a part of you and so institutionalized in your symbols and your groups and your gangs that you have to hate in order to belong to your people." She pauses, takes a breath, and actually reaches across the table. She covers his hand, which is palm-down flat on the table, and squeezes it. He looks at her, clearly skeptical but not resisting.

171

Owedia goes on, "We all need to belong, Roger. You don't need to hate to belong. Follow the one symbol on your chest that means something. Follow the cross, Roger. Follow Christ. Follow love."

Roger looks away, a small embarrassed smile on his lips.

The sun sets behind us as Owedia and I drive back to town. It is one of those slow Indiana sunsets that smears the horizon with color for an hour or so, then shuts down fast into night.

Ahead of us lights shine prettily in the windows of those few tall buildings that make up the downtown of Indianapolis.

Owedia stares out the side window, and I feel depleted and too sad to speak. It is as though Roger has come between Owedia and me in ways that make no rational sense yet cannot be avoided. His face is so much like mine, and his attitudes so like mine once were, that I want to disown him, for her, repudiate him, for her.

What's worse, he's told us nothing that brings us closer to the identity of Mr. E.

I drop Owedia in the parking lot of the deaf school. As she steps out she takes my hand and says, "Try and make it to hear Rev. Jones on Sunday."

"I will," I lie.

22

On my desk Monday morning there is a note from Tammy reminding me that the judge needs to respond to the petition for rehearing in *Hinton.*

I find the petition buried beneath a stack of opinions and other paperwork in my in-box. I have not looked at it since it arrived, and I cannot bring myself to look at it now.

I attach a Post-it to the front of the petition, and on it I scribble, "Recommend denial."

A foregone conclusion, and now it is done.

That evening, Owedia calls to ask if I will come with her to visit Je-Taun, who is home from the hospital. She reminds me that we owe her that courtesy, and I agree to come.

I pick up Owedia at her apartment at 7:00 Wednesday evening. I have been curious to see where she lives, and I am surprised that it is an apartment in an old building in the Fall Creek area of town, a dilapidated section where light industry, Victorian homes, apartment buildings, and retail businesses share the blocks in unzoned chaos. In my mind I had seen her in a pretty townhouse near the canal downtown, something cheery and neat, suitable for a teacher.

Outside the front door to her building, I press a button next to her name. A buzzer sounds, and I am admitted to the dank front hall, where a hand-lettered sign warns me that I must push the front door shut behind me.

Her apartment is up two flights of steps; when I reach her landing she is standing in her open doorway, looking composed and lovely as ever.

"Welcome," she says, "I'll be just a moment." She disappears and I enter into her kitchen.

The floor is painted wood planks and the room is lit by a bulb inside a paper lantern. The plaster of the walls is cracked and buckled; there are pipes in the corners running from floor to ceiling; and a radiator under the kitchen window, which overlooks a supermarket roof next door, shrieks every few seconds with a burst of steam. There is a claw-foot tub in a corner, a refrigerator, stove, sink, and table, cat food and water bowl and litter box on the floor.

There is just enough space to walk through these things into the next room, where I see a metal-frame day bed, prettily made up with flowered linens and covered with an array of pillows and stuffed animals.

She stands in the next room putting on a jacket and looking at herself in an oval wall mirror. I knock on the door frame and step inside as she smiles. There are bookshelves against all the walls, some houseplants, a television. Above the bookcases the artwork of her students is displayed—finger paintings, collages, and pencil drawings. On one bookshelf there are pictures—of her family, I presume—and there is a sculpture of hands clasped together in prayer and a wood cross on a stand.

It is a poor person's apartment, though clearly she has tried to make the best of it, and I know I should compliment her on her place, but I cannot.

It occurs to me as I look out her bedroom window, which also overlooks the supermarket roof, that she lives here because this is what she can afford, that the salary she earns as a teacher at the deaf school must be pitifully small.

"I didn't picture you living in a place like this," I tell her.

"I never pictured me living in a place like this either," she says.

The place where JeTaun lives is a modern two-story garden-apartment complex, and inside it looks like a seedy motel, a step down from the tenement seediness of Owedia's place.

JeTaun greets us pleasantly, looking much improved, her bruises having faded and only a speckling of scabs remaining on her face. She reintroduces us to her mother, a stooped older woman with thick glasses, and to the three of her kids who are sprawled on the floor in front of the TV.

Before we can respond, JeTaun commands Owedia to sit in a chair JeTaun has placed in the middle of the living room.

"It's time to do something about that hair," she announces, and without waiting for Owedia's approval, she shakes out a sheet and covers Owedia up to her neck. "We gonna trim you up a bit and then we gonna give you a color so you don't look like no clown." She holds out three boxes of hair color for Owedia's inspection. "What color you like, honey?"

Owedia glances at me and laughs. "Should I trust this woman with my hair?"

I smile. "I don't think you have a choice."

JeTaun shakes her head. "Can't be worse, honey."

Owedia picks the dark chestnut shade, and as JeTaun sets to work, I tell her I'm sorry she got hurt because she spoke with us.

"It was Sammy done made somethin' of it. Sammy snitched on me for snitchin', and that's some shit. What does he know about it?"

"Who's Sammy?"

"He's the bartender at Sugar Street," Owedia informs me. "JeTaun didn't consider that he pours drinks for a lot of people connected to the Indy Boyz."

"So somebody beat you up for snitching?"

"Shit, yeah. He didn't ask who I was snitchin' on. He didn't know I was snitchin' on fuckin' Vipers. I wasn't snitchin' on no Indy Boyz."

"Do you know for sure that Sammy was involved in hurting you?"

"As close to for sure as shit."

"Did you tell that to the police?"

"No way. I ain't gonna snitch to the police. And they know that."

"But they're the ones who beat you up."

"If I snitched to the police I'd get worse than beat up."

Owedia looks worriedly at me. "Are you sure it was black men who beat you up? Not Vipers?"

"It was brothers all right. I heard a voice on one of 'em, and I could just feel it. They was brothers."

"You told me you knew a Viper named Freeze. Would you say he was one of the leaders?"

"Yeah, he is, 'cause he's the one with the money. He's the one got the big spread up in Carmel."

"Do you know his real name?"

"Uh-uh. No."

"Do you know where he lives?"

"Uh-uh. I been there, and it's one of them big stone mansions with the columns and the pool in the back, but I sure as shit couldn't tell you where it is or how to get there."

JeTaun's mother suddenly comes to life and says, "What place is that with the pool?"

JeTaun ignores her. "One thing you wouldn't forget about this place is they got statues all over the place. Like ladies, you know . . . naked . . . and some weird shit too . . . like metal all stuck together every which way."

"When were you there?"

"Maybe three, four years ago now. We brought Freeze some shit. Then hung there a while. His folks was away. Like in Europe or someplace."

"He lives there with his parents?"

"Yeah, it's their place. And I don't know if he's still there."

Owedia asks, "What does Freeze look like?"

"Like not much. He's a fat boy. Fat and mean, 'specially with the shaved head, you know? And they all so pale, like worms."

"And does he have the snake on his neck?"

176

"Yeah, sure, they all got it."

"What about other tattoos?"

"I think he got the Nazi sign on his arm. Lots of 'em do. They love that shit."

Two hours later, I drop a transformed Owedia in front of her building. JeTaun has done splendidly—Owedia's hair is now the color of black coffee, shiny and soft. She is no longer startling and she is somehow less beautiful, but she is *lovelier*.

As she waves good night, Owedia smiles and tosses her head as if she truly feels lovelier.

"Call me," I tell her, and I hurry uptown.

When I step into my bedroom fifteen minutes later, the message light on my answering machine is blinking.

The voice is Owedia's, telling me that she's been mugged.

I telephone her back immediately.

"There were three of them," she says, her voice quaking, "wearing ski masks. They ran into the building before I had a chance to close the front door all the way. They came up behind me . . . they *swarmed* me and shoved me against the wall by the stairs. It was awful."

I sigh. "Owedia . . ."

"So one guy took my pocketbook, and he said, 'We just want your money, sister.' He took out my wallet, took all the money and credit cards, and another guy reached over and pulled my necklace off."

"Oh, Owedia."

"But then the first guy said, 'Sister, we warning you. Leave it alone. Don't go messin' with no Indy Boyz, you hear me?' "

"Oh, shit."

"Yeah."

Owedia is silent a moment, breathing loudly, and then I hear her start to cry. "I wanted to do *something!* I wanted to hit them and yell at them and tell them how wrong they were! But I couldn't! I just . . . *cowered* there and prayed they wouldn't hurt me!"

"That was the right thing to do. You might have—"

"I wanted to rip their masks off," she goes on, even more passionately. "I wanted to spit in their faces for what they'd done to Dexter. I wanted to knock the fear of God into them!"

I can't help but laugh. "I'd love to see you do that."

"Me too."

"But you know you did the right thing, right?"

"Maybe."

"I shouldn't have driven off until I was sure you were safe inside your building. I'm sorry."

"This has never happened to me before. I wouldn't have thought to ask you to wait."

"Have you called the police?"

"Yes. They're on their way. But it's over now, I'm okay, and I don't think they're in any rush."

"Are you going to tell them this is connected to Dexter's case?"

"I don't know. Maybe I should. Maybe it's time to tell the police what we know."

"I think you're right. But if you do, you can't tell them about my involvement in the case."

"I don't see how I can avoid it."

"My job and maybe my career depend on it."

"You know," she says, "I really don't understand this thing about you working for the state. Why is it such a big deal?"

I open my mouth to speak, on the verge of telling her the whole story, when I hear her apartment buzzer in the background.

"That's the police," she says. "I'll call you later."

"I didn't tell them about Dexter," Owedia says twenty minutes later. "I couldn't. I just didn't want to open that can of worms."

I am hugely relieved, and at the same time horrified to realize that I may be protecting myself at the expense of finding the real killer.

"So just what do you do for the state?"

"Listen, Owedia," I say. "I'm thinking about heading down to my father's place this weekend. Would you like to join me? I think it may not be a bad idea for us to get away for a few days."

She hesitates, then says she is flattered by the invitation but that she could not miss seeing Dexter on Saturday or attending church on Sunday. "And next Wednesday is Christmas. I've got some serious shopping to do."

"Do it tomorrow," I tell her, "And I'll speak with Carl. We'll make sure he gets there on Saturday. We could ask Mr. Williams to go with him."

"Yes . . . but I really must go to church Sunday."

"Rev. Jones takes a Sunday off once in a while, doesn't he?"

"Well, there are times when he is at other churches."

"So you could do the same, Owedia. And it's only fair that you give my church a try."

I call my father the next evening to tell him that I will be coming with a friend.

He says, with a joviality entirely unlike him, "That's fine, darlin'. That's a terrific idea."

"Are you all right, Daddy?"

"I'm doin' just fine," he says. "How are *you* doin'?"

Just fine, I say, and now I know there is something strange going on. "What's goin' on?" I ask him.

He says, "There's somebody here you ought to say hello to."

For an instant I can't imagine who—one of my siblings is the likeliest guess—but then it occurs to me, fearfully, who it must be.

Her voice is abruptly there, lower than I remember it, hoarse from so many years of smoking, a rural voice, a voice more like mine than I like to admit.

"Hey, Nora, this is your momma. How 'ye doin'?"

And I have only one way to respond to her. "Shit, Momma, what the hell are you doin' there?"

"Well, I needed to spend some time with your daddy," she says defensively. "I just need to put some things to right."

"How come, Momma? What's going on?"

"I'd rather not say now, honey"—and now her voice is cracking, a bit too theatrically—"Let's just see how things develop, all right?"

179

"How long you been there with Daddy?"

"Oh, a week or so."

"How long you stayin'?"

"I don't know, honey."

"I was thinking about coming down this weekend to visit Daddy. With a friend. But maybe this is not a good time for company."

"You know you're not company here, honey"—as if it were her home—"and any friend of yours ain't company neither."

"If you and Daddy need the time to yourselves—"

"Uh-uh, no, you should come down. Now, is that a boyfriend?"

"No, momma. A woman friend."

"Oh. Just the girls, huh?"

"That's right, Momma."

I might have known that it would happen, that she'd turn up when there was no place else to turn. It had been a good long run this last time—nearly seven years since I'd seen her. But she'd never actually come back and moved in before—that was the strange thing. That, and the subdued tone of her voice. I wondered if something really bad had happened to make her come crawling back like that, and to do it a week before Christmas.

On Friday at 3:00, just as I am about to walk out the door, Tammy calls me on the interoffice phone to let me know that she has received the concurrences of the other judges in our denial of Dexter Hinton's petition for rehearing. The order will go out Monday, she tells me, and it is clear in the drawn-out way she says the words that she knows how much I care about this case.

With the denial of the petition, Dexter Hinton is gone from our chambers.

23

Owedia has dressed for the country, and I am startled to find her waiting for me in front of her building in jeans and a big sweater, a green parka thrown over her shoulders, sunglasses, and a brown felt hat.

I'm wearing jeans and a big sweater too, but on me everything looks ratty and at least twenty years old. She looks like she just stepped out of an L.L. Bean catalogue.

Owedia carries a shoulder bag, and there is a large hard-shell suitcase on the sidewalk next to her. I jump down from the cab of my pickup, embrace her, then strap her bags down in the back next to mine. She climbs in the passenger side.

It is a clear early winter afternoon, sunny and brisk, the kind of crystalline day that doesn't seem to belong to the days before or after it.

When I get into the cab, she says, "Let's hit the road, girlfriend."

We are quiet as we drive through town to Route 37. I am thinking of Dexter, of the odd sense of closure I feel now that his appeal is forever out of my office. I am thinking about the deception I've played on Carl, Owedia, and the rest, and I am wondering if I have the strength to tell Owedia the truth.

I tell myself that in a matter of months I won't be working for the judge and this will all seem like a distant memory.

Maybe I don't have to tell her the truth after all.

Owedia looks out the passenger-side window as we stop for a red light on our way out of the city. Following her gaze, I see the usual collection of young men on the street corner, some holding bottles in bags.

"Lord, I hate to see the wasted lives of those men," she says. "What hope do they have? What good could possibly come to them?" Turning to me, she takes off her sunglasses and rubs the bridge of her nose.

There is a purple half-circle bruise around the outer edge of her left eye.

"I thought you said you weren't hurt," I say.

"That's what I said," she replies.

Leaving Indianapolis, moving now at seventy-five miles per hour, the farms and strip malls rushing past us, I begin to feel good again and I can see Owedia start to relax. I put the radio on; it's tuned to my usual country station, and they are playing an old Conway Twitty song about talking to the man in the moon.

"Can you stand country music?" I ask her.

"No," she laughs.

"Then find something you like."

"Christian music all right with you?"

She tunes the radio to a particularly soulless woman singing about the new man in her life—Jesus.

"Hey, look at those baby cows with their momma," she says cheerfully, pointing to a large Guernsey sharing a field with a flock of goats.

"Uh-huh," I say. "Sure are cute."

> *Jesus rings the bell*
> *Once I fell, now I'm well*
> *Jesus is enough*
> *Lift me up, fill my cup*

"Things may be a bit uncomfortable in my folks' house," I tell her. "My parents have been separated for a lot of years, but now my mother's back, at least for a while."

"Oh." She glances worriedly at me.

"I didn't know about it when I invited you down. I'm sorry I didn't tell you about it before we left town."

"That's all right," she says. "Except I didn't know you'd been through that. I just assumed you grew up in a happy family."

"Well, I didn't. But I tried to make it a happy family for my brothers and sister."

"You raised your siblings?"

"Mostly."

"You shock me."

"Why?"

"I never thought of you like that, that's all."

"Did you grow up in a happy family?"

"Yes, I did," she replies. "And we're still happy. My parents and my two brothers are coming into Indy next week for Christmas. I can't wait to see them."

As twilight comes, Owedia tilts her head back and closes her eyes. The cab of my pickup is less than comfortable for that kind of sleeping, and after a moment Owedia leans against her window.

"Do you mind if I shut my eyes for a bit?" she asks.

"No," I say, and I reach over to squeeze her hand.

Thoughts of the Vipers and the Indy Boyz recede as I cruise southward into the night, Owedia asleep at my side, and my mind turns toward Unity.

I wonder what Owedia will think of my parents. I could not have told her the truth about the racism in my family, not if I'd wanted her to come with me, and it occurs to me with some guilt that she will suffer terribly when my father's attitudes—and my mother's—become apparent. To my knowledge there has never been a black person in that house, and I cannot recall ever having seen my father or mother in conversation with a black person.

And my mother. I accepted long ago that there was something wrong with her mind that made her incapable of love, of loyalty, or of any of the emotional components of parenthood. It would not occur to her for a moment to set aside a desire of her own, a whim even, for the sake of one of her children. As a young child I knew what a selfish woman she was, how unlike other people's mothers, and by the time she left, my hatred for her was something I had lived with so long it had been embroidered upon in my mind into a complex and beautiful fantasy. I wished her dead so many times and in so many ways; so often I imagined myself withholding the antidote to the poison she'd just swallowed or refusing to extend my hand to pull her up from quicksand.

It wasn't until I was in college that I was able to put a name to her illness—manic-depressive syndrome—and to have the slightest sympathy for her. It was the disease that made her evil, and I pitied the emptiness of her life. What a terrible thing it must be to be a slave to oneself.

But by then, she was long gone from my life.

Owedia awakens when we pull off the highway and onto the two-lane road that wanders up and down hills into the heart of Unity County. She shakes her head sleepily, then cups her hands against the passenger-side window and peers outside.

"It's awfully dark out here."

"No streetlights in the boonies," I tell her. "There's no sense in keeping the cows and corn awake."

Owedia puts her hands behind her head, stretches her neck and torso, and says, "Have you ever been in love, Nora?"

I laugh, surprised by the question. "No, I can't say that I have. There's been boys that I've loved. Or gone out with. Guys I've enjoyed being with. But nobody I've felt like I couldn't live without." I glance at her; she is staring out the windshield wistfully, waiting for me to ask, "What about you?" So I do.

"I just had the funniest dream about a guy. A guy I knew for a short time last summer. I met him at church. He was a divinity student, just there for the summer, and then he was going to Atlanta to study theology at Emory University."

"Did you go out with him?"

"No. But we used to have long talks after church. He sang with the choir, and sometimes I would see him at Rev. Jones's house."

"So what did you dream about this guy?"

"It was something like . . . I was working in Carl's garden, digging a hole in the ground and I was very tired and dirty and sweaty, stinking so much that I was disgusted with my own smell, and then he walks up, perfectly clean in his suit, and he looks down at me, smiling, and I look at myself and realize that I am waist-deep in this muddy hole, and I am so ashamed, I just *burn* with it."

"Sounds like a sex dream to me."

She giggles. "God, no!"

"Can I ask you a very personal question?"

"You can ask."

"Have you ever had a lover?"

Owedia erupts with laughter. "What?! Are you asking if I'm a virgin?"

I feel myself blushing. "Well . . . you being so religious and all . . . I wouldn't know."

"For your information," she says, still laughing, "I am not a virgin. But I'm not the type to sleep with a lot of guys either. I'm twenty-four, and I've only had three serious boyfriends." She sighs. "And I was in love with each of them. Or thought I was."

"Maybe you should plan yourself a trip to Atlanta."

"What about you? Have you had a lot of men?"

"Mmm, I don't know. Somewhat less than twenty." Or maybe somewhat more.

"And all that without being in love?"

Her words cut deeper than I like to admit. "Afraid so," I say, "but like my grandma used to say, cold soup is better than going hungry."

The door opens and she is there, Betty, my mother, smiling ear-to-ear and looking better than I could possibly have imagined—trim-waisted, dressed in one of those flowery country dresses she always favored, her hair well-Clairol'd and neatly turned up at her shoulders.

"Hey, Momma," I say, the words catching, despite myself.

"Darlin', I'm so glad to see you," she says, embracing me. "And who's this?"

"Momma, this is my friend Owedia. Owedia, my momma."

Owedia smiles gently and extends her hand. "Hi, I'm very pleased to meet you, Mrs. Lumsey."

"Betty, please," she says. "And I'm delighted to meet you!"

My father comes up behind, himself looking oddly better than he has in years. He has shaved, for one thing, and he is wearing a clean flannel shirt, new jeans, and suspenders.

He introduces himself to Owedia, shakes her hand heartily, then hugs me close.

I look around to make sure we're in the right house.

Dinner is ready and waiting, and Owedia and I are ushered to the dining-room table, where my momma has set out cornbread and a bowl of her homemade applesauce. In a moment pork chops are served, along with mashed turnips and sugar beets. Owedia smiles at me in bemused surprise, thinking, no doubt, that this feast is in our honor.

And dinner proceeds so swimmingly well I can hardly speak. Here are my mother and father, reunited and behaving like Mr. and Mrs. Midwest America, politely inquiring of Owedia's life and work, fascinated by the fact that she is a deaf teacher, and relating whatever stories that have anything to do with deaf folks they've known or seen on TV.

It is all too much as if there is something to prove, and the warmer the hospitality gets, the more nauseated I feel.

After dinner, we drink coffee and eat my momma's Christmas-tree cookies coated with green sugar crystals. And at long last the conversation turns to me.

"I was so proud when Daddy told me you'd become a lawyuh,

honey," my momma says. "You always was the smartest one, we knew you'd go places."

"I worked hard for it, Momma," I say. "Being a lawyer has less to do with smarts than with motivation."

"Daddy tells me you work for the court, is that right?"

"Ahh . . . yes." I had wanted to tell Owedia everything this weekend, to find a quiet moment walking my father's land to explain it all. If my mother hadn't been here I could have done that; my father wouldn't have said a word, and with a sinking feeling it dawns upon me that I had not considered this, had not given a moment's thought to the inevitable fact that my mother would ask about my job and that Owedia would be there to hear it. Lamely, I add, "I work for the state."

"You work for a judge on the court of appeals, don't you?" She smiles at me in a motherly way, as if to prove that she has asked about me, that she cares enough to know about my life. "You write the cases for the judge, isn't that right?"

"Yes." I look at Owedia, who watches me silently, her face impassive. "But I'm hoping," I go on, "to quit working for the state and get a job with a law firm. I'm eager to start practicing law."

"You're going to make a wonderful lawyuh," my mother beams.

When the coffee is done, my parents mosey into the den to drift asleep in front of the television, and Owedia and I say our good nights and go up to the guest room, where we are to sleep in the single beds that were once mine and my sister's.

I begin to undress, summoning the words with which I must tell her everything. Silently she takes her bag and goes into the bathroom. Five minutes later she reenters the room in a long white nightdress.

She looks very beautiful.

I sit cross-legged in a T-shirt and panties on the bed I slept in as a child.

She sits on my sister's bed and takes a Bible out of her bag.

"Owedia."

"Yes?"

Her expression is guarded, but kind. She is ready. I am ready. And so I tell her what I do, for whom I work, and about my role in writing *Hinton v. State*. She listens attentively, her hands folded in her lap.

"If it were to become known that I had any contact with the parties to this case either before, during, or after the time that I was working on the opinion, I would lose my job—for certain—and I would probably be suspended from the practice of law, and possibly disbarred. I could not tell you. I shouldn't be telling you now."

"Why did you do it?"

"I don't know. It was stupid. I shouldn't have done it."

"Why did you do it?"

For some reason, I start crying, and I just feel so miserable and lame, but I cannot stop crying to speak. I tell myself that it's because I am home and because my mother is here and I'll be damned if I'll cry in front of her, but I need desperately to cry and this is as good a time as any to do it.

Owedia sits watching me cry.

"Why'd you do it?" she repeats, her voice hard with anger.

"Because Carl lives two houses away from me. And because once I got to know him, and Dexter, and you . . . I could not keep my goddamn nose out of it."

"So you're telling me you wrote an opinion reversing Dexter's conviction, but that you could not convince the judge that it was the right thing to do?"

"Yes."

"And so you wrote the opinion that's keeping Dexter in prison?"

"Yes."

"How could you do that knowing it was wrong? Knowing that under the *law* it was wrong?!"

"Owedia," I say. "That's my job. Right or wrong, I serve the judge."

"And this is a job you care about keeping?"

"Justice is a set of rules, Owedia. The rules are made by people—they're not handed down by God. And the decisions are made by people. Judges aren't gods. They're fallible. But the system has ways of correcting mistakes. That's why we have appeals. And a supreme court if the appeals court is wrong."

"That may be," Owedia says, now furious. "But the trial court starts off presuming that the prosecutor wouldn't be there if he didn't have a good case. And the appeals court presumes that the trial court knew what it was doing. And the Supreme Court thinks that if the trial court and the appeals court say everything's okay, then it's okay. When does somebody stand up and say, hey, something isn't right?"

"I tried to do that, Owedia. It's part of my job to tell the judge when I think he's wrong."

"But you didn't do it well enough. That's why Dexter is still in prison and I'm getting beat up on a wild-goose chase after some skinhead."

For an instant I wonder if she is speaking of the bruise around her eye, and then it is clear that she has not told me everything. "What do you mean . . . beat up?"

She stands and lifts her nightdress, revealing dark bruises on her legs, her hips, her ribs and lower back. "They knocked me down and kicked me," she murmurs. "I lay on the steps and curled up to cover myself, but I could not stop them from kicking me."

"Owedia . . . why didn't you tell me?"

"I don't know," she says softly as she lowers the nightdress. "I should have. But I was worried that it would scare you. And that you would give up helping me find Mr. E."

"I won't do that," I say, and now I go to her and put my arms around her. "You're lucky you weren't killed. Or raped."

"I know."

We hold each other for a moment, then we climb into my bed and I lay with my arms around her, so much like I did with my sister when she had been frightened by a nightmare.

I awaken to the weekend morning smells of my childhood, of biscuits baking and sausage frying, smells that have a more vibrant quality on country air than they do in the stuffy confines of my city kitchen.

189

Owedia and I have rolled apart during the night, and she is there sleeping facedown, the pillow clutched to her head like a child.

I pull on my jeans and go down to the kitchen, where I know I will find my mother, alone.

She is there at the sink, washing utensils as she cooks.

When she sees me she smiles and says, "Hey, darlin', you're up early."

"It smells so good I couldn't sleep."

"Can I get you some coffee?"

"Yes, Momma, thanks."

She fills a cup from the percolator that has sat on the kitchen counter since I was a child, then turns to stir the crumbled bits of sausage she's got browning in a skillet.

"I suppose you think you've got a right to know what I've been doin' the years I've been gone."

"No. And I don't think I want to know. It's none of my business."

"Well, I would like to talk to you about it, honey. So's maybe you'd understand and you wouldn't hate me so much."

"I don't hate you."

"Sure you do. Maybe you don't even know it, but you do. You'd have to, being the woman you are, caring for your daddy."

She opens a sack of flour, dips a tablespoon in and sprinkles flour over the sausage. While she does this I go to the refrigerator and take out the carton of whole milk, then put it on the counter for her.

"Well, the thing is," I tell her, "I guess I do want to know where you've been. But what's more important to me is why you're back. And what you intend to do with Daddy."

She opens the oven and pulls out two tins of biscuits. She presses the tops for firmness, then puts the tins on the counter behind her and turns off the oven. After wiping her forehead with her sleeve, she pours some milk into the skillet and scrapes the bottom to make gravy.

"When I last saw you, you'd started college, isn't that right?"

"Yes."

"Well, as I remember it—and honey, there's a lot I don't remember—I was living in Louisville then and I'd had just enough of winter and so I thought I'd try living in a warmer spot, so I went with a friend of mine who had a job in Brownsville, Texas, which is about as warm as you can get in this country. He was with the army. I was with him for three years, and when he got shipped over to Germany, I said, that's one place I don't ever want to live, so I let him go and I stayed in Brownsville but another six months because that town suddenly seemed to me an awfully ugly, dirty little place, which is what it was. So I went to Tampa with another friend of mine. He was in the resort condominium business, sold condominiums all over the country. So I went to Tampa with him, and that didn't last but a few months. I liked Tampa, though, so I stayed on there another year. The best I could do there was some receptionist job with some light typing, and I thought maybe I'd do all right as a secretary, but the jobs are hard to find and don't pay shit, I don't mind telling you."

The gravy has thickened, so she turns off the flame and covers the skillet. Then she pours herself some coffee and leans against the counter as she speaks.

"So I went over to Orlando and tried to get a job at Disney World, but they didn't want me, so I took what little money I had and came back up to Louisville, where I still had some friends. I got myself a job selling makeup in Lazarus in the Northgate Mall down there, and it was pretty good for a while. I had my own place, I had a new boyfriend, Tom, a floorwalker at the store. And I had some money.

"But then I started having blackouts, where I'd find myself in my car a hundred miles out of town and I wouldn't know how I got there. Or in a bar somewhere. Or with some man." She looks at me quizzically, as if I might know why. "I would lie to Tom about it. Then I lost my job. And him. And then one day I found myself in the airport at the ticket counter trying to buy a ticket to Miami with a stolen credit card. And so I had myself committed."

She takes a pack of cigarettes out of the kitchen drawer and offers me one. "First today," she says. I take one and we stand there smoking together for the first time in our lives.

"I was in the state mental hospital at Crawfordsville, Kentucky,

191

for ten months. It wasn't fun, but I was so glad to be there, to be taken care of, and to know where I was going to wake up in the morning. Your father must've heard I was there, 'cause after a while he started coming to visit. He brought me clothes, books, things to eat." She pauses to sniffle. "He loves me, I guess." She looks away. "And I love him. And I'm on medication now. I've only been out a couple of weeks, but I'm feeling pretty good. I think I could make it."

I embrace her gingerly, both of us still holding the cigarettes.

"You're the first of the kids I've seen," she says. "I sure hope the others are as nice about it as you."

They won't be, I think, not by a long shot.

She takes my hands in hers. "You see, honey, I've always been reckless and stupid, but I never knew why. I never knew there was something wrong with my mind. It's just like when I married your daddy—Christ, you have no idea—how we loved each other secretly . . . and then it was too late and we had to get married."

I nod, having figured out the math years before.

"But now look at you! A lawyuh! God, I'm so glad you're not reckless and stupid like me!"

I could argue with that, but I just smile and change the subject: "So how do you like Owedia?"

"She's a lovely young woman," she says without missing a beat. "But not the type of girl I'd expect you to be friends with."

"Why do you say that?"

"She's such a young thing, she seems so innocent and fragile." That's all.

"Not like me," I say.

"No. Uh-uh," she says, as we hear a stirring upstairs. I turn and see Owedia toddle sleepily into the kitchen, smiling beautifully and looking just as childlike as my mother had painted her.

After breakfast, Owedia and I put on our jeans and flannels and I take her for a tour of the farm, my father's rifle balanced in my hand and his old .45 pistol and some ammo in a shoulder pouch. It is a sunny morning, brisk but not impossibly cold. The coldness of the fields is nothing like the bitter cold of the city, where the wind seems accelerated by the obstruction of buildings, whereas here on a day like today the wind blows—not blasts—and it is possible to be outside.

We go first to the barn and the horse paddock, where I promise Owedia a ride, then we walk along the south side of my father's soy field, just hard, turned-over earth now, toward a patch of woods where I liked to read in solitude as a child, when she says to me, "Your folks are awfully nice."

It is such an odd thing to say, and so untrue, to my mind, that I stop in my tracks, not knowing whether to laugh or yell.

"No, they're not, not really," I tell her. "They're awful racists, if you want to know the truth. They always were. When I was growing up my father would always go on about the niggers this and the niggers that. He hates black people."

The look on her face is of sadness and consternation, and I immediately regret having told her.

"I've had members of my family in the Klan," I go on, unable to keep from confessing. "And in this county, there's never been a black person who lived here. The people here just won't sell to blacks." She watches me pitifully. "I was raised to be one of these people, and somewhere inside me, and not very deep, I *am* one of them."

"Your folks are awfully nice," she repeats. "And so are you." She offers her hand.

I place my hand, hot with shame, in hers.

"You think I haven't dealt with racists? You think I don't know what hatred looks like? And I'm not talking about people like our friend Slick, with his tattoos. I'm talking about otherwise nice people who either look at you like you're beneath contempt or they're scared of you! They really are scared!" Her eyes are lit up with conviction, and I don't know when I've seen her so powerful. "But the amazing, beautiful thing is that people change. They really do. It's one of God's miracles, and you're living proof of it. Maybe your folks aren't the racists they were when you were growing up."

"And pigs can fly," I tell her.

"Do you know the story of the hymn, 'Amazing Grace'?" she asks, with her schoolteacher's directness.

"No."

"It was written more than two hundred years ago by a man named John Newton, who was an English slave trader. He had not yet given up the slave trade when he wrote the hymn, but he later devoted his life to outlawing slavery. For me, 'Amazing Grace' is about being reborn out of hatred and racism. It's about coming to view all people as God's children." She smiles. "Listen to the words." And she sings, her voice achingly pure in the still air.

> *Amazing Grace*
> *How sweet the sound*
> *That saved a wretch like me*
>
> *I once was lost*
> *But now I'm found*
> *Was blind*
> *But now I see*

She has never held a gun before and she is reluctant to do it, but I want her to shoot with me; in fact I insist upon it, rudely, and she agrees.

Together we haul a crate of bottles out of the barn, then I hand her the rifle to hold.

She handles the rifle gingerly, aiming it toward the sky as she runs her finger up the barrel. "I hate guns," she says. "I hate the very idea of them."

"But a gun is just a tool. Hating guns is like hating knives."

"But you can't make salad with a gun. You can only hurt things."

"We're just going to hurt some bottles."

I leave her to get acquainted with the rifle while I walk the hundred yards or so away and set up the bottles. When I turn around again I see her standing there, legs apart, holding the rifle site to her eye and following a bird across the sky, her finger curled around the trigger.

"You look like you know what you're doing," I call to her.

"Do I? I guess anybody who's ever watched TV knows how to hold a gun."

"Yes, but there's a little more to it than that," I say, now directly in front of her. "Stand at about a ninety-degree angle to the target with your legs about a foot-and-a-half apart, with your weight evenly distributed so you don't fall over." She moves her feet. "Good. Now, when you hold the rifle, you want it in what they call the butt cradle, just below the collarbone and above the chest muscles. You want to hold it so you just have to lean your head over a little to see through the site. Good."

Owedia grins as she adjusts to the weight of the thing, the feel of it in her hands. It is thrilling to hold something so powerful and destructive, and it is frightening in a giddy, nutty way. Introducing Owedia to this feeling is as weird to me as if I had turned her on to pot, and we are both strangely excited.

I show Owedia the safety, and I release it. I move behind her to steady her, and I put my arms around hers. "When you're ready to fire, take a deep breath and let it out slowly. As you let it out, increase the pressure on the trigger. The rifle should fire when you're about halfway out of breath."

Owedia inhales slowly, aims for a long moment, then presses the trigger, so slowly that I am surprised when the rifle fires and the shock of it hits us like the clanging of a bell.

Owedia is rewarded with an explosion of glass.

"Good shot!" I yell, clapping her on the back.

"Beginner's luck." She holds the rifle down, engages the safety, and as she touches the barrel, feeling its warmth, the pleasure in her eyes seems to dissipate.

We take turns shooting, with mixed success. After a time, I show her how to shoot with the .45—it is a long-barrelled western model—but after half-a-dozen misses, Owedia's ambivalence begins to wear on me, and there is no fun in it for either of us. We walk meanderingly back toward the house. The cold air and the shooting have exhausted Owedia, and I am relieved when she tells me she would like to lie down and read before lunch.

My mother is in the kitchen baking. It is as if she has chained herself to the kitchen, perhaps because she knows she has a place there, and when I come in, rifle in hand, she smiles broadly, hugs me, then hands me a list of things she needs for lunch.

"Why don't you and your daddy ride into town together and pick up these things, hmm?"

We take my truck, my daddy and I, and I drive us into town. He opens his window despite the cold air so he can smoke, but it just means that I get cold, smoky air blown in my face the whole way into Unity.

He talks about his eagerness to retire, he talks as ever about selling the farm, he talks about his progress rebuilding his antique tractor. It's not until we're on our way back with eggs, bacon, turkey, lettuce, grits, and the rest of it that I ask him, "So how do you feel about Momma being back?"

He shrugs and says, "Hell, I'm glad of it."

I let that rest a while, then say, "But aren't you angry with her?"

"She didn't come to me, honey. I'd heard she'd gone to the hospital in Louisville and I went there because I just had to see her. And after I'd done been there a few Sundays, I knew I wanted her to come home. If you want to know the truth, I begged her. I begged her to come back."

"But aren't you afraid that you're going out on a limb for her and she'll just end up leaving again?"

"Honey, it was the Christian thing to do." A tiny smile forms on his lips. "And besides, she's family."

When he says that I freeze for a shocked instant, but then I start laughing, harder than I have laughed in years, and he laughs too, a ridiculous, pathetic laughter that has him clutching the dashboard for support. We keep laughing, far past the point where it is painful, and we cannot stop it. I am fearful of running off the road, but I do not, and after a time the laughter dies into bursts of giggling, the sound catching achingly in our throats.

It really isn't funny.

I find it infuriating. Their apparent happiness, their normalcy, my father's tender, wormlike acquiescence, my mother's ascendancy to domestic goddess. I know that it cannot last. No way.

Lunch is, like our breakfast and dinner, a lavish spread of salads and sandwiches and cornbread and grits. Owedia floats through it all grinning, eating with tremendous appetite, oblivious to my pain, and I find myself thinking the nastiest racist thoughts as I watch her eat, as if the eating itself were a degrading activity and having a good appetite made it even more disgusting.

There is an image in my mind, perhaps from a package label dimly remembered, of a black child pressing a block of cornbread into his mouth, his lips wide open around it, yet somehow grinning, crumbs all over him.

I cannot eat.

That evening, after dinner, when my father and mother have settled down in front of the television, Owedia and I put on our coats and head out into the winter night—Owedia wants to see how brightly the stars shine out here.

So we go, and though it is too cold to walk, we trudge along the fence past the barn to the horse paddock, where we lean with our heads back and gaze around the vast, bright starry sky; it is a clear, still night of uncanny transparency, and there is not an inch of sky without stars.

"Of course, you don't wish for me to tell Carl or Dexter," she says suddenly, but it does not seem like a non sequitur.

"I wish you wouldn't. I suppose they'll have to find out sooner or later. But they would hate me, I think, and not understand that I did all I could."

"I think it's the deception that's the problem, not what you could or couldn't do."

I sigh; she is right, of course.

"How long can you keep it from them?"

"I don't know. Perhaps they'll never find out."

"They'll find out. But I'll keep your secret for as long as you can keep it."

"Thanks," I say, irritably. "So what do we do next?"

"We find Mr. E."

"Easier said than done."

"The first thing to do is to find this Freeze. And how hard can it be to find a fat white guy named Freeze with a shaved head and a snake on his neck and a swastika on his arm?"

"I think it's time you went to the police, Owedia. The IPD has a gang task force. They've probably got pictures of all the Vipers."

"I could ask Barbara Jones to do it. That way it wouldn't be connected to the attacks on me and JeTaun, and your name would be kept out of it."

I agree, though I find something intangibly worrisome about Barbara Jones. "But what then? Suppose we find a name and address for Freeze? Do we just go to him and say, 'hey, who really shot that old lady?' "

"Yes, we do that," she says. "But we also find Joe Baker. And we tell him we know everything. About Freeze and about Joe shooting that informant."

"Yeah . . . and then what?"

"And then we convince Joe to testify against the real killer in exchange for leniency."

"You're assuming an awful lot. What makes you think Joe would agree to that?"

"I think I could convince him. And I think—I mean, I feel it, I really do—that he knows he's got to be punished. That it's time to stop running."

"And what about the prosecutor's office? They have to decide Joe's worthy of credibility. And leniency."

Owedia shrugs. "I don't know. But how can they not want to see justice done? Knowing that Dexter is stuck in jail?"

She holds out her hand, palm up, and waits for mine to clasp it gently, as I do.

"Have faith," she says. "Have faith and all this will happen."

Sunday morning, when Owedia and I come down to the breakfast table, there are packages awaiting us, one on each of our plates, small boxes store-wrapped in pretty red metallic paper.

Owedia and I make a fuss over them, smiles and hugs and you-shouldn't-haves, and we open them to find two sets of earrings, not the same but almost so, each one a teardrop of gold with a pearl hung within it.

I have in my suitcase a gift I had intended to give my father before leaving. It is a book on wood carving and a new carving knife. I bring them down now and present them to him, and he accepts the gift with much manly reticence.

I have nothing for my mother. I could not have bought a gift for her, not feeling the way I do, and she seems to understand that. When I embrace her and wish her "merry Christmas," there is no bitterness in her eyes.

Later, in Brother Jesse's congregation, Owedia sits between my mother and me. Hers is the only black face among the fifty or so faces here, and though she participates in the service as spiritedly as the occasion will allow, I can feel her discomfort. There is something unwelcoming here, and it is not just the stares or the plainness of the service or the spartan coldness of the pews or Brother Jesse's frightening manner; there is something inherently exclusionary about this church, this religion. Owedia is not welcome here, not the least bit welcome, and though there is talk of charity and of opening our hearts to our neighbors, it is only to those who comprise our small community.

These are rules that are understood, and I have violated them.

My parents know this, and yet they have allowed me to bring Owedia here without a word of discouragement. I don't know if this is because they have developed a social conscience, or because they want to punish me.

Yet when the organ music swells and we are bid to rise, Owedia sings and for a moment there is beauty in this place.

>*And he walks with me and he talks with me*
>*And he tells me I am his own*
>*And the words I hear whispered in my ear*
>*None other has ever known*

24

Big-boned women are above petty emotions—we are simply too big for that—and we take no pleasure in the failures of others.

So I feel nothing in particular, no kind of satisfaction, when I find among the junk mail waiting when I return to Indy a card from Paul with the words "It's a Boy" splashed across its face and the bad news inside. It turns out he didn't get the job with the public defender.

The card also mentions that he's the proud father of a son, Matthew Mark, all of six-and-a-half pounds, born at 9:25 P.M.

There's not a word about my hospitality. Under other circumstances I might be insulted.

Monday the denial of Dexter's petition for rehearing is handed down without opinion. I go to Carl that evening, and we sit quietly in his living room, just the two of us. I allow him to tell me the news of the denial as if I had just happened to drop by to say hello, and once he has told me I talk to him about the two options still open to Dexter—the petition to transfer the case to the Indiana Supreme Court and the petition for postconviction relief. He listens wearily, and my offer to help him is accepted with a shrug.

"I hoped somethin' would come of the appeal," he says. "I didn't

think much of this rehearing business, 'cause I can't see a judge changing his mind after takin' so long to reach a decision. But it hurts. It
really does."

"*Dura lex sed lex.*"

He looks at me quizzically. "What'd you say?"

"It's Latin. It means 'the law is hard, but the law is the law.' "

" 'The law is hard, but the law is the law,' " he repeats with a frown.
"Ain't that the truth."

"It's what courts say instead of 'tough shit,' " I tell him.

Owedia calls me every night to be sure I am safe in my house, and
when she does not call me I call her. On Christmas Eve I give her my
number at work, and I tell her that I am thankful for this honesty and
for her friendship.

"You didn't have to wait so long," she says, and she asks if I will be
at church tomorrow.

"No," I tell her, "I'm not good at holidays."

"What are you doing for Christmas?"

"Spending this one alone. I'll catch up on some reading, house-
work. What about you?"

"After church, I'm going with Carl and my parents to see Dexter,
then we're all going out for dinner. Why don't you join us?"

I decline, though not without guilt. After subjecting Owedia to my
family, it would only be fair for me to sit through dinner with hers.

But they're a happy family.

And I couldn't bear that.

That night I walk to the vacant lot a few blocks from my house,
where some men have been selling Christmas trees out of a truck.
They are now at half price, and I buy myself the smallest tree they've
got, just big enough to put on the end table in my living room. It's a
token Christmas tree, enough to provide a Christmassy smell and
satisfy my minimal expectations of the holiday. As a child, it was my
siblings who were to be kept from disappointment at Christmas, not

202

I. It was I who bought the presents and wrapped them, and that included presents for my brothers and sister from my father and presents for my father from my brothers and sister. Most years, I was told simply to buy something for myself.

Lowered expectations have always served me well.

On Christmas morning, Haberman calls and invites me to join him at the mall for lunch and a movie. It is his habit, he tells me, to go to the movies on Christmas. He says it used to be that the theaters would be empty on Christmas but for Jews looking for refuge from the holiday; now, everybody goes, everybody needing refuge from their families.

I accept Haberman's invitation, glad to escape my four walls. Before leaving, I call my father, get no answer, and then I call each of my brothers and sister and leave Christmas greetings on their answering machines.

Two days after Christmas, Owedia calls to tell me that she spoke with Barbara Jones and asked her to get in touch with her contact in the IPD's gang task force. Barbara agreed enthusiastically—maybe too enthusiastically. I am apprehensive about her involvement; she strikes me as a gossip and a busybody, and maybe dangerous. Her job, if she can manage it, is to get mug shots or any other kind of shots of Vipers that we might show to Dexter, and to find out names and addresses of known Vipers.

Owedia asks me to join her and Carl to see Dexter on Saturday, but I cannot see Dexter now when I have so little hope to give him.

By Sunday we have heard nothing from Barbara, and I give in at last to Owedia's gentle badgering that I come to church.

It is a warm sunny day, a day too much like spring for the last weekend of the year, a day of false hopes. On this day every seat is filled and the doors at the back of the sanctuary are left open so that the ranks of those standing can extend out into the lobby. The ushers mill around nervously, trying hopelessly to keep the aisles clear.

I stand behind the last row of seats, counting myself lucky to have a good view.

> Mystery of mysteries! That God should have given to man his only begotten son! Mystery of mysteries! That Jesus Christ walked among us so that we might be free! Mystery of mysteries! That our lord Jesus Christ gave his life so that we might be saved! Mystery of mysteries! That Christ was resurrected so that we might be reborn!

Rev. Jones paces solemnly, cordless microphone in hand. The crowd is hushed, anticipatory, and at the end of each line an "amen" rises out of the congregation. Listening to the pleasant drone of Rev. Jones's words, I watch Owedia sitting with the choir behind him. Her hands lay restlessly in her lap, and sometimes I think I see in the tiny movements of her fingers a wish to be signing.

After the service, Owedia, Carl, and I collect our coffee and cake and wait for Barbara Jones to enter the fellowship room. When she does, as part of Rev. Jones's usual entourage, she glances at us, but immediately turns away and joins a conversation on the other side of the room.

"Is she avoiding us?" I ask Owedia. "Isn't she going to tell us what the IPD had to say?"

"I had hoped she would."

The three of us move toward her, and as we approach the cluster of women with whom she is speaking, I become aware of Rev. Jones nearby, his eyes fixed on me. When we are at Barbara's back, Owedia says, "Good morning, Barbara."

She turns and smiles quickly. "Owedia, good morning. Hello, Nora."

"Good morning."

She shakes my hand. "And good morning, Carl."

"We've been eager to speak with you, Barbara," Carl begins, but she ignores him and turns to Owedia.

"Owedia, I'm sorry," she says in a rush, "but I have had no time to get over to speak with the police. And I'm not sure when I will have the time."

"Oh. Why is that?"

She takes a deep breath, and says with evident reluctance, "To be perfectly honest, I think it's best if the church doesn't get involved in particular cases. I think there is much we can and should do to discourage young people from joining gangs, but I cannot help you find gang members."

Owedia's expression turns incredulous as Barbara speaks, and Owedia looks at her imploringly and says, "I thought you wanted to help us. That's what this is all about. This case. This particular case. Of this child, Dexter Hinton. What about him?"

Barbara tightens her mouth. "I can't help you, Owedia."

Abruptly Rev. Jones is at her side, and for the first time I am close enough to see him well. He is not a tall man, and he is very round, but he has an enormous head and large, compelling features. I cannot take my eyes off him.

"What is it, Barbara?" he says, at the same time reaching out his hand to shake Carl's hand, then Owedia's, then mine.

"I'm Nora Lumsey," I say, without waiting for Barbara to answer him.

"I'm happy that you've come again," he says kindly.

"I was just explaining to Owedia," Barbara says, "that as much as we want to help Dexter I cannot become involved with the police."

"Of course not," he says, gently scolding Owedia. "We're not private investigators or investigators of any kind. If the police think that we have a particular ax to grind, they may not be so receptive to us when we have the needs of the whole community in mind."

Owedia holds her breath, her whole body trembling with fury. "But . . . if we can't put the weight of the church behind any particular case . . . Forgive me, but what good can you do for the community if you won't stand up for one member of the community?"

"Owedia," he says, taking her hands between his, "it's important for us to keep lines of communication open between us and the police and between us and young people, both gang members and those who are not gang members. If either of those groups feel that I am a threat, I will alienate them, and the community cannot afford to let that happen."

"What about Dexter?" Owedia withdraws her hands from his and says, helplessly, "Rev. Jones, we need your help."

"You have my help. As much as I can give it. And you have my prayers."

We leave the church then, our mouths shut with anger and shock.

"Oh, he talks a good talk," Carl says, finally, as the three of us walk toward the parking lot. "But he hasn't a lick of courage."

Owedia is simply too upset to speak.

"We'll just have to get the information without Barbara," I say. "Owedia and I will go to the police."

Owedia looks at me and says somberly, "I won't let you endanger yourself."

On Tuesday, December 31, a half day for the court, I call in sick because I have neglected my little house, my home, and because there is just too much shit to be done: inches of dust to be wiped away, my token Christmas tree to be dismantled, piles of clothes to be washed, the bathroom to be rid of all the flora growing there. Out with the old.

I accomplish what I need to with the stereo blasting out the music I love best, Patsy Cline and Dwight Yoakam and Suzy Bogguss. By 8:00 that evening I am spent, sweaty and stinking in my T-shirt and sweatpants, and I am sitting on the floor of the living room, rewarding myself with a cold beer, when I hear three loud knocks at my door.

The knock is so much like Paul's that I brace myself for the unpleasant confrontation where I tell him it was fun, but not again, thanks, not even on New Year's Eve.

But when I look out the side window, the man at my door is Joseph Baker.

He stands bathed in moonlight with his hands in the pockets of his leather jacket. He sees me at the window, and he says in a low voice, "I need to talk to you."

I should be afraid, I know, because I am alone and he could easily overpower me and murder me or rape me, but there is something in his tone that makes me trust him.

I open the door and ask him to come in. He steps inside, tilting his head oddly, shyly, as if to signify that he is not a threat. The first thing I notice is that his style of dress has changed; instead of the quasi-military look, he is wearing a green sweater and black dress pants under a sleek black leather coat. The second thing I notice is that there is no look of appraisal; instead, he appears nervous and strangely depressed.

I am a tall woman but he is nearly a head taller than I am. I stand away from him so as to take all of him in, fold my arms over my chest, and I ask him what he wants.

"I'm goin' away," he says softly, "I know what you tryin' to do for Dex and I got to say a few things before I go."

"Why me? Why not tell it to Owedia?"

" 'Cause she wouldn't listen. She's mad at me from way back and I don't need to get into that." He hesitates a moment, then says, "Same with my grandfather. So I want you to tell 'em that you saw me and that I had to go away."

"Where are you going?"

"Far away, and that's all I'm gonna tell you. Some nasty shit is flyin', and I got to go."

"What kind of shit?"

"I'm in trouble." With this, his voice goes up in pitch, and he looks like he's about to cry. "You don't know what you're playin' with."

"Tell me."

"There's a lot of money involved, there's cops involved, there's people all over the country tied into it."

"I don't give a shit about those people or what they do, all I want is to get Dexter out of prison."

"It ain't that simple."

"Who is Mr. E, Joe?"

"Who?"

"Who was in the car with you and Dexter the day the old woman got shot?"

"That's what I'm here to tell you. But you got to know that the one you're looking for is too important to these people to let you or the cops or anybody else have him. And that's why I'm gettin' the fuck out of town. If he gets caught and the prosecutor gets him to talk in exchange for a plea bargain, then a lot of people go down. And they ain't gonna let that happen. They'll kill him first themselves before they let that happen. But before they do that they gonna hurt you so you stop lookin'. Then they gonna hurt you some more."

"And what about you?"

"I'm dead already." He folds his arms across his chest, as if to imitate me, but he hugs himself tightly and struggles to maintain composure.

"Who killed the old woman, Joe?"

"His name is John Bowman."

"Is he a Viper?"

"Yeah."

"Is he the one who goes by the name Freeze?"

"Yeah, that's him."

"Did he fire the shot?"

"Yeah."

"I was told that if I heard that it was you who shot that woman, I could believe it."

"Did JeTaun tell you that?"

"No," I lie.

"Well, I told some people that I did it. 'Cause I thought if I said that maybe nobody would bother about Freeze. And I'm damn good at hiding. The cops ain't never found me yet for anything I done, and ain't nobody gonna find me this time."

"Where do we find Freeze?"

He reaches into the pocket of his coat and takes out a scrap of newspaper with the name *John Bowman* and a Carmel address scribbled on the back.

"He be there most of the time. Freeze only come downtown when he wants some excitement."

"Like killing somebody."

"Yeah, and all kinds of other shit you don't wanna know about. He's a sick motherfucker. I think he killed that old woman just because Dex was there, 'cause he wanted to show off, maybe, or 'cause he wanted to mess Dex's head up."

"Does Freeze live alone?"

"Yeah. Sometimes his father be there and sometimes there's other Vipers there. It's a big old place."

"What's Freeze's father got to do with all this?"

He looks down, then away, and says, "I'm gonna fuck my shit up good if I tell you that."

"I thought you said you were dead already."

He laughs. "That's just an expression."

"Uh-huh."

"If I was dead I wouldn't be here talkin' to you."

"Uh-huh."

He smiles and says, "I may have to run further than I planned."

"Thanks," I say.

"Freeze's old man sells drugs—the legal kind, mostly. He works for one of those big drug companies, you know? And he spends a lot of time in South America. It ain't nothin' for him to get cocaine— pounds of the stuff—and him being so clean and upright, they don't look twice at him when he comes through customs."

"And Freeze sells it for him?"

"Yeah, but not only that, he handles payoffs to the cops, he deals with gangs and dealers in other cities, he deals with people who turn the coke into crack . . . he got his fingers in so much shit, if he ever gets caught, he ain't gonna serve no time. No way. But a lot of other people will."

"So why'd he do something so stupid as to kill that old lady?"

" 'Cause he can't believe he'd ever get caught. He thinks he can do whatever the fuck he wants and not get caught." He frowns. "And maybe he's right."

"No, he's not," I say, looking at the address in my hand.

"How you gonna prove it? I can't stick around to testify."

"I don't know," I tell him honestly. "But we will find a way."

"I got to go," he says abruptly. "You do whatever you want with what I told you, but I'm done. It's over and I'm leaving this town and I don't plan on comin' back." He opens the door behind him. "Ain't nothin' I can do about what happened to Dex," he says pitifully. "Tell him I'm sorry. Tell Owedia I'm sorry. Tell my grandpa I'm sorry."

"Happy New Year," I say, and I hold out my hand.

"Yeah, it could be," he says, shaking my hand quickly before slipping out the door.

I watch him run off across my lawn and down the street, where there is no car waiting for him.

I call Owedia immediately, and when I've told her everything, she says, simply, "He must not leave."

"I don't see how we can stop him," I say, "and he's probably right that he's in danger if he stays."

"Without Joe, there's no way to prove Dexter didn't do it."

"Unless Freeze confesses."

"Why would he do that?"

"In a plea bargain."

"In a plea bargain for what? What has he done that's worse than murder?"

"If the prosecutor wants his testimony badly enough, he'll find a way to reduce the charge."

"So now that we know who this guy is and where he lives, what do we do?"

"You have to take the information to the police."

"Where should I say I got the information?"

"Tell them Joseph Baker came to your apartment."

"I can't lie like that."

"Why not?"

"You want me to lie to the police?!"

"Why not? Don't you know how to lie?"

"Yes, but I get stomachaches when I lie."

"Then just say you can't tell them where you got the information."

"I'm not good at this kind of thing. I'm not good at confrontation."

"Sure you are."

"It would be a lot easier if you were there."

Of course it would. But I cannot do that, not now, and I am vaguely annoyed at her sudden lack of toughness. I suggest that she take Carl with her, and she agrees that she will go with Carl on Thursday and tell the police what we have learned.

On January 2, as I walk through the State House on my way to work, I see the governor standing outside the door to his office surrounded by a crowd of young children, third-graders, perhaps. He has an aide at each side, young men in dark suits who are handing out pamphlets to the children. The governor signs the pamphlets and shakes the children's hands.

As I walk by he glances up and smiles at me. Embarrassed, almost blushing. I wonder if it is because I have caught him doing such a blatant politicianlike thing or because I've seen him truly enjoying himself.

He is such a pretty man, our governor, projecting so much goodheartedness, it's easy to see why he was elected. What's hard to understand is why he has to spend so much of his time trying to get reelected.

I look at him and I feel the hate rise in my throat and I think no, it's not fair—if the affirmation of Dexter's conviction benefits this man, it's not his fault, it's just politics.

After all, he came to Dexter's church. He grieved with us. Didn't he?

I watch his face beam as he chats with the children, and he looks at me again, with a look that lingers too long. I fantasize for an instant that I could approach him about Dexter, but just then he turns away, as if sensing that I have something more on my mind than admiration.

At 5:00 that evening, Haberman and I are both still at our desks. This has never happened before. I do not know why he is working late, but I am more than a little irritated by the sound of the keyboard clicking steadily under his fingers. I have been dawdling too long on my utilities case, and I have promised the judge a draft by Friday. I don't know what the hell Haberman is writing, but his speed in writing it makes me want to choke him.

I do not want him to be here when Owedia calls, but when the phone rings, at 5:15, Haberman reaches for it first.

These are, after all, his chambers. He puts the call on hold and turns to me, smiling, and says, "It's for you."

I thank him and take the call. "Hello."

Owedia says, "You're not free to talk, are you?"

"No. But tell me what happened."

"I called the IPD this morning and asked them what to do if I had new information in a case. They asked me how old the case was and if it had resulted in a conviction. When I told them, they told me I would have to petition to get the case reopened. So I told them there wasn't time for that, that the guilty one wouldn't wait around for them to decide about a petition. So they told me to come down to the central station and fill out the petition form, and they would take a look at it. So I picked Carl up, and the two of us went down there. I felt bad for Carl. He put on a suit and tie, as if what they thought of him mattered. Maybe it does, I don't know. . . .

"So we went down and filled out the forms, and you know, I had been wrong about the case being closed; it isn't. The case against Dexter is closed, but not against Joe Baker. So I told them I had new information in that case, and then we got to speak with a Lieutenant Brown. Who was involved in the original investigation of Cora Rollison's murder."

"Wow."

"No, not wow, not really. He was interested in what I had to say, but it was like I was an old friend he hadn't seen since high school. He was interested, but he's moved on. Cora Rollison was a hundred murders ago. He's got other priorities. And while he'd like to bring in Joe Baker, the murder is solved as far as he's concerned."

"Even after you told him everything? About . . . you know"—now I am whispering into the phone—"the Vipers and the drugs and John Bowman?"

"He told me he'd pass the information on to the narcotics division. But there was no enthusiasm there, not even a pretense of hope. And I think he only promised to do that because Carl was sitting there, looking really depressed."

When I get off the phone, Haberman turns his head to me and says, "Not bad news, I hope."

I shake my head. "No, it's just that . . . some things seem to take so long to happen."

"You were so quiet on the phone, I was worried something was wrong."

"No. But thanks for asking."

He turns around completely. "Do you often work this late?"

"Now and then."

"The judge is worried about you, you know."

"Really?"

"Yes. He thinks you're still upset about the Hinton decision."

"I guess I am."

"He wishes you'd get over it already."

"I know. But I can't. Not yet."

Haberman smiles wistfully. "Sometimes I wish I cared the way you do. In all my time here, I've never fought for a defendant, never gone to bat for a principle. Maybe it's time I did something I care about."

"And what would that be?"

"I don't know."

I laugh, he shrugs, and I feel sorry for him.

"One of these days, I'm going to put my résumé together and start looking for a real job."

"You mean that?"

"Yeah, I do. I'm stale as hell, and you've helped me see that. Thank you."

"You're welcome . . . I think."

A moment later, Haberman puts on his coat, mumbles good-bye, and with a sad smile, he is gone.

I work until 10:00, later than I have ever labored for the judge. I am worried about his disapproval, embarrassed about his expression of concern to Haberman. He has become too much like a father to me—not like my own father, who was helpless except when he was farming—but like a father who controls through fear. I realize then how much I yearn to get out from under his thumb.

25

Sometimes the taste of whiskey is like a spoonful of dirt in my mouth, raw and foreign, sickening, to be spat out fast if I had any sense. Other times it's hot and soothing or cold and bracing, sometimes sweet like caramel or bitter like kale.

It's manna.

It's my drink.

When I get home, I curl in my big rocking chair and let the whiskey slip around my tongue and I surf the news on TV.

It's a slow news day. The fortunes of our teams top the news, as ever, the Pacers and Colts and Purdue and I.U., all we here really care about.

And then there's Roger Swango's face in a little box to the left of the anchorwoman's head.

He's been found dead.

I cough abruptly, the whiskey turned to shit in my mouth.

". . . was stabbed to death in the shop facility at Pendleton. Several inmates are suspects in the killing, which is believed to be gang-related. Questions are being raised tonight about security at Pendleton, where a work stoppage last year by corrections officers resulted in the largest . . ."

I grab the remote and mute her, unable to bear the yammering, and I watch the anchorwoman's lips move as I work at slowing my heart.

Dearest Roger! Fucked-up, crazy Roger! I had dared to believe there was a glimmer of hope for him, I really did, and I tell myself I might have done something about it, maybe gone to see him, talked to him, taught him something about moving on from hate . . .

Dear God, forgive me, I whisper.

Owedia is in bed, I am sure, reading something uplifting when I call with the news. She is silent for a long time; then her voice is calm as she says, "Maybe it had nothing to do with us."

"Yes," I murmur, trying not to sound morose.

"I pray it had nothing to do with us."

"Yes, of course, me too."

"It's the gangs . . . with the drug deals and all that. Dexter—and us—we're just not that important."

"Yeah, sure . . . So why were you attacked . . . and JeTaun . . . and why is Joe Baker leaving town? And why does it feel like we're right smack in the fucking middle of a gang war?"

She is silent.

I say, "It's kind of funny . . . that here we are a white woman and a black woman on the edge of this fight. And you and I have worked so hard to be more than what we came from. Me, comin' up from hillbilly trash, no different from what Roger Swango came from, and you—"

"But I'm not that," she says sharply. "I'm trying to be the fulfillment of what I came from, to live up to my heritage, and not be dragged down by evil."

"Yes, of course," I say, embarrassed. "I'm sorry."

"I'm worried about Dexter," she says abruptly, her voice catching.

"So am I."

"The security in the Boys' School is no better than at Pendleton. If they can be tattooing each other without the guards knowing, they could be . . ."

She is crying now.

"I know," I say. "Maybe Joe had the right idea in getting the hell out."

"Joe?! He *abandoned* his brother. You think that's the right idea?"

"I only—"

"Dexter is worse than abandoned. He's been thrown to the lions."

"I know."

"More than ever, now, Nora, we've got to get him out of there."

"I know."

Before hanging up, I tell her, "Lock your doors and windows."

"Yes, I will, and you do the same."

After a sleepless night, I lumber through a dreary Friday, quietly oblivious to the work in front of me. I am shocked to find myself fighting tears, dizzy with emotion, not only with worry over Dexter but *grieving* for Roger Swango. His bruised face hovers in my mind, his bad teeth, his unembarrassed grin. It is odd, but in contemplating that face, an increment of guilt is washed away, and I am freed from anguishing over whether Roger was killed on our account.

It was the grinning ugliness inside him that killed Roger.

By 4:30 I am exhausted with sorrow and worry, but I cannot go home; this night, the first Friday in January, is a special night in Judge Albertson's chambers, a night that any clerk in her right mind would anticipate with nervous pleasure. It is the night Haberman and I are to be the judge's guests at the yearly banquet of the Inn of Court, and it is a chance to hobnob—and network—with the elite of the city's legal community.

The Inn is modeled after the English Inns of Court, where the education of barristers and solicitors was once carried on exclusively. Here, it is a members-only social club for judges and lawyers. The Inn meets once a month for drinks, dinner, and a seminar on a legal topic, and Judge Albertson never fails to attend. On those evenings, he works until 5:00 instead of going home, and when he departs the office it is with the look of a satisfied, successful man about to enjoy himself immensely.

Tonight is the only night of the year when guests are permitted at the Inn, and it is a tradition for judges to bring their clerks. Haberman has attended these occasions seven times before, and so he is entirely blasé about it; but as he and I put on our coats and follow the judge through the corridors of the State House, my tiredness begins to leave me, and I am thankful for a night's relief from the horrors of thinking about Vipers and Indy Boyz.

The night is bitingly cold and windy, and I hold on to Haberman's arm as we trudge the few blocks from the State House to the Columbia Club, the city's oldest and most prestigious men's club—though now of course women are permitted. Haberman smiles at me, surprised at the contact, and I marvel as ever at how easy it is to give a man pleasure.

We pass under the long red awning of the Columbia Club to the entrance, where a doorman, perhaps the only full-time doorman in this city, cocks his head stiffly as we enter. The judge leads us past a sitting room with a massive fireplace, a smoking room now with signs declaring it smoke-free, and up a flight of red-carpeted stairs to the mezzanine banquet room. Above us, crystal chandeliers glitter and tinkle softly.

Haberman and I exchange bemused glances.

It's all too much, too laughably elegant for this overgrown farm town.

In the banquet room, the members of the Inn—mostly men in their fifties and sixties, but including more women than I might have imagined—huddle in cocktail-party formation, each elder of the tribe surrounded by his gaggle of starry-eyed youth.

That would be me, and yes, my eyes turn starry too, as I recognize the Hoosier luminaries who are among our company this evening.

The chief justice of the Indiana Supreme Court is here, along with the chief judge of the Court of Appeals—Judge Albertson's boss—and several federal judges. There are name partners from the city's biggest firms, the county prosecutor, and a number of high-profile criminal defense attorneys.

The judge leads us to the cash bar, where we buy our drinks—mine a whiskey and soda, appropriately ladylike—and set off into the crowd. There are about a hundred or so people here and the room is small and overheated, so Haberman and I must excuse ourselves repeatedly as we follow the judge single file like obedient ducklings, pausing when the judge stops to shake somebody's hand, stopping now and again to be introduced to one or another of his buddies from all his years in practice and on the bench.

We're networking, I remind myself. At that moment, I am bumped from behind while attempting to walk and take a sip of my drink. As a splash of whiskey and soda dribbles down my chin, I look behind me and there's the chief justice.

"Sorry about that," he says kindly, and he whips out a handkerchief so stiffly starched it resists being unfolded.

"It's all right," I say. "My fault."

He is very tall, Lincolnesque in stature, stooped and awkward, with wide-set eyes and a big beak nose. He has the kind of ugly beauty that is captivating.

"You must be Nora Lumsey," he says, glancing over me toward the judge, who has continued on through the crowd. "I'm John Hohlt."

It takes me a rude moment to register that he knows who I am without ever having laid eyes on me, and while I wonder about this I blot my chin, refold the hankie, and hand it back to him.

"I'm delighted to meet you," I say, shaking his hand, "and I'm flattered that you know who I am."

He laughs. "You needn't be. Judge Albertson has been raving about you for months."

"Raving . . . in a good way?"

"Raving in a good way, yes."

There's nothing I can say to that.

"I understand you and the judge locked horns over *Hinton versus State*. Well, I must say you ended up doing a hell of a good job."

Hell of a good job?

"Forgive me, Chief Justice Hohlt," I say, gathering courage. "But how can you comment to me on a case that may come before you?"

He shrugs. "I don't see a problem with what I just said. You're a clerk who worked on an opinion, not a party to the case."

"Yes, but—"

"And I just complimented you on a job well done." He's smiling, but he's obviously annoyed.

"Forgive me," I mumble.

"I think I've hit a tender spot." He reaches out, squeezes my shoulder once, and turns away.

Nice going, Lumsey.

I wander in search of Haberman and the judge, embarrassed at having made such an ass of myself, but angry that the judge would allow me to go on feeling so insecure about my work, yet would say nice things behind my back.

We do not lock horns. He makes use of my enthusiasm and need for approval, yet regards me as so far beneath him that he needn't make the effort of praise.

I hate him for that, and for taking me so lightly as to joke about me with his buddies. I want to yell at him, make him feel what I feel—that *Hinton v. State* is not about points of law and not about getting the best of his clerk in a battle of locked horns. It's about a young life, the best part of which will be spent behind bars, thanks to his ego.

"You're overreacting."

I look up to find Haberman in front of me and another whiskey and soda being substituted for the empty glass in my hand.

"Bumping into the chief justice is a religious experience, I know, but snap out of it, Nora, you're starting to attract attention."

I sip my drink, stealing a glance around me, and yes, there are more than a few people gazing at me—that peculiar big girl alone in the middle of the crowd, staring.

Haberman puts an arm around my shoulder and we walk.

"It was Jeremy Bentham who said"—Haberman says, gesturing expansively with his free hand—" 'The law is not made by judge alone, but by judge and company.' Here we have gathered in this room many of the judges and much of the company who make and interpret the law in this state. Rather grand, isn't it, when you think about it?"

"Yes, and I have the distinct feeling I don't belong here. It's too fucking grand, and I don't know shit about the law."

"Why be so down on yourself? Nobody expects you to know anything about the law. In fact, occasions like this are designed to knock the arrogance out of you. It's a profession, not a religious order, and the people doing it are human. Even the chief justice puts his pants on one leg at a time."

"Yeah, they all do."

Haberman babbles on, comfortingly in his way, as we walk through the crowd toward the judge, who I am surprised to see engaged in spirited conversation with a much taller, much younger man.

The young man's back is to me, and I laugh to myself to see the judge standing with his head at this man's sternum, gazing up earnestly as this man speaks down to him, quite literally.

Then I see the side of the man's face, his smooth baby-face cheeks, and my heart begins to thump like mad when I realize who it is.

On their own, my feet stop moving.

I see then what I have refused to see for so long, and my embarrassment and anger rush up in me, throbbing hot and cold for an instant, and then I am just cold.

Haberman glares at me. "What's up? The program'll be starting any minute."

"I—"

"Come on."

"No."

He takes my arm, but I wrest it away and with an annoyed look he hustles over to the judge, colliding with one local lawyer-celebrity after another as he goes.

I cannot, will not, move.

It is like stumbling upon the truth, like watching your lover in conversation with another woman and knowing suddenly from the looks on their faces that he's sleeping with her too.

And then just as quickly I don't believe it. Would the governor have dared ask the judge to affirm Dexter's conviction? Would the judge have agreed?

And is that why the judge assigned me to draft the opinion? Because he knew there was a reversible issue and thought I wouldn't catch it?

I am moving now, almost running, because I want to get close enough to know if what I'm thinking could be true.

Suddenly I am there, standing at the judge's side. Close up, the governor's face looks almost real, with a shade of stubble here, an enlarged pore there, a certain crookedness to his lower lip. There are hairs out of place, and a hair or two growing out of his ear. But he is still impossibly beautiful.

"Governor Doyle, I'd like you to meet my other clerk," the judge says jovially. "Miss Nora Lumsey will be with me for this year."

The governor's blue eyes shift toward mine as we shake hands.

He pronounces, "Good evening, Nora," and he gazes at me with what looks like love in his eyes.

"I'm delighted to meet you, Governor," I reply coolly.

"Judge Albertson is one of our finest appellate judges, and before that he was one of this state's finest criminal defense lawyers," the governor says amiably. "You can be proud to be working for him."

"Well, thank you," the judge says, not giving me a chance to respond. "But that was before you were out of diapers."

"I hate to say it," the governor jokes, "but you happen to be right."

The judge laughs and squeezes the governor's upper arm as we break and move toward our tables for the seminar.

"Nice to meet you, Mr. Haberman," the governor says, stepping slowly away. "And you, Nora."

He says my name with frightening clarity. I twist my head to look at him, but he has already turned his back to us.

The judge pulls out a chair for me.

I say to him, my heart still pounding, "Do you know the governor very well?"

"Of course. I see him here now and then, and at political functions. I've been to the governor's mansion on occasion for dinner."

"The governor was very interested in the Hinton decision . . . he and Furness were talking about it for weeks."

The judge picks up a dinner roll and splits it open with his fingers. "Yes, that's right."

I take a dinner roll and the judge and I stab together at the butter plate. "Has the governor ever said anything to you about the case?"

"What do you mean?"

"Would he ever say anything like, 'Hey, Judge, nice decision?' "

"Sure, we've talked about it. It's an important case."

"Did he know that you were the judge who was writing the opinion in the case?"

"You mean before the decision was handed down?"

"Yes."

He takes a sip of scotch, then sets about buttering his roll. "Of course not. The identity of the judge to whom a case has been assigned is kept confidential."

"Sort of like the hood on an executioner."

The judge drops his wrists noisily against the table edge and stares forward for an instant before turning to me. "Miss Lumsey, I find your bluntness occasionally charming, and I find your naïveté . . . an interesting challenge. But I will thank you to say no more to me about the Hinton decision. It is done. You were wrong. End of story."

With that the judge puts down his knife and the dinner roll and glances quickly around the room. Then he stands and addresses the table. "If you will excuse me," he says, "I have some business to discuss with Judge Baird and I will be moving to his table. Enjoy your dinner." And he takes his scotch and is gone.

I turn to Haberman, who gazes heavenward and shakes his head slowly. "You amaze me," he says. "You don't know when to shut up."

"No, I don't. I know I don't. And I don't care."

"There's an old Yiddish saying . . ."

"Oh, God, no."

He smiles. "There's an old Yiddish saying, 'A man who is destined to drown will drown in a glass of water.' "

I look at him, angry, and I don't want to hear any more.

"Don't drown," he says.

A waiter comes around with wine. The chief justice gets up from his seat on the dais and goes to the podium.

The evening's entertainment, he tells us, will be a brief talk on jury selection and the "race card"—how lawyers try to influence the outcome of cases by affecting the racial composition of the jury.

If I were in my right mind, I'd be very interested; it's a topic that's near to my heart.

But I'm not in my right mind.

And Haberman isn't helping. When my wineglass is empty, he motions discreetly to the waiter and asks him to leave the bottle; the waiter does, and Haberman fills my glass, grinning sweetly.

I like Haberman. I want to tell him everything.

I don't hear a word the speaker is saying.

I know there is a second bottle brought, and I know how incredibly stupid it is to get drunk here among my potential future employers, but it's too late now, and Haberman is filling his glass too, so abjectly depressed about his own chances for further employment, and there is intermittent laughter around our table, but I don't know what it's about.

As the speaker drones on, I spy on my colleagues—the other law clerks and their judges—and I watch the judge sitting morosely with Judge Baird, the judge's eyes half-closed, his face slack with drink.

Off in a dimly-lit corner of the room I see a black man sitting alone. I do not recognize him at first, but I know I know him, and so I clutch Haberman's shoulder and lean toward the man and squint, and then I see the black frames of his glasses and the gray hair and with a jolt I know it is Ralph Sawhill.

He is sitting at a table with several others, but the seats on either side of him are empty. As I stare at him he neither moves nor speaks, while the others at his table engage in animated conversation.

I feel for him, for how sad and lonely he looks.

Later, over dessert, I ask Haberman, "Do you know anything about Ralph Sawhill?"

"You mean the lawyer in the Hinton case?"

"Yes."

"You never stop, do you?"

"What do you know about him?"

"He's one of the greats. Or used to be. The Hinton case was certainly not a high point for him."

"Does the judge know him?"

"I imagine so."

"It must be difficult for a judge to be impartial when he knows the lawyers."

Haberman chews his cheesecake slowly a moment, composing his thoughts. "Honestly, I doubt it's ever an issue. Every case is important to the parties involved and sometimes to many others as well. But it's a job, Nora, honest to God, and as far as I can see the judge does his best for justice. It isn't personal. Of course, if he knew one of the parties to a case, that would be completely different. As a judge, he'd be hopelessly compromised. But as for knowing the lawyers, hell, he drinks and plays golf with these guys! He knows their wives and ex-wives and children!"

My head is spinning. I smile at him, thinking there isn't a thing he could say that could possibly make me feel any worse.

"You've heard of a concept called the separation of powers, right? In the United States Constitution? It mandates an independent judiciary. That's to prevent the kind of extrajudicial pressures you're talking about. Not that it isn't felt in intangible ways. Don't you think the judge felt sorry for the Hinton kid? But that's where integrity comes in. And professional detachment."

"Professional detachment? Isn't that a way of saying, 'if we close our eyes and ignore the truth, maybe it'll go away?' "

"No," he says, "Not to me. But clearly you're not ready to exercise that level of detachment. I hope for your sake you get there soon."

He's right. I'm foolish and naive and sentimental and maybe paranoid. I must think very little of myself and of lawyers in general if I don't believe we can exercise professional detachment.

I've never been detached about anything.

I watch the governor sit laughing with the chief justice and a number of other stellar figures, oblivious to me, and it galls me so that they are enjoying themselves while Dexter is suffering God-knows-what in the Boys' School.

The judge's chin is on his chest as talk chatters on around him.

And I feel such an aching disappointment in him. Here is a man who boasts of the purity of his justice, a judge so devoted to process that he would not deign to raise an issue *sua sponte* to save the life of a child. If it is true that he affirmed Dexter's conviction as a favor to the governor, even if he believed unequivocally in Dexter's guilt, it is a betrayal of everything he pretends to stand for.

Haberman drives me home. I am too drunk to drive, but not drunk enough to invite him in.

I like Haberman. I want to tell him everything.

26

I know God is a big-boned woman because God is kind and fair, despite being strong enough to *fuck anybody's shit up good* if they were to be bad. But She doesn't do that. God is strong, but restrained.

She gives hangovers occasionally, but She doesn't punish, not really. Folks who do bad things don't get struck down dead, don't get cancer, and don't pay for it—unless people make them pay.

That's what Justice is for. Justice does the punishing because God won't do it—until the next life, maybe—and people simply can't wait that long.

And it's clear that Justice is not the big-boned woman she's represented to be, a woman strong enough to hold up those scales eternally, eternally blindfolded, a woman strong enough to need to exercise restraint.

I need to exercise restraint.

I awaken the next morning raw inside and out, and there is a numbness in me now that doesn't go away, not with coffee, not with a quick shot. This is not my usual hangover. I don't even want to cry.

It's a fucking dead end.

Owedia calls. We are all going to see Dexter today, she and I and Carl, and I agree to go, if only because she will drop me off at the State House on the way back so I can pick up my car.

Carl is dressed as if for church. He is always neat, even when working in the garden, but today he is beautiful in a blue suit and herringbone overcoat and black fedora.

Owedia whistles at him as he walks to her car.

He grins, turns once, and says, "I will not let the middle of winter turn me into some kind of hibernating creature."

He has packages for Dexter—belated Christmas presents from friends. It occurs to me with a guilt pang that I have not bought a present for Dexter, have not even thought of doing so, and I wonder what is wrong with my heart that Christmas has come to mean so little to me.

It's worse than that, really. The whole holiday season makes me angry.

I help Carl pile the presents into the car, and then I let him sit in the front seat while I scrunch myself into a corner in the back and quietly watch the scenery go by.

Dexter is bad today. He is petulant, morose, and nearly obnoxious. In fact, he's acting exactly how I feel.

He accepts the presents that Carl brought. They are all in open bags for inspection by the corrections people on our way in. Without a word, Dexter examines the contents of each with disdain. They are books, mostly—*Goosebumps* books, science books with gadgets built into them—books to feed his aspirations, and today he has none.

"It's a new year," Carl says to him, and Dexter signs, "For you, maybe. One day is the same as the next here."

Dexter tells us that there is a program that his teacher is trying to get him into that would let him work on a farm in the spring and summer. Carl and Owedia think this is a wonderful idea, and I guess

I think so too—considering the wonderful things that growing up in the fresh air did for me—but I just sit there and watch his face maturing—his mouth growing around his big teeth, his peach fuzz turning dark. And I want to scream.

Today, I am mute.

In fact, I say hardly a word all morning, and when Owedia drops me off at the State House, she asks me if everything is all right.

I tell her it is, and I apologize.

"I'm out of sorts today," I say, too embarrassed to tell her I have a hangover. "Postholiday blues, I think."

"Let me help you chase those blues," she says. "Have dinner with me tonight. There's a new vegetarian place over in Broadripple I've been wanting to try."

"You're not a vegetarian, are you?" If Owedia were to become any more righteous, she'd be glowing.

"No, but I've been thinking of converting."

I agree to meet her there, though the thought of going to Broadripple conjures an image of Ralph Sawhill, and my heart kicks nervously.

The restaurant is in a huge, old Victorian house just off Broadripple Avenue, and Owedia is sitting on a velvet-cushioned bench in the lobby when I arrive.

"Hey," she says, and she hugs me. She smells very good, of rose water. "You're looking much better than this morning."

"Thanks," I say. "I napped."

We stare at the menu a long time; there is nothing familiar here, no dishes I've ever eaten, though the vegetables are mostly recognizable.

The good news is that they have a liquor license, and I immediately order a Jack Daniel's on the rocks.

Owedia tells the waiter, "Water will do."

When he's gone, Owedia takes a breath and, gesturing enthusiastically, tells me why she had asked me to dinner. "I've been thinking," she says, "that maybe we've been beating our heads against the wall because we're going about this all wrong. I mean—we don't have the resources to hunt down gang members. That's crazy. It's Dexter we've got to focus on. We've got to press the authorities to release him."

I hear this and I see the fear in her eyes. Roger Swango's death was a powerful message, and I can't deny it's sent me spiraling down too. Yet—

"Dexter won't be eligible for parole for twelve years," I tell her, "and I don't see any other basis for getting him out. Maybe he could file some kind of civil rights action against the state under the Individuals with Disabilities Education Act, but there's really no basis for it—he's got Mrs. Martell three times a week, so you can't say he's not getting an appropriate education for a deaf kid."

"What about taking it up to the Supreme Court?"

"We're doing that. I'm going to help Carl with the brief, but like I've said, the chances of getting it reversed are slim."

"What about that post-conviction relief thing?"

"For that, you need new evidence. And that means finding who did the killing."

She spreads her fingers along the edge of the table. "What about this judge you work for? Isn't there something he can do?"

"What do you mean?"

"I don't know what I mean," she says irritably. "He's a *judge*! Can't you talk to him about the case, show him he was wrong—"

"What do you think I tried to do?"

"—and maybe he could talk to somebody on the Supreme Court."

"You don't understand the way the system works. It's all done with briefs and arguments. Judges from different courts don't talk to one another about cases." Except when they're off-duty.

"All I know is, in the beginning you were hiding the fact that you work for this judge. Now you're hiding *behind* the fact that you work for this judge. What's the difference? You tell me you can't do anything. Well, I don't know whether to believe you or not."

It stings to hear it, but she isn't far wrong.

"I guess I deserve that." I down my drink quickly and order another. "But you've got to believe me that it's completely out of my judge's hands now. And mine, as far as the judge is concerned."

Owedia buries her face in the menu, and when the waiter returns with my drink, she orders squash stuffed with pine nuts and sun-dried tomatoes. I order the polenta and sauteed vegetables—figuring that anything resembling cornbread can't be all bad.

When the waiter leaves, Owedia and I stare at each other for a moment, a kind of ocular handshake, a truce. Without shifting my gaze I take a sip of my drink. As the whiskey hits my mouth, I feel a little numb spot at the back of my head and realize that it's my second on an empty stomach.

"There's something I ought to tell you," I mumble, unsure if I have the courage to say it. "I don't understand it all, but I believe the governor may be behind the affirmation of Dexter's conviction."

Her eyes widen, and then glisten.

"What are you saying?"

"I'm saying I think the governor asked Judge Albertson to affirm the conviction. I think he did it because he knows that if Dexter is released and given a new trial, Emmett Furness would turn Dexter into a symbol of Doyle's weakness on law and order."

She stares at me, disbelieving.

I say, "Do you remember at the church the governor said that Furness was trying to turn Dexter into another Willie Horton?"

"Yes."

"Do you know who Willie Horton is?"

"Yes, he's the man who was released from prison on parole in Massachusetts and went out and raped a woman."

"That's right."

"And it may have cost Dukakis the presidency in 1988."

"The governor plans to be president some day, and he's afraid Dexter's going to haunt him the same way. And he can't afford to lose the white conservative voters."

"And this judge of yours would go along with that?"

"I don't know."

"But you think it's true?"

"I don't know!" I yell. "I just feel it. The judge has spoken to me at times about . . . the politics of the judiciary, and then I saw him and the governor together last night at a dinner, and the way they were talking, I *knew!* Then I asked the judge if he had spoken to the governor about the Hinton decision. And he said yes, although he denied that the governor knew he was deciding the case before it was handed down."

I finish my drink and order another. "And then I've been thinking about how the governor and Reverend Jones are tight, how Reverend Jones helped save the governor's career when he was mayor. I think about Michael Taylor and Burnett and the others and how there was the perception that the police were out of control when Doyle was mayor and how the mayor tried to mend fences with blacks through Reverend Jones. I think about Doyle urging restraint when Dexter was arrested and then suffering the most vile backlash, and you can be sure he said to himself I'll never make that goddamn mistake again!"

"If you're right, it means it's completely hopeless. Because the Indiana Supreme Court is going to do the same thing."

"Yes." I whisper, my throat so tight I can hardly breathe.

She reaches across the table and squeezes my hand.

"You're drinking an awful lot," she says.

I nod.

"You shouldn't."

I nod. Of course I shouldn't.

"I didn't want to say anything in front of Carl this morning, but I knew you were hung over. I know what alcohol smells like on a person the next day—it's like it's coming out of your pores. I used to smell it on Dexter's mother when she'd bring him to school."

I am perverse enough to want to tell her that I'd already had a drink this morning when she picked me up, but why pick a fight? No, I sit there politely and take the scolding.

"I'm just worried about you," she says—of course. "I think that drinking is your way of coping with the stress of all this."

I have to laugh at that. "Drinking . . . is my way . . . of achieving happiness. It feels good to be drunk. Not too drunk. But drunk. That's all, honey. That's all."

In that instant I have become my mother, and with her meanness I reach out and squeeze Owedia's hand sarcastically.

"Don't—"

She pulls back her hand. The waiter brings a loaf of crusty peasant bread and takes my empty glass and asks me with a tilt of his head if I'd like another. I nod, avoiding Owedia's glare, and I say, "I think you need to get yourself on a plane to Atlanta."

"What's that supposed to mean?"

"You need to get away, have yourself some fun."

"That's not what you mean."

"No, that's not what I mean."

"Do you see how much fun you are when you're drunk? It makes you just a *wonderful* person."

"You're so right. And maybe if you weren't so fucking self-righteous you could relax and have a drink or get laid once in a while instead of acting like some goddamn Mother Teresa. As if being a saint is going to help Dexter—well, honey, it ain't!"

"Stop—"

"And as if kissing the Reverend Jones's ass is gonna convince God to reach down and pluck Dexter out of prison!"

"Nora—"

"And you think because I work for the fuckin' judge I can *do something*? Shit!"

The waiter tiptoes toward us with my drink and wincingly tells us dinner will be right out. He is about to scurry away when Owedia grabs my drink and calls to him.

"Take this back, please. I think my friend has had enough."

"What the fuck are you doing?"

I stand and reach for the drink before the waiter can grasp it.

"I have *not* had enough."

"Nora, please—"

She pulls hard on the drink and my fingers slip on the wet glass and it splashes all over her, the entire contents of the glass, all over her

233

lovely sweater. She watches this happen, disgusted and angrier than I've ever seen her, but she calmly puts down the glass and starts dabbing herself with her napkin.

"Now I'm going to smell like you smell," she snarls, and she throws down the napkin, picks up her coat, and leaves the restaurant.

I sit there a while.

The waiter cleans up the mess on the table, sweeps the scattered ice cubes into a dustpan, then asks me, "Do you think your friend will be returning?"

There's nothing I can do.

Nothing for Dexter. Nothing for myself.

She's right. Drinking does help me cope. It's helping me cope with the pain of sitting here alone right now.

The waiter brings me a fresh drink—"on the house."

It's obvious I need it.

I can quit drinking any time.

I pull into my driveway at 10:30, blind with exhaustion, thankful to the deities for seeing me home safely. I leave my car next to my front door rather than attempt to guide it into my garage; all I want is to be undressed and in bed with a book. I already have a head start toward oblivion.

But as I turn my key and push my front door open, I sense a shadow move behind me, and within an instant there is a force against my back, pushing me in—not a hand or a fist, but it is like a strong wind, irresistible, and it is only after a moment that the force takes the shape of a man and there are his fingers grasping my throat, his arm snaking around my waist, and suddenly there is a hand holding a gun to my cheek.

27

He stinks. That the first thing, after the shock—his rotten odor, his breath at my face reeking of cigarettes, beer, and decay, and his body giving off a feral unwashed smell. Then there is his fleshiness against my back; he is heavy, taller than I am, and his hands are soft, sweaty, slimy.

"Get on the floor. Face down." His voice is high and clear, like a boy's, and it is a country voice, with inflections I recognize instantly.

He holds me by the collar. The barrel of the gun is now planted behind my ear. My hands go out as I lower to one knee, then the other, then let myself down to the dusty wood floor.

He follows me down, putting one leg on each side of me until he is sitting on my buttocks, leaning over me as I lay flat.

"You don't get it, do you?" he says, rubbing the gun against my skin.

"What do you want?"

"I want you to stay out of where you don't belong. You mess with the Vipers, you get messed with, and you get hurt. Bad."

As he says this he taps the gun against my skull, harder each time, and my skull rings maddeningly.

"Stop that. I get the message."

"I could kill you now. I don't know why I don't."

So it has happened. Lying there with my face on the floor and this man on my back, his gun against my skull, I can't help but think, through my terror, that it feels just like when my brother and I would wrestle on the living room floor. Occasionally, to keep the peace, I would let him win, but I always was the strongest of my siblings, and the biggest.

And the meanest. After my mother left, I had an anger inside me that would not leave me alone and would not let me be dominated, not for real or for play, not for a moment.

And I am angry now—about Dexter, about Carl, about JeTaun and Owedia, about my ass of a mother, about Paul, about Roger, about the judge, the governor, and Reverend Jones, and about me and my idiot heart.

Perhaps he expected me to whimper, cry, or beg, but I cannot, and what scares me most is that this clumsy boy will shoot me inadvertently. So I remain still while he makes up his mind.

For a long moment he strokes my skull with the gun, then apparently he decides that he has accomplished what he was told to do— not to kill me, rape me, or rob me of anything but my sense of security. Holding the gun to the back of my head he lifts his weight from me and murmurs, "Don't move, bitch."

It's those words that set me off. As he says them I recall seeing them in so many transcripts of trials for rape; they are the cliché of the rapist, the parting shot, the final humiliation, the word *bitch* used to crush whatever molecule of self-respect is left; *bitch* equals *animal* equals *whore* equals less than nothing.

He lifts himself from me, shifting his weight to his left hand and also to the gun boring painfully into my head. As he gets up I feel the gun lift away, and then I move.

Quickly, I reach back and get his gun hand in a lock with my right arm so that his gun is pointing toward the floor. I roll to my left, onto him, my back to his chest, knocking him flat over.

"Bitch!" he cries out, and the gun, now pointing into the air, fires into the ceiling. With my free hand I grab the gun out of his hand, then roll to my right and into a crouch.

When the dust settles I am holding the gun with both hands extended in front of me, and he is lying on his back with his hands palm-up at either side of his head, like a dog wanting his belly scratched.

"Don't shoot!" he says.

Don't shoot.

It's so pathetic I almost laugh.

Holding the gun firmly in front of me, I rise to my feet, back up to the wall and flip on the light switch.

There on the floor is a large child, a fleshy white kid with a shaved scalp, dark eyebrows, and flushed cheeks. He is a big-boned boy, thick and barrel-chested. He also appears quite stupid.

"What's your name?" I ask.

He says nothing.

It occurs to me that I have never pointed a gun at another person, and it is a remarkable and terrible sensation. I want to pull the trigger. I want to shoot the gun, and there is a weird irritation growing inside me, a physical need that is so much like the need for sex that it momentarily scares the shit out of me.

How I would love to shoot this boy, but just enough to satisfy me, not to kill him.

"Your street name, then," I say. "What do the Vipers call you?"

He says nothing.

"How about Pretty Boy?"

His eyes flash angrily.

"Now, don't fuck with me, Pretty Boy, because I know how to shoot."

Now he's sullen, impatient.

I back up to the kitchen, pick up the wall phone, and dial Owedia's number.

She answers with a guarded hello, and I realize with some guilt that she must have known it would be me.

"Owedia, I need you to come to my place. Right now."

"What is it?! What's wrong?"

I cannot tell her, not yet, not knowing yet myself what I will do with my captive. I have an idea that I must use him to put a stop to this, all of it.

"An emergency has come up."

"What is it?! Is it Carl?!" she shrieks.

"No, no. It's okay. Just please come now."

"Tell me."

"I can't," I say, and I hang up the phone.

He is staring at me sullenly, the little brute, resentful, no doubt, of being toyed with now, of having the tables turned so dramatically.

And I am enjoying this far more than I have a right to. My mind seems suddenly unnaturally clear. I feel his gun vividly in my hand, as if I had never held a gun before. It is big and heavy, warm and slick now with the heat and sweat of my hand. I want to look down at it, examine it, smell it, hold it up to the light, feel the power of this terrible thing.

He is watching me, waiting. Maybe he is thinking that he can run away, but I won't let him. No way.

He is an ugly thing, but it occurs to me momentarily how holding this gun I could make him take his clothes off. How holding this gun, I could violate him. How he is just a child, but I hate him so, I could kill him.

Then an image of a plastic shovel enters my mind, a child's drawing with red crayon spots for blood, of the carefully filled-in outline, a child's drawing of violation.

I feel a rush of sadness, recognize it as exhaustion, and I find my eyes closed for an instant.

I look up to find him on his feet and sprinting toward me across the room.

My finger, there on the trigger, comes alive without the necessity of thought and before I am aware of it I have aimed and fired and there is a hole in his shirt below his shoulder.

He stops, startled, and the look on his face is much like that of a frightened cow.

The sound of the gun echoes loud against my plaster walls.

And then he starts to bleed.

As a child I once helped my father put down a calf whose spine had been broken in a fall into a sinkhole. Poor thing lay still and heavy, barely able to breathe, eyes fixed forward as if knowing, waiting for release.

My father, thinking it the right thing to do to teach his children the reality of the responsibility we take on when we care for livestock, gathered the four of us together around the doomed creature. Being oldest, it fell to me to pull the trigger, which I did with my father's arms around mine, my back nestled into his big chest, my arms straight in front of me with the barrel of the gun, my father's old .45, pressed up against the side of the calf's head.

My sister and brothers had gaped enviously until I pulled the trigger; then the calf's head jerked once and shook as her body spasmed and blood trickled from the bullet hole and pooled beneath her head. All our faces went blank, and we seemed to feel collectively faint, as if we too were falling away from life and the heat would soon leave our bodies.

I feel it now, that hot rush of relaxation that quickly drains, leaving a chill. I watch him step back, still amazed, and stumble against the wall and down to the floor.

I am thinking about the bullet hole that I see now in the wall behind him, and about the blood on my wall and floor. I wonder if I should offer him the comfort of a chair or my bed, but whatever he bled into he would ruin. Selfish bitch that I am, I let him sit there on the floor with his back against the wall and one hand pressing the wound.

He is starting to breathe hard, and I can see that he is manfully stifling the pain and trying not to cry.

"I . . . wasn't kidding," I say, as if it would answer his pitiful look.

He takes his bloody hand from the wound, looks at it, and says, "You got to get me to a hospital."

I shake my head slowly, knowing somehow that he will not bleed to death, and I say to him, "You're going to take me to John Bowman."

He stares, his face reflecting the slow process of his mind as he considers this demand.

"My friend will be here in a moment," I tell him. "She'll dress that wound and then we'll get in her car and go."

He stares. It's too much for him.

Owedia screams. She is there in my open door screaming at the sight of the bleeding boy on my floor and I must drag her into the house and shut the door to avoid alarming the neighbors.

It is a moment before she sees the gun in my hand, the boy's shaved skull, and the sullen look on his face.

"Dear God," she murmurs, her voice erupting tremulously from her throat.

In a matter of minutes we are in Owedia's car heading north on Meridian Street through a starry night, the air hard with cold.

I am in the backseat leaning against the car door, holding the gun pointed out from my belly at the boy slouching quietly on the other side of the car, his hands bound behind his back, a big piece of duct tape neatly covering his mouth. The fight has gone from his eyes, and in the light of the passing street lamps I can see that he is getting sleepy.

Foolish boy. After dressing his wounds, Owedia had given him three codeine-laced painkillers from my medicine chest, enough, we thought, to render him weak, not enough to knock him out. We were wrong. By the time we cross Eighty-sixth Street, he is asleep.

It is just as well. I know where John Bowman lives, and I do not need the boy awake to make an example of him.

Owedia drives with her lips set tight, afraid to speak in front of the boy and afraid no doubt that I have lost my mind.

Still, she drives carefully toward Carmel and the address Joe Baker had given me. She has a map on the seat next to her, but she has not had to look at it yet.

When the boy is asleep I tell her so.

She starts to cry silently, tears suddenly running thick, shining in the headlights of oncoming traffic.

"Why are we doing this?" she says. "It would be better to wait for the police to do it."

"You said yourself they're not likely to do anything soon."

"What are we going to do when we find John Bowman?"

"We're going to ask him about the murder of Cora Rollison."

"He'll just say he wasn't there."

"Maybe. Or maybe he'll admit to the murder."

"Why would he do that?"

"Because he's an arrogant bastard."

"So what will that get us?"

"We'll know the truth. And we'll have looked him in the eyes."

"Is all this worth that?"

"It is to me. Isn't it to you?"

"Yes . . . I think so. But I'm scared that boy's going to die in my car."

I can't help but laugh.

"What on earth could be funny now?"

"I was worried about him bleeding on my wall."

She shakes her head. "Why don't we just drop him at an emergency room?"

"Because he's not dying. And we'd never get out of there. And because I want the pleasure of delivering him to Mr. E."

"Aren't you afraid that something could go wrong?"

"No."

"You have a gun. Anything could happen."

"I'll be careful with it."

"No, really."

"I know."

"And what happens if something goes wrong and the police have to get involved?"

"I don't know."

"There's no way you can disappear, now. You're in it as deep as Carl or Dexter or me. The police are bound to know about you."

"Maybe."

"They'll find out if they haven't already. You'll have to tell the judge. You'll lose your job and God knows what else is going to happen."

"I know."

"Are you willing to let that happen?"

"It's happened already."

As we pass 116th Street into Carmel the road gets darker and the houses get bigger and more set apart from one another; at 120th Street we pull over to the side of the road and turn the light on to look at the map.

The address is 11549 Admiral's Isle, and according to the map it is in the Admiral's Harbor subdivision. And this in a place a thousand miles from any ocean.

From 126th Street we take Amish Farm Road, the artery that links the many subdivisions carved out of what might once have been an Amish farm; suddenly the sign heralding Admiral's Harbor is there at a gate festooned with decorative anchors. Owedia takes the turn at a surprising clip, and I am nearly thrown onto my sleeping captive.

We drive past a series of cul-de-sacs, and we discover that this place is nothing but a series of cul-de-sacs, and then, finally, there is Admiral's Isle.

It is a stem leading to a wide circle with only three houses on it, and there, at the farthest point on the circle, and occupying the largest portion of it, is the house JeTaun had described.

There is a circular driveway. The place is huge and built of gray-colored brick and its exterior is lit by lights embedded in the lawn. There is faux-Greek statuary on the lawn and some strange welded-metal sculpture, lit up like at a cheap suburban catering hall. It is an opulent crime against taste, and it seems a more-than-fitting home for a wealthy skinhead.

Owedia turns into the circular driveway, parks in front of the house, and turns off the ignition.

"This is crazy," she says quietly. "It's too dangerous. We don't know who's in there. And nobody knows we're here."

"They don't know that."

"We should drive to a pay phone, call the police and have them meet us here."

"And tell them what?"

"Tell them anything! The truth, maybe!"

"I'm going in. If you want to wait out here, that's fine. But I need to go in there now and look this man in the face and find out if he was in that car with Dexter and Joe. I've been attacked. You've been attacked. JeTaun was attacked. And Roger Swango is dead. It's going to stop now."

I open the door and step out swiftly, knowing that Owedia is right and that this may be the most foolhardy thing I have ever done. Yet in a moment I hear her door open and close softly and in an instant she is there beside me. We walk up to the beveled glass door together, and as she presses the doorbell, I keep my right hand firmly on the gun in my pocket and glance quickly back at our sleeping Pretty Boy.

We wait. We spend five minutes there at the door watching our breath condense against the glass, but there is no response, no sound from within, no lights. No one home.

Owedia is practically dancing for joy.

"It always pays to call before dropping by," I say. "Would you mind if we sat in the car a few minutes to see if someone shows up?"

Owedia agrees, though clearly not pleased with the idea. I slip into the backseat next to my prisoner, who is out cold; I touch his forehead carefully with my hand to be sure that he is not dead, and no, he is not, his skin is warm and I cannot resist feeling his bristly head. I find the soft stubble strangely fun to touch; it's like stroking a pig.

Owedia sits in the front staring forward quietly at first, but then looking around at the big homes and humming to herself. I don't know the tune but it sounds like a gospel song, and just the bare melody of it is enough to make me feel hopeful and to make me believe that perhaps we have not done such a foolish thing by trying to get to the truth ourselves.

After a time, Owedia stops humming and turns to gaze out at the lawn sculpture.

"I'm sorry about dinner tonight," I tell her.

"So am I," she replies, without looking at me.

"I've got to lay off alcohol for a while."

"That's exactly right."

About seventeen minutes later, at 11:53 P.M., a car pulls into the cul-de-sac.

In the rearview mirror I see that it is a big black boat of a car like the one that picked up Joe Baker at Carl's house the night the opinion was handed down. It slows as it rounds the curve of the cul-de-sac, its headlights sweeping across the house behind us.

Owedia turns to me, her face contorted with panic. The car, a shiny new Cadillac, enters the circular driveway behind us, its headlights glaring into Owedia's car. I do not know whether to duck down or stare back, but before I can make up my mind the Cadillac draws back, then pulls forward onto the grass and drives around us.

"Put on the headlights," I yell to Owedia, and in an instant the interior of the Cadillac is brightly illuminated.

Revealed in our headlights is the head and neck of a fleshy boy like the one asleep beside me. The tattoo on his neck is as clear as could be, and a second after the light hits him, he turns and glares at us.

It is, I am sure, the face I have waited so long to see. It is a well-made face on a squarish shaved head, with attractive dark eyebrows and deep-set eyes. What is surprising is how pleasant a face it is, and in that fleeting second I regard him, I wonder if there is something really good behind those eyes or if it is merely an accident of facial composition.

"Good Lord," Owedia says. "It's him."

The Cadillac skids on the grass and swerves into the street.

"Follow him," I say.

"What?!"

"Follow him! We can't lose him now!"

"You're out of your mind," Owedia grumbles as she hurriedly turns on the ignition and throws the car into gear. "You are really out of your mind."

Owedia pulls the car quickly out into the street and accelerates like mad to catch up with the Cadillac, which has disappeared from the cul-de-sac. We catch sight of it speeding toward the entrance to Admiral's Harbor, where it turns right onto Amish Farm Road, leading away from the city. Owedia grips the steering wheel and floors it, and in a matter of seconds we have pulled within trailing distance of the Cadillac.

Owedia is clearly agitated, and through gritted teeth, she says, "*Why* are we chasing him? We know where he lives."

"Now that he knows we've found him, he may disappear. I'm not turning back until I've spoken with him."

"We could just send the police after him!"

"We can't do that until we know more."

"How much are we going to find out if he won't talk to us?"

"The question is, why is he trying to get away from us? What does he think we're going to do to him?"

"You've got the gun, girl, you tell me."

Amish Farm Road is a straight line north across land as flat as anywhere on earth, and the further we go from the city, the more snow there is glowing faintly on the fields that extend on each side of the road to the horizon, where the trees are silhouetted against a starry sky. There are no street lamps here, just two lanes of road in our headlights and the pinpoints of red taillights beckoning us onward. We are travelling at better than eighty miles per hour, yet we could be soaring through the air on wings for all we feel the speed.

That is, until the Cadillac makes an abrupt turn. In the distance we see a tiny image of the arc of his headlights sweep across a barbed-wire fence, and then we see his lights move westward. Ours are the only cars on the road, and in the dark on this land we can see so far it is as if we were pursuing him along a grid.

"Where's he going?" Owedia asks as we reach the intersection where the Cadillac turned; it is a one-lane gravel road, rutted with tracks and chuckholes, and as soon as the car hits that gravel, it starts bouncing like mad and Owedia has to slow down considerably to avoid running off the road. "Shit!" she cries, and it is the first time I have heard her use that word. "Is he going somewhere or is he just trying to get away?"

"Damned if I know."

The Cadillac gains distance on us quickly—it is perhaps a half-mile or more up the road—but Owedia accelerates once she has the feel of driving on gravel, and we begin to make up the difference. The sound of stones banging against the bottom of the car is thunderous, and I keep a close eye on Pretty Boy for fear that the noise will awaken him. That does not seem to be an immediate danger; he jostles about limply as the car swerves and jolts, but his eyes stay closed.

"Shit!" Owedia repeats when the car hits a particularly nasty chuckhole, and I am afraid to talk to her. She is driving with amazing tenacity, and I am grateful for her wholehearted commitment to my folly. I want to thank her, but I cannot, not now, and it occurs to me as I look at her huddled over the steering wheel that this is a payback for the risk I've taken in choosing to help Dexter.

I reach forward and give her shoulder a squeeze.

She screams, slams on the brakes, and twists her head around abruptly.

"Shit!" she cries again, "What the hell are you doing? I thought that was *him!*"

"Sorry."

Owedia resumes driving, but we have lost valuable seconds. The car is perhaps a mile from us now, when suddenly its lights disappear from the road.

"For Christ's sake, Owedia, step on it! If he turned, we may lose him!"

"Watch your mouth," she says sharply, as if in self-rebuke. "And I hope we do lose him."

Still, she floors it, and as the car accelerates it skitters and slides in the gravel and it is all I can do to hold on to the seat in front of me and keep the gun on Pretty Boy.

Seconds later, we reach a sharp bend in the road, and there, up-ended on its side in a ditch next to the road, is the Cadillac.

Owedia skids to a stop, and we avoid falling into the ditch ourselves by inches. I throw open my door and run toward the Cadillac, but looking up I see silhouetted against the snowy field a figure running laboriously through the snow, his shaved head shining unmistakably in the moonlight.

I leap across the ditch and climb gingerly over an old barbed-wire fence; it is only waist-high, but it is slippery and I am awkward gripping the snow-covered fence post with my bare hands, in one of which I am trying to hold tight to Pretty Boy's gun.

Mr. E is not far from me now, and though the snow is wet and the ground beneath it seems soft, I feel him within reach. Glancing back quickly, I see Owedia caught on the barbed wire, a sleeve and the side of her jeans snagged in such a way that she is halfway over with one arm underneath a leg, with nowhere to go and nothing to do but fall over into the snow.

I run, my heart pounding like mad. I am strong but I am not in any shape to run for very long, and though I see that he is tiring too, if he does not slow down I will lose him. The field seems endlessly wide. There is a stand of trees and the lights of a farmhouse off in the distance, maybe three or four hundred yards from me. I wonder if he

247

is heading there. I wonder why he is running from us. I wonder what he has done, who he thinks we are, why he thinks we are chasing him.

I am so tired. I am cold and my clothes are wet from splashing myself with wet snow and from sinking into the not-quite frozen mud and slush with each step. The fact that I am still wearing the clothes I wore at the office—skirt, stockings, and low heels, fortunately—does not help, and I am not oblivious to the fact that I am destroying one of the four decent sets of work clothes I own.

When I glance back again Owedia has extricated herself from the barbed wire and is coming after me. She's a tough woman for a city chick, I think, tougher than I give her credit for.

When I am a hundred yards from Mr. E, the earth changes, becomes harder beneath the snow, and suddenly I am able to put on speed. I am now close enough to see his face when he turns to check on me, and when he does I can see that there is blood on his face flowing darkly from his skull and spattered across his cheeks and forehead.

He slows down abruptly, and when I am close enough to throw a ball to him he stops, turns quickly, raises a gun and fires at me twice.

I feel a hot pain explode in the space below my rib cage on my left side. It is like a sudden terrible nausea at first, and then it is the biggest fucking hurt I could imagine, an *ow* of such intensity that I sink to my knees, and as I continue to go down I manage to twist so that I fall onto my side and then my back so I am not facedown in the snow.

The blood is warm rushing out of the hole in me, warm in the clothes against my back.

I feel even worse for having shot Pretty Boy. I hadn't known how much it hurt.

After a few seconds it doesn't hurt anymore. I realize I could die here, that it is quite likely I will die here.

The stars above me are pretty and it is all very quiet and I don't feel cold anymore, but . . . Oh, shit. I really don't want to die here.

Owedia's face passes quickly above mine, her movement a blur against the radiant stillness of the sky. I feel her slip the gun from my fingers and then she is standing above me, straddling me, arms out in front of her, elbows slightly bent, the gun cradled in the palm of her right hand.

Two shots shatter the air, echoing against the snow. And the smell of the gun on her fingers against my cheek is the last thing I remember before blacking out.

28

I am awakened by a sharp-voiced black man in an orange uniform; he is calling me "Miss Lumsey" again and again and there is something big and plastic on my face with cool air coming out of it and I am to nod beneath the mask if I hear what he is saying.

I hear what he is saying.

There is a helicopter there, an ambulance, and police cars, policemen, policewomen, police lights, and the smell of exhaust.

Owedia is watching me; we make eye contact, though I cannot move or speak, and then she is waving to me as I am lifted into the helicopter and within seconds we ascend clamorously from the ground. The man pushes my hair out of my face and I see now that there are tubes connected to my arms and that there are two other paramedics examining my midsection, one of whom is cutting away at my clothes with a large scissors.

And then it occurs to me that even if I live, I will not be needing these work clothes much longer.

I am alone in a curtained stall in an intensive care ward when I awaken. I see from the tag on my hospital gown that I am in Presbyterian Hospital. I am groggy and I sense that there is a terrible throbbing pain where the bullet went in, but it is as if I am floating a mile above the pain, observing it in detached contemplation.

Whatever drug they've given me, it's good.

After a time the curtains part; doctors come in and police too, but I am so numbed and high I cannot speak. I am awake but I am dreaming, drifting, and the faces come and go, examining me, sniffing me, attaching and reattaching tubes and wires.

Owedia is there for a time, holding my hand. I am so glad she is there and unhurt, but still I cannot speak.

Later, Owedia sits at my bedside holding my hand and tells me that John Bowman is alive and under police guard in a place called ward D, a secure area the hospital uses for institutionalized and incarcerated patients.

"I got him twice," she says, without the slightest hint of pride. "Almost killed him. The doctor says he's going to wear a colostomy bag for a while."

My lips form the words, "nice shot," and I squeeze her hand, understanding how badly she feels.

"But he'll be well enough to stand trial for attempting to kill you. And for the murder of Joe Baker."

I squint at her, disbelieving, and after sipping some water I am able to whisper, "Joe? He killed Joe?"

"The police found Joe's body in the backseat of the Cadillac. He'd been shot in the forehead. Lieutenant Brown says they won't know for sure if Bowman did it until they compare Bowman's gun with the bullets they took out of you and Joe."

"But why? Why Joe?"

"I don't think they know. They found thirty thousand dollars in an envelope on the front seat of Bowman's car. They think he took it from Joe, but they don't know where Joe got it. The lieutenant said there's been a gang war brewing for some time."

"Did the Vipers know Joe came to see me?"

"I don't know." Owedia hesitates a moment, then looks squarely at me and says, "I should tell you that the police are also going to check Bowman's gun against the bullet that killed Cora Rollison. If it matches . . ." She looks away, overcome. I hold her hand next to my cheek.

"The lieutenant told me he was going to call your chambers. I guess they must know by now."

I nod.

"I'm sorry."

"It's okay," I croak. "I really didn't want to be a lawyer anyway. Tell me, how's Pretty Boy?"

"Who?"

"Pretty Boy. The kid I shot."

"Pretty Boy? You're kidding, right?"

"Yeah. So how is he?"

"His name is Kevin Nunn—also known as Speed—and he's in ward D. He'll be fine, thanks to me. I can't tell you how many compliments I got from the nurses on my patch-up job."

"Have you told Carl?"

"No. I haven't even been home yet."

"What time is it?"

"It's ten-thirty in the morning."

"What day is it?"

"It's Wednesday."

She bends down and kisses me on the cheek, then signs something at me.

"What's that mean?"

"Get well soon," she says.

By 3:00 that afternoon my head has cleared sufficiently that I am able to give a recorded statement to Lieutenant Brown. A very dark-skinned man who sounds like he just stepped out of a TV cop show, he sits solicitously by my bed and leads me gently through the events that have brought me here. I tell him everything, the whole truth of it, because there is nothing else I can do.

Sometime later Tammy, Haberman, and the judge arrive. Tammy

252

has brought me a metallic helium-filled balloon with a happy face and those words "Get Well Soon," and the three of them offer their expressions of concern as if I were a coworker who had been injured in a car wreck.

When I can't stand it any longer, I say to the judge, "You know why I'm here, don't you?"

He nods.

"You know that it's all wrapped up in Dexter Hinton's case?"

"Yes, I know," he says. He gazes sadly at me. "I'm sorry for what's happened to you, and I'm sorry you've gotten hurt as a result of your involvement in a case that came before the court, regardless of the fact that your involvement was *ultra vires* and irresponsible." He touches my shoulder gently. "There will be consequences. This is not the time to discuss them."

"I am resigning my position, Judge, if that makes it easier for you."

He shakes his head. "It's more complicated than that, Nora. We'll discuss it when you're out of the hospital."

Haberman steps forward and leans on the bed's guardrail. "I should be incredibly pissed off at you," he says.

"You have a right to be."

"I can't believe you kept such a secret for so long."

The thing to do is to apologize, I know, but I cannot. After a long silence, I say, "I couldn't tell you."

Looking down at my hands, he says, "There's an old Yiddish saying, 'You can't dance at two weddings at the same time.' "

"What the hell does that mean?"

"It means, it would have been better to choose to be truthful to everyone."

Throughout the evening, cops come by from ward D to check up on me and flatter me with comments about the balls it took to hunt down Bowman. I learn from them that Joe Baker was killed trying to consummate a final deal, a double cross in which he betrayed both the Indy Boyz and the Vipers.

It was a simple plan that only an experienced go-between could execute. Joe told his connection in the Indy Boyz, a crack manufacturer and dealer named Shamar, that he had an opportunity to score a half a kilo of cocaine from a source in the Vipers. Joe had made this kind of deal dozens of times, so it was no problem for Shamar to lay twenty thousand on Joe to buy the stuff. At the same time, Joe told John Bowman that several kilos of pot were available from a source in the Indy Boyz, and he was in the process of collecting ten grand from Bowman when something went wrong. The cops didn't know what happened—Bowman wasn't talking—but it was clear from informants in both gangs that I wasn't the only one Baker had told about his plans to quit the scene and disappear. And someone must have tipped-off Bowman.

Owedia comes with Carl, briefly, and he cries pitifully, admonishing me for my reckless behavior.

"I lied to you," I whisper, choked with shame. "I'm sorry, Carl."

"I don't know how you could have done what you did," he says. "And I don't know how you could have done otherwise. I'm not angry with you. Except when I think how lonely it must have been for you. You should have told someone."

At 10:00 that night I am starting to drift off to sleep when Lieutenant Brown arrives with the results of the ballistics analysis. The bullet that was removed from the muscles of my lower back was from the same gun used to kill Joe Baker. And Cora Rollison.

"I've spoken with the prosecutor's office, and it's likely that Bowman will be charged with Rollison's murder," the lieutenant tells me. "Dexter Hinton may still be charged as an accessory, but his conviction for murder is likely to be overturned. And then the prosecutor's office will have to determine whether or not to file new charges."

Now I cannot sleep. Feeling vaguely like a hero, I call my father to let him know what has happened.

When I reach him, he is drunk and alone.

"What in hell is wrong with me that I let her do me like that" he cries, before I can even tell him where I am. "You know she don't even

254

tell me where she's goin'. Not a word. Just gets in her car and goes. Happened two days after Christmas."

I ask him if he needs anything.

"I don't need anything," he says, and he hangs up the phone.

29

I am awakened the next morning by Pat, my nurse, an obese white woman in her fifties with a puff of gray hair around her head. She hands me the *Indianapolis Standard,* open to page A5, where a single column, just five paragraphs' worth, tells that a Joseph Baker of 2913 Rutherford Avenue was killed and that John Bowman of Carmel was arrested for the murder. Owedia and I are named as witnesses to the murder, and it is mentioned that I am in stable condition at Presbyterian Hospital with a gunshot wound to the abdomen.

"At least they got yer name right," Pat says as she helps me with the bedpan, or tries to; she is so heavy she has trouble moving me. I attempt to lift myself up, but the pain is too intense, so together—her pushing, me pulling—I manage to get the thing under me, and I pee with a great deal of agony.

There are muscles in my side and back that I won't be using for a while.

It isn't until later that I am told that my left kidney was nicked by the bullet and that the whole damn organ is in a state of panic; it is irritated, sore, and in danger of becoming infected.

A crew of young doctors, babes every one, takes turns examining my wound, changing the bandage, palpating my skin. If it didn't hurt so much I might enjoy the attention.

Pat keeps close surveillance on the doings behind the curtains of my stall; I think she's afraid I'm going to drag one of these boys into bed with me.

That afternoon, Lieutenant Brown pays a visit, and he tells me that the *Standard* and the TV news are eager to speak with me, but he would prefer if I did not speak with reporters until John Bowman is charged with Cora Rollison's murder.

"Owedia Braxton has agreed not to talk," he adds.

"I can't see that I'd ever want to speak to the *Standard,*" I tell him.

The next day a story on page A2 of the *Standard* reports that an anonymous source within the police department has confirmed that the bullets taken from Joe Baker and myself match the bullet that killed Cora Rollison.

The day after that I am moved to a private room, where I am offered a telephone. I refuse it. There is no one I need to speak with but Owedia, and she is there every day at 3:30. When we are together we sit quietly and commiserate about me: my job, my kidney, my future. I ask her to move in with me and help pay the mortgage for a while.

"I may also need some help getting to the bathroom," I tell her.

She agrees to be my roommate, and she will move in this weekend, just in time for my release from the hospital, which is expected to be Sunday.

The day after that the *Standard* carries a front-page story announcing that new evidence indicates that Dexter Hinton was framed for the murder of Cora Rollison, and that the child had been coerced into confessing by Indianapolis police. For the first time the story gets the facts right about the roles Owedia and I played; evidently Lieutenant Brown had felt secure enough to release the truth—omitting my employment with the Indiana Court of Appeals. Now we are the *good citizens,* John Bowman is the *evil drug dealer,* Joseph Baker is the *one who tragically got what he deserved.*

Cora Rollison, nearly two years dead, is still the *elderly white lady.*

The paper quotes a statement released by Governor Doyle lauding the Indianapolis police for resolving the case and noting without irony that "the system works."

On the lower half of the page there is a full color picture of Dexter, not the menacing Dexter but now an old school picture of a smiling Dexter, pulled from God-knows-where in the paper's files.

On Sunday, the *Standard* carries an editorial calling for Dexter's release:

> A society is judged by the quality of its justice, just as a man is judged by the quality of his character and a city by the quality of its heart. In judging Dexter Hinton, this city may have been moved more by fear than reason, and in failing to hear a deaf child's voice, seeing only the violence done too often by children of his age and his race, an injustice was done.

His age and his race. Dexter Hinton is still the *black boy*, but now he is the *young victim of his race; after all, it couldn't be helped.*

I am weak, so weak, yet happy to be riding in the front seat of Owedia's car, which still smells so much of Pretty Boy that I can almost see him back there serenely sleeping.

I have lost weight. I am smaller everywhere—the size of my legs and even my hips, my belly and arms and face and breasts have all shrunk, miraculously, and it is as if my bones are smaller; I do not have that starved-cow feeling that I have had so often after dieting—that my skin, hanging on my enormous skeleton, looks pathetically deflated.

Five days of hospital food and painkillers will do that to a body.

Carl is there, broom in hand on my front steps, when we arrive. He grins, and I am so happy that we have come to this moment together that I don't mind feeling half-dead.

30

It is Wednesday before I am able to go to see the judge, and as I walk through the State House, aided by a hospital-issue wooden cane, each step on the marble floor sends tiny shock waves through my still-tender left side. I am aware with great sadness that this is the last time I will be coming here as an employee of the court. The architecture of this place is so grand and powerful I feel as though I am losing a love; I don't want to stop coming here.

Perhaps Owedia is right—I do need to find a church to belong to.

When I enter the chambers Tammy smiles sadly and says, "Nora, honey, we're going to miss you."

Haberman looks up from his computer terminal and says, "Christ, Nora, you could have rested for another week! You look like hell!"

I thank him as he stands and hugs me gently, and then he and I set to the task of cleaning out my desk.

The judge's door is closed and remains so, though I know he must be aware that I have arrived.

Haberman sits at my desk, leaning into the depths of my file drawer; it contains no files, just a stack of drafts of opinions, xeroxes of cases, and hundreds of pages torn from legal pads covered with my jottings.

I never throw anything away. Now, because I cannot bend or lift anything heavier than a sandwich, Haberman is doing it for me.

"Now here's something you might want to keep." He hands me a coffee-stained early draft of *Hinton v. State*.

"Case closed," I tell him, and he adds it to the recycling pile.

At the end of the half hour it takes to pack everything away, I knock on the judge's door. After a few long seconds, he says, "Yes, come in."

The judge rises when I enter, and he reaches out his hand prematurely; I move toward him, my own hand extended, as quickly as I am able, but it seems an eternity before our hands reach each other for a very brief handshake.

"Please sit down," he murmurs, and I do.

"I've accepted your resignation effective as of the end of this week," he says softly, with a glance at his desk calendar. "That's January seventeenth. You've been here for five months, which means that you have earned five vacation days, for which you will be paid. I've requested that the court administrator continue your health insurance coverage through March thirtieth. That will take care of most of your medical bills, won't it?"

"Yes, thank you."

"The matter of your ex parte communications with the appellant, Dexter Hinton, will have to be brought before the Disciplinary Commission of the Supreme Court of Indiana. Do you understand how that works?"

I shake my head.

"An investigator for the commission will conduct interviews and determine the facts of the case. A report will be submitted to the commission, which then examines the facts, gives the attorney an opportunity to respond, and submits a recommendation for action to the supreme court. Do you understand?"

I nod my head.

"What you've done is a flagrant violation of judicial ethics. Your conduct will be evaluated under the standards applied to judges because as my clerk you stand in my shoes. You are expected to conform to the highest degree of judicial discipline in refraining from improper contacts with those who come before this court. The reason for that is simple: In order to uphold the principle of equal justice before the law, a judge must be impartial. A judge must not be tainted by potentially prejudicial contacts with defendants, with the state, or with any litigant."

"I know that," I say, and before I open my mouth I know I am about to say too much. "And I know that what I did was wrong. But I also know that it is wrong for a judge to be tainted by potentially prejudicial contacts with elected officials for whom the outcome of a case has political significance." The words come out as I have rehearsed them a thousand times, never daring to believe I'd say them.

He glares at me, surprised and pained. It's the same look Pretty Boy gave me when I shot him.

"I know the governor asked you to affirm Dexter Hinton's conviction," I say, unable to stop even if I wanted to. "Don't ask me how I know, and I can't prove it. But the circumstantial case is too strong to ignore."

And then he begins to relax, and I see him almost look to heaven.

"I don't know why you did it," I go on. "I think you thought Dexter was guilty and so it really didn't matter if the rules were followed to the letter. The governor was afraid that if Dexter was released it would jeopardize his reelection and his chances for the presidency. The pressure for you to affirm must have been tremendous. So you did the governor a favor, and it didn't cost you a thing."

The judge follows me with his eyes, patient, impassive. I move forward in my seat, leaning on the handle of my cane, and stare him down.

"And I wouldn't have minded, I suppose, if Dexter Hinton had been guilty of the crime." My voice begins to crack, but I'll be damned if I'll shed a tear in front of him. "Or if you hadn't made me feel that I was wrong for raising *sua sponte* that Dexter's conviction was constitutionally flawed. I was *right,* goddamn it, I was *right!* And not just about Dexter's innocence, but about the law! And in rejecting my work you squashed every bit of self-esteem I had worked so hard to build in three years of law school!"

I am losing it, making an ass of myself, as ever, and I don't care. Unable to stay seated any longer, I push myself up on the cane and lean toward him. "I can't forgive you for what you did to Dexter, and I can't forgive what you did to me. You did this!" I yell, raising the cane. "You sent me on that . . . insane chase to find the real killer because *you* didn't have the integrity to do what was right!" Now I'm pacing, completely beyond control, and I'm waiting for him to call security. "You spoke to me about justice as process—what kind of bullshit was that?! Yes, we have a process, but it's implemented by *people!* People who put their pants on one leg at a time, as you old boys are so fond of saying. And the people who are supposed to do justice in this process should be balancing the dictates of process with reason, compassion, and . . . faith. Process is not to be hid behind. It's not an excuse for obeying the dictates of . . . politics."

When I finally shut up I hear my heart pounding in my eardrums. The judge simply licks his lips, looks thoughtfully at his desk for a moment, then comes back at me.

"Sit down, Nora," he says, and, exhausted and in pain, I comply. "You are my employee," he continues, "not my master or my judge. You have not even been out of law school a year. You think you understand the relationship between politics and the judiciary. You don't know the half of it."

He gets up from his desk and goes to the window. "I have absolutely no interest in justifying or explaining my actions to you. It's none of your goddamn business. But I will say this: There was only one perfect being, Nora. And they crucified Him. I'm not volunteering for the job, and neither should you. The truth may be as elusive to you as it is to the rest of us."

As he speaks I can almost hear my pretensions collapse. I fear he is right. I have thought too much of myself, blundered in my outsized way into matters far more important than I have a right to know.

"I don't have a judicial temperament," I tell him, groping toward an apology. "I shouldn't have taken this job. I'm not cut out for it, and I've been shitty at it. I'm sorry." I stand up, and reach out my hand to him.

He pushes himself up in his chair, a look of impatience on his face, and he shakes my hand slowly. I am about to turn and leave when he says, "I'm not quite done, Miss Lumsey. Please sit down."

We both sit, and he leans his elbows on his desk and gazes earnestly at me. "The penalties for conduct such as yours, were it committed by a judge, would range from suspension from the bench for a certain period to complete disbarment. The supreme court makes the decision, but I will be consulted. I am going to recommend that you be suspended from the practice of law for six months."

Six months. It is a slap on the wrist, hardly punishment at all, really, and I bow my head automatically, servilely, and I am about to thank him when the judge continues.

"I shouldn't be telling you this," the judge goes on, frowning, "but I have heard through the grapevine that there is an opening at the public defender's office. You could not work there as an attorney, obviously, but they may hire you as a law clerk for the duration of your suspension. Call them."

And now a job, Paul's job. The judge has obviously made calls on my behalf, trying to mitigate the sting of the suspension. I am grateful, thinking not of my convictions, not of my fear of becoming as corrupt as Paul, but of my mortgage, my student loans.

"I also want you to know that I have issued an order vacating my decision in the Hinton case and remanding the case back to the trial court. Now it's up to the prosecutor's office to determine what to do about this evidence . . . you've uncovered."

He tells me this with a tremble in his voice, his face flushed, a too-direct stare. It is a mask of authority, but transparent. Oh, no. Oh, *shit.*

"You son of a bitch," I hear myself murmur. "You fucking hypocrite, how could you?"

"*Thank you* would have done nicely, Miss Lumsey," he says without smiling.

I turn and go and I close the door quietly behind me.

There is surprisingly little for me to take away; my law dictionary and the few other books I brought with me fit into a single shopping bag, which Haberman carries down to my car.

"So what are you gonna do now?" he asks as we walk through the State House.

"I'm thinking about working for the public defender, if they'll consider a lawyer who can't practice."

"I hear they specialize in selfless crusaders. Under the circumstances, I'd say you were a shoo-in."

"What about you, Larry? Got that résumé worked up yet?"

"Not yet," he mumbles. "I've got to hang in there at least until the judge replaces you. Then, who knows?"

He slides the bag of books onto my backseat, then holds out his hand. "I'm going to miss you, Nora."

I slip past his hand, put my arms gently around him, and kiss his cheek. "You're all right, Larry," I tell him. "You're a good guy. And you were right, you know."

"Oh? About what?"

"About justice requiring faith."

"Ah."

"Thanks for everything."

"Dinner sometime?" he asks, blushing, pointing a finger as if scolding me. "When you're strong enough to match wits with me."

"I could do that in a coma, Larry."

It is odd to have a roommate. I have not had a roommate since my first two undergraduate years, and now I am sharing my pretty little house with a young black woman I hardly know.

We each have a bedroom, but there is only one bath, and so it must be shared. Our two sets of cosmetics now stand side by side in the medicine chest and the bathroom cabinet. It is peculiar how different our needs are; for her there is the universe of products for black skin and black hair, none of which are the least bit useful to me, and for me there are those few things I use, reluctantly, to make myself socially acceptable.

She, who would be beautiful without the least effort, spends a good half hour each morning applying makeup.

With only one bathroom, and with my need for assistance caring for my simplest needs, we quickly dispensed with shyness. Now we are free to be naked in front of one another and for one to use the toilet while the other is at the sink, and throughout our time together we talk constantly, lonely, friend-starved as we have been.

My weight is coming back, slowly, along with my strength, and it has become a daily ritual for Owedia to comment, in an exaggerated black-inflected speech, "You lookin' fat today, girlfriend." To which I respond, in my best white-trash accent, "Ah ain't near as fat as ah orter be."

But on this day, a Wednesday, a week and a half after my return from the hospital, we bathe and dress in silence, and there is a solemnity and awe in the space between us that we somehow cannot disturb with words.

It is the day Dexter is to come home.

Things have moved quickly, as they always seem to when the *Standard* puts itself behind a cause, and within days of the public announcement that John Bowman had been found in possession of the weapon that killed Cora Rollison, Bowman was charged with the murder and the wheels were set in motion for Dexter to be freed.

On Monday, the prosecutor's office, after making a public display of consulting with the family of Cora Rollison, announced that it would petition the court to reverse Dexter's conviction. On Tuesday, the court granted the petition without a hearing, and the Department of Corrections subsequently issued a statement that Dexter would be released after spending one last night in the state's custody.

We are dressed for church, Owedia, Carl, and I—there may be reporters there, perhaps the television news, and we want to look our best—and as Owedia drives, Carl sits stiffly next to her, trying hard not to wrinkle. I sit in the back looking at the two of them.

"I got three angels now," Carl says, turning his head just enough to let me know he's talking to me. "You two and Dexter. Lord! How blessed I am!"

My stomach is churning painfully. Though I need it less and less, I have brought the cane to help me walk the distance between the parking lot and the visitors' center, and now I am glad simply to have it to hold for comfort's sake.

"You're the angel," says Owedia, smiling at Carl, and in the set of her teeth I see that she is as nervous as I am.

There are papers to sign while we wait. Carl and I stand at the counter in the principal's office as a secretary takes pages from an open file folder and turns them to us for Carl's signature. I glance through each of them before Carl signs, explaining terms and the import of each document. I have become his lawyer.

Owedia stands behind us in the narrow alley between the counter and the row of chairs that lines the wall, her gaze fixed on the heavy metal door at the back of the office. Through the small window in the door, a metal grating can be seen, part of an inner door, perhaps. Above the door, a clock on the beige plaster wall reads 10:07 A.M.

At 10:23, the door opens and Dexter emerges, trailed close behind by a tall white corrections officer wheeling a dolly stacked with two cardboard boxes—apparently containing the sum of Dexter's personal possessions.

Dexter is dressed in new clothes—navy corduroy pants and a purple plaid shirt, still showing their packaging creases. He holds the straps of a red, white, and blue knapsack in his hands, dangling it at his side, almost touching it to the floor.

When he sees us his expression does not change; there is no smile, no joy. He looks like a kid getting out of public school after a particularly hard day.

Owedia signs something to him, but he does not respond.

We wait and watch on our side of the counter as he shakes hands with the principal, a chubby blue-suited man in his sixties, who, with great effort, forms a few signs for Dexter.

Owedia whispers, "He's saying, 'We'll miss you, but don't come back.' "

Dexter ducks his head oddly, and I can see now that he is overcome with emotion, so much so that he can hardly move, let alone sign. Yet he signs briefly, with great firmness and seriousness, back at the principal.

"What's he saying?" the principal asks of Owedia.

"He is saying, 'I will never come back here,' " Owedia replies, signing as she speaks.

Dexter shakes hands with the corrections officer and with the secretaries, his expression loosening as the women smile and wish him luck. Then a door to our left is buzzed open, and Dexter comes through.

Dexter walks slowly into Carl's arms like it was the thing he'd been wanting most in the world to do, and he silently puts his arms around Carl, pressing his face into Carl's chest as Carl bends to him, tears streaming down Carl's cheeks, and Carl kisses the boy's head repeatedly. After a moment Owedia moves in to touch Dexter's back, and then he glides into her arms, and then she is grinning and crying, her hands touching Dexter's hands, the two of them signing by touch.

Owedia must have signed something to Dexter about me, because he takes his head from her breast, leaving spots wet from tears, and comes to me and puts his arms around my big body, not pressing his face into me but looking up at me and smiling broadly, his eyes sparkling with tears, but sparkling.

I smile back at him, dizzy with the intensity of the moment, and all I can think is, here I am holding Dexter Hinton, the fearsome child who rose from a page in a transcript to transform my life.

In the parking lot, a gang of reporters pursues us as we walk toward Owedia's car. They are mostly women, and they are behaving as gently as one would hope, but this is not the time for us to stop to answer questions. The photographers run in front of us to take photographs, but move away politely as we trudge forward.

As he walks, Dexter moves with his head practically turned around behind him, his gaze cast back toward the school buildings, furtively scanning the windows for signs of his ex-classmates. Before getting into Owedia's car he stops and looks for a long time at the structure of interconnected brick buildings that is the Boys' School; it is a place that would look like any urban high school but for the bars on the windows and the high barbed-wire fence. Yet there is no sign of life evident from where we stand—no faces pressed against the windows, no hands waving good-bye.

I think he is hurt by this lack of ceremony, and he stands for such a long time that it seems that he does not want to get into the car to leave. It reaches me then that this is his world now, that after spending two years here it is the place he feels most at home. I wonder then if the hard part for Dexter begins now, with freedom.

Before we get into the car Carl touches Dexter on the shoulder, then gestures as I saw him do the first time we visited Dexter together—his arms, fists clenched, breaking free of chains. This time Dexter does not repeat the gesture but nods, a bit sadly, and turns away from the school.

A week later, life looks different.

Dexter is back at the deaf school, and, with Owedia's help, he has begun to take stock of the catching-up he must do. Living three doors away has made it easier for Owedia to work with Dexter in the evenings, and it also enables her to keep an eye on him.

The *Standard* issues periodic bulletins on the fate of John Bowman and Kevin Nunn, both of whom await trial on a long list of charges. It is noted that John Bowman, Sr. remains at large somewhere in Colombia. No mention is ever made of Roger Swango.

Following Dexter's release, the paper runs a series on Indianapolis's youth gangs, of which the Indy Boyz and the Vipers are but two of more than twenty local gangs, with an increasing presence from national gangs like the Bloods, the Crips, the Vice Lords, and the Disciples, in all having a combined membership of well over a thousand teenagers and young adults. The gangs operate like kid-sized organized crime syndicates, earning considerable fortunes from prostitution, gambling, drug dealing, theft, and extortion. Indianapolis gang members are regularly before the courts on charges related to their illegal businesses, but also for rape, assault, weapons possession, and, increasingly, murder.

And the city is, the paper reports, in the midst of a cycle of escalating gang violence over territory and power, fueled by the city's increasing racial polarization. The white gangs—whose members are a peculiar midwestern breed of the sons of rednecks, religious cultists, and race extremists—model themselves on the citizens militias, layering political rhetoric onto the old pastimes of pursuing quick money and harassing blacks. The black gangs too, have become better armed and better organized, espousing a social agenda that borrows elements of Islamic militancy and the Black Power movement of the sixties. But when it comes down to it, it's drugs and money, just drugs and money.

The black gangs wage war against the white gangs, and vice versa, and when they are not fighting they do business, form alliances, make treaties; their members live and die for each other and for the gang.

And now I can't see a group of four black teenagers walking together down the street without wondering. And I can't see a car full of white teenagers drive by my house without feeling a jolt of fear.

The following Monday, I interview with the public defender's office.

I am here despite my misgivings. I've been bought, I know that. But I must work, and if there is any work I was meant to do, this is it.

The work of the public defender is good work for meddlers and big-boned women; it is work that requires fortitude and an unyielding itch to keep the justice system honest.

I am trying not to feel like a coconspirator. Pursuing this job makes my hands as dirty as the judge's and the governor's, and I am as compromised as the Reverend Jones. Still, I go.

I am famous. They've heard about me, being maybe the only judicial law clerk that has ever been fired in this state. And they don't seem to mind.

I am interviewed by the same man who interviewed Paul the morning I threw him out of my house. His name is Donald Parrish and he is a talkative, funny, white-bearded sixties throwback, an intelligently idealistic man who embodies everything Paul pretended to be.

He smiles a lot. He likes me. He offers me the job on the spot.

I may have a hard time not falling in love with him.

And right now I think I need to be in love. It's long overdue.

On a sunny Sunday a month after Dexter's release, we throw a block party to celebrate Dexter's homecoming. The party is at Carl's house because it is bigger than my house, and everyone is there—the Cumberbatches and Williamses and JeTaun and Barbara Jones—without Reverend Jones—and the Pattons and Johnsons from across the street; classmates of Dexter's from the deaf school, and teachers, colleagues of Owedia; Haberman comes, to my surprise, and even seems to enjoy himself, shmoozing, as he says, with the men tending the stove.

The stove. Elston Cumberbatch is at the center of it, with Carl at his side, and the two men are fretting over two huge pots, one containing a Caribbean stew of pork and black beans, the other containing a spicy mixture of rice and vegetables.

I sit in a corner of Carl's living room for a long time, sipping a Diet Coke and taking it all in, watching Dexter in particular; for a while he was having fun playing video games with his friends, but all day there has been a worried look in his eyes, and now he clings childishly to Owedia, not touching her but standing very near and very quietly as she speaks with other adults. Dexter looks so distracted at moments that he seems about to start sucking his thumb.

JeTaun comes over and crouches down next to me. "Shit, girl, you either drinkin' too much or not enough. What's makin' you so unhappy?"

"I'm all right," I tell her, forcing a smile. "I can't help worrying about Dexter. He needs a lot of support right now."

"Looks to me like he's gettin' it. You couldn't have done more, honey. You saved that boy's life, you and Owedia. And now look at everybody here. These people love Dexter and they're looking out for him. It takes a village to raise a child, right? Well, this child's got his village. Right here."

She holds out her hand, palm up, and I take it in my hand and we squeeze.

"Yeah, you're right," I say, "but there's a lot of shit the village can't protect him from. And I mean all the shit he suffered at the Boys' School that he's got bottled up inside him. And all the shit that goes on on the streets of this city every day."

"You're gonna kill yourself worrying about shit like that. The shit that's inside Dexter is somethin' maybe you can help him with. But if you're gonna worry about the streets of this city, you oughtta run for mayor."

On a Friday evening five weeks after the block party, Owedia and I are working with Carl on flower beds in front of his home. He has purchased two flats of posies, petunias, and impatiens, and this is to be our first formal lesson in home gardening. It is time, Carl says, for him to pass on his knowledge before his back gives out completely.

It is a cool evening, early-spring sweater weather, and Dexter is dribbling a basketball with great concentration in the driveway as we work.

The world subdues as the sun slips away, leaving a peaceful gray twilight, quiet but for the rhythmic ringing bounce of Dexter's basketball against the asphalt.

We are so intent on the task at hand, the flowers and the mulch and our fingers pressing into the cool moist dirt, that we do not hear the car approach Carl's driveway and slow to a crawl. Dexter is so intent upon maintaining the rhythm of the basketball moving between his hand and the ground that he does not see the shiny blue car with the young men inside it, and he does not see the gun in the passenger-side window, and he cannot hear the three shots fired from that gun.

We hear them.

We hear them like thunder with our faces bent close to the dirt, our hands packing soil around roots, and we are wrenched upward, our hearts bursting with the horror first of anticipation and fear and then of the reality of the sight of Dexter curled up convulsing on the driveway, his head and chest bloodied.

The car is already gone by the time Dexter's basketball bounces into the street.

Carl is on his knees by the boy praying.

Owedia puts her hand under his head and kisses him, runs her hands over him, tries to keep him warm.

I run inside and call 911.

By the time I get outside Dexter has stopped moving and there is raised such a cry of despair, of anger, and of disbelief, that I stand, unable to move, and watch the three of them there in the driveway, Carl and Owedia shaking, keening, crying over Dexter, whose blood flows impossibly fast from his still form and trickles down the asphalt and into the street.

31

The choir has black robes for funeral services. I had not known this, having seen them on Sunday mornings only, singing in Sunday clothes.

Now they look like singing judges, and Reverend Jones, pacing in front of them in his black suit, resembles a lawyer making an argument to the court.

It is standing-room only whenever a service is held in this place, but today the place is packed tighter than I have seen it packed, and there are television trucks outside and white people, dozens of them, milling eagerly at the periphery of the crowd.

Haberman and I sit in the third row at the front of the church, with Carl and the rest of us who are Dexter's family. Haberman's eyes are red from crying—he's been crying all morning, the poor soft-hearted son of a bitch—but I cannot cry.

And now the choir is singing, of all things, "Just a Closer Walk with Thee."

Owedia is there in her usual spot in the second row, her voice ringing out as fervently as ever. I had asked her why she would sing when she needs to grieve with the rest of us, and that even if she could not grieve for herself, Carl would need her strength beside him.

"Singing is the only way I can get through this," she said.

And yes, she is singing her heart out, her face wet like everybody's but mine.

"You ask me where was Jesus when our Dexter's life was snuffed out! When even Jesus cried out, 'My God, my God, why hast thou forsaken me?'

"Where was Jesus when our Dexter's life was snuffed out? Who can tell me?

"And where was our Lord Jesus when that boy was put in prison? Who can tell me?

"And while we're at it, where is our Lord Jesus on any day of the year when innocent children die by gunfire, pawns in the gang wars and the drug wars? Who can tell me?"

I look to my right down the pew, past Mr. and Mrs. Williams, to where Carl sits crying, his whole body shuddering. Somehow he becomes aware of my gaze and he turns to me, still crying violently, and extends his hand toward mine.

"Do you know what it means to forsake someone? It means to abandon them, to cast them off, to desert them. Lord knows, people forsake each other. We see it every day and it breaks our hearts. Fathers who forsake their children. Children who forsake their elderly parents. That's not the kind of behavior we approve of. And not the kind of behavior we expect of God. Or of Jesus."

I take his warm hand in my cold one, and the shock of his skin touching mine sets me crying too. But I am crying stunned. Stupefied. Angry.

To think that for a moment I believed I held Dexter's fate in my hands.

"But I know where Jesus was when Dexter was cut down! And I know where Jesus is whenever a child dies!

"He is with those children. Loving those children. Because as we know God did not forsake Jesus! And as we know Jesus does not forsake his children!

"It's men who forsake, not Jesus! It's men who forsake, not God!

"Our son Dexter is with Jesus now.

"Praise Jesus! Praise Jesus!"

274